T0107360

Sisterhood
of Lake Alice

Mari M. Osmon

iUniverse, Inc.
New York   Bloomington

Sisterhood of Lake Alice

This is a work of fiction. All of the characters, names, incidents, organizations, and dialogue in this novel are either the products of the author's imagination or are used fictitiously.

iUniverse books may be ordered through booksellers or by contacting:

iUniverse
1663 Liberty Drive
Bloomington, IN 47403
www.iuniverse.com
1-800-Authors (1-800-288-4677)

Because of the dynamic nature of the Internet, any Web addresses or links contained in this book may have changed since publication and may no longer be valid. The views expressed in this work are solely those of the author and do not necessarily reflect the views of the publisher, and the publisher hereby disclaims any responsibility for them.

ISBN: 978-1-4502-6292-7 (pbk)
ISBN: 978-1-4502-6294-1 (cloth)
ISBN: 978-1-4502-6293-4 (ebk)

Printed in the United States of America

iUniverse rev. date: 11/4/10

Dedications

A special thank you to my husband, Roy, who introduced me to this magical little town of Fergus Falls, Minnesota. I immediately fell in love with its tree-lined streets and easygoing residents.

I also want to thank Kelli, Traci, Eric, Chad, Lauren, and Samuel for the joy they bring into my daily life.

A special thanks to Judy and Dee for their inspiring friendship, which is filled with laughter, tears, hugs, and comfort that only true friends can give to each other. Also to Marlene, a wonderful example of what being a volunteer is all about.

JUST FOR TODAY

Just for Today, I will box up my worries, cares, and concerns.
I will place them in my box with its strong lid and lock.
I will lock them up and tuck the key away—Just for Today.

Just for Today, I will be kind to me and know this is well deserved,
I will allow all my gentle thoughts to simply flow from me and
I will be free to be happy—Just for Today.

Just for Today, I will be kind when logic says I should not be,
I will find some way to make this a better day for all who come my way.
I will give smiles instead of frowns—Just for Today.

Just for Today, I will learn to be better than I am right now.
I will fill my mind and soul with one great inspiration.
I will give myself the gift of knowledge—Just for Today.

Just for Today, I will look for beauty in everyday places.
I will smell a flower and look at the evening stars.
I will find pleasure in what I already have—Just for Today.

Just for Today, I will love someone who simply needs to be loved.
I will show a child, a loved one, or a friend that I cherish and honor them.
I will give the gift of ME—Just for Today.

Just for Today, when I reach for my box of worries, cares, and concerns again,
I will take out my key and lift up the lid.
Peeking inside, I will find my box empty, and I will be free …
Just for Today.

Mari M. Osmon

Prologue

Welcome to Fergus Falls, 1955

Welcome to Fergus Falls, Minnesota, population 12,460 proud Americans—at least that is how the sign reads that greets people entering town. There are 10,026 assorted types of Lutherans and 1,130 Catholics, and the rest of the people are considered "the others." This little town lies in the middle of beautiful and abundant land with rolling green hills. It is about fifty miles east of Fargo, North Dakota. A scenic little place, the town is surrounded by farms that have the blackest dirt you have ever seen. The cows almost seem to smile. Aside from the regular Fergus Falls residents, almost every Saturday the farmers and their families come to town to bring something in for trade, shop, visit relatives, or just have a cup of coffee and a piece of pie. They talk about the wind and the weather. The town resembles a mix between a Norman Rockwell and a Currier & Ives painting, with tree-lined streets and flowerbeds of daisies, mums, and roses everywhere you look.

Only four blocks long, downtown Fergus offers you every kind of shop you can imagine. For example, City Café and Bakery serves some of the best coffee and Danish pastries around the area. Viking Restaurant boasts of the best, big, juicy burgers, rich, thick chocolate malts, and blue-plate specials known for miles. Victor Lundeen's bookstore is the place to buy a book, candles, or writing paper—or to just run into someone and chat for a while. All the women in town shop for dresses, hats, aprons, and other necessities at Norby's, O'Meara's. and Gambles department stores. Claire's Dress Shop is the only place where women would think about going to buy their special occasion and fancy clothes. Many of the men in town go to Claire's to buy their wives a surprise gift for a birthday, anniversary, or Christmas. Claire makes a point of knowing almost all the women in town. She keeps a card file with the women's names, sizes, special dates, favorite color, and what would be the perfect gift for her.

Olson Furniture and Funeral Home takes up half a block. They were the first in the area to start selling television sets. They keep one turned on in the front display window at all times. There always seems to be a crowd of people standing around watching a TV show from the sidewalk. Then, there is St. Claire & Rovang, where the men go to buy their one going-to-church and funeral suit. The store also carries overalls, blue jeans, and flannel shirts in the downstairs shop.

The Fergus Theater is right next to Olson's. A Saturday afternoon matinee costs ten cents, and another ten cents will buy you popcorn and a small pop or a box of candy. Eddy is the head usher and always on the lookout for a troublemaker. He wears a fifteen-year-old navy blue jacket, which is many sizes too small for him, with his name embroidered on it. No one has ever seen him smile. Rumor has it that he lost all his teeth from eating too much candy. He is mean and loves to throw kids out of the movies. By some unknown magic, whenever he does kick kids out of the show, their parents always find out about it. Once that happens, it normally means you are not going to the movies for a few weeks.

Fergus Falls just installed the only two automatic stop signs in town. They are both downtown—one on the corner of Union and Lincoln, and the other at the intersection of Mill and Lincoln. They sit right in the middle of Lincoln Street on a six-foot block of wood. Two sides of the block are painted red, and the opposite sides painted green. Every three minutes the block turns. All the drivers obey the color in front of them. Everyone seems to have an opinion about the stop signs. Some folks feel all you need to do is to just be polite and wait for your turn. Nevertheless, when an outsider hit Doctor Burns's car, nearly injuring Anna Burns, everyone knew the time had come to do something. Change is good, at least once in a while. Within a few weeks, Kenneth, the town handyman, invented the two automatic stop signs.

On the Friday after Thanksgiving, with all the stores competing for the prettiest and most creative windows, the town always celebrates the beginning of the Christmas season. It was a perfect time to introduce the new automatic stop signs. Everyone in town came to witness the event. People clapped as they all watched the signs slowly move into action. Kenneth's picture appeared on the front page of the *Daily Journal* with the mayor and a few of the important downtown businessmen. The mayor let Mrs. Burns cut the ribbons that were tied around the new stop signals. It was quite a big change for Fergus Falls. Change does not happen fast or without some pain in this town.

Most of the houses in Fergus Falls are well maintained and often have vegetables gardens in their backyards. Mighty oaks and graceful elm trees line the streets. During the summer, the trees keep most of the houses cool. During the fall, the leaves turn incredible shades of red, gold, and orange. As the leaves fall from the trees, they are raked into huge piles that sit on the curbs waiting for the street cleaner machine to come and get them. In the meantime, it is a great place for the kids to take a running start, throw themselves into the middle of a pile, or play a game of hide-and-seek covered with leaves. It smells so good during the fall when the air is crisp and clean.

Fergus Falls is a small enough town that everyone seems to know each other's business. There is the group of rubbernecks, the town gossips who can send a story around town faster than the *Daily Journal*. The only real outcasts in town are the people who drink too much at The Spot. Sometimes the hoboes hang around behind the train station. If the police find them, they take them to the city jail, where they get a hot shower and a good homemade meal, which Millie Moody makes for them. After a good night's sleep, they go on their way with a brown bag lunch. Everyone figures that it is a nice thing to do for the hoboes.

Another wonderful part of Fergus Falls is Lake Alice, which is only a few blocks from downtown. A tiny lake, probably more like a big pond, it's beautiful anytime of the year. All the kids and even some adults go ice-skating as soon as the water freezes and the green light on the lamppost tells them that it is safe to skate. From the small warming shed, you can hear the music playing over the loudspeaker. Not one fish lives in Lake Alice, but lots of ducks, geese, and even an occasional swan glide through the murky water. People bring stale bread or crackers to feed them. Some of the biggest and most beautiful houses surround Lake

Alice on Lakeside Drive. Most of the residents of these houses are doctors, dentists, lawyers, and businessmen. Everyone knows this is where the rich people live.

It seems as though there is a church on almost every corner in Fergus. All of them take great pride in their beautiful stained-glass windows, steeples, and huge wooden doors that weigh a ton, making them hard to open. There is even a Catholic church in town. Our Lady of Victory is a huge church and has the only private grade school in town. Everyone gets along okay; however, the silent rule is that Catholics and Lutherans do not mix socially. Each group seems to have their own way of doing things. For example, the Lutheran women make and sell lefse several times a year. They have a big celebration in May, called *"Sitnamae,"* which is a meatball dinner with all the fixings to raise money for their needy causes. The Catholics have bingo games, "smokers" for the men where they have beer and cigars and play cards, and New Year's Eve dances that are all capable of raising thousands of dollars while having a good time.

Recently, Fergus Falls decided it was time to merge two small hospitals into one big one. Lake Region Hospital is the new name, and there are many plans for it to become an impressive place in the next few years. The most beautiful building award in Fergus Falls goes to City Hall. Covered in gold tin, its tall steeple can be seen from miles away. The Post Office building is the biggest building, with beautiful marble floors and a statue of someone that no one knows. Surrounded by churches on each corner, the courthouse stands in their midst as a reminder to the "criminals" in the jail on the top floors of the building to mend their ways. Almost all of the churches are Lutheran: there is German Lutheran, Norwegian Lutheran, Free Lutheran, and just plain Lutheran.

Everyone enjoys a simple and good life in Fergus. You can feel safe walking down the streets at any time of day or night. The kids ride their bikes on their secret routes, taking them through the unpaved alleys all the way to downtown. The winters are hard, with temperatures often going below zero and many feet of snow. Ice-skating on Lake Alice or going sledding down Old Smokey are the favorite ways to pass time during the long winters.

There are many ways to celebrate the arrival of springtime in Fergus. Everyone opens their windows to air out the house of the stale winter smells. The clotheslines start to reappear. It is a time to start hanging laundry outside and smell fresh, clean sheets again. In most backyards, the men start to plant the gardens, while the women work on their flowerbeds.

Summer is fun because of the many lakes around here. You could go to a different lake each day and still not make it to all the lakes by the end of the summer. The summer is warm but never humid.

When fall arrives, it is time for homemade apple cider, caramel apples, and warm sweaters. The air captures the smells of pot roast cooking, leaves burning, and the first hot chocolate being made. Anyone is welcome to take free apples and squash from the baskets outside the stores.

Yes, Fergus Falls offers all who live here an uncomplicated life. They are not fancy people, but they sure are friendly folks. Life is basic here, with a strong sense of belonging. The fact that everyone in town knows each other has proven to be both a blessing and a curse to most of us at some time in our lives. Some of the young people dream about moving away to the big cities of Fargo or Minneapolis. However, it seems that after you leave for a while, Fergus Falls always calls you back home to the joys of a pretty town with lots of nice people waiting to welcome you home.

Chapter One

Emily Larson

The Meyers moved to Fergus Falls in the early forties. Ralph Meyers owned a large construction company, which had been awarded a contract to build the new Lake Regional Hospital. Ralph and his wife, Ruth, soon became an important part of the community. They often donated large amounts of money to the city for many worthwhile causes. Their twin daughters, Joyce and Julia, were pampered and spoiled. Many thought they were self-centered; however, the town learned to accept them for who they were.

It came as no surprise when years later, Joyce Meyers announced her engagement to Dr. Howard Larson. Dr. Larson was not known for a warm, caring manner; however, he was considered one of the best surgeons in town. He was also the town's most sought-after bachelor. In fact, merging the two small hospitals was only accomplished because of his insistence. The new hospital became Dr. Larson's pride and joy. Shortly after it opened, Dr. Larson took the position of chief of staff.

Joyce Meyers's wedding was the event of the year in 1947. All twelve bridesmaids were dressed in flowing, lavender satin dresses. Two flower girls wore a miniature version of the same dress and scattered white rose petals as they paraded down the long aisle. Dozens of perfect white and pink roses delivered from Fargo filled the church with their soft fragrance. Joyce's softly draped satin dress was created by a famous designer from New York City, with an Italian lace train more than twenty feet long. The dress had a sweetheart neckline covered with pearls and lace. She looked like a princess with a stunning tiara sitting on top of her mass of curls and veil. Dressed in a formal tuxedo, Dr. Larson looked cool and aloof. The mother of the bride, Ruth, wore a deep purple dress with matching gloves and shoes. To everyone's surprise, she also wore a tiara.

A large crowd filled Bethlehem Lutheran Church. A few important people from Fergus were invited, but the rest of the crowd was out-of-town strangers. The governor of Minnesota and both senators attended the two-day celebration. Pictures of the wedding appeared in newspapers all over the state. Dr. and Mrs. Larson were definitely celebrities in this little city.

After a month-long honeymoon to Europe, they returned home to their newly purchased home. The beautiful old Victorian house, which overlooked Lake Alice, had been elegantly restored. It was professionally furnished and filled with priceless antiques. While on their honeymoon in Europe, they purchased tapestries, Persian carpets, and artwork to add to their collections.

People often drove past the house, especially in the evening, just to marvel at its style and beauty. It became the site of many parties and charity events. When Joyce discovered that she was pregnant, she was extremely upset. After the first three miserable months, Dr. Larson surprised her with a trip to New York, where she bought one-of-a-kind maternity clothes. In June, the doctor informed Joyce that she was carrying twins.

Joyce Larson expected perfect twins, just like her and her twin sister. She had been on bed rest for several months. That did not stop her from ordering two of everything she could think of for the babies' rooms. Her husband had little time or patience for all the chaos that had been caused by the upcoming births. As soon as the pregnancy was announced, he arranged for a live-in nanny. She would arrive one month before the births so that she could take care of the details of preparing for the arrivals. Dr. Larson seemed to be gone more than he was home these days.

Dr. Larson was in Minneapolis when Joyce went into labor. Julia, her sister, drove her to the hospital. She tried to keep calm while waiting patiently for the news of the babies' births. Within a short time of arriving at the hospital, it became apparent that there were some serious problems with the delivery. Joyce was quickly wheeled into the delivery room. Julia was advised to contact Dr. Larson and tell him that there were complications with the birth of the twins.

Emily Catherine Larson was born October 8, 1950, weighing six pounds thirteen ounces. She had soft blonde hair, big blue eyes, and long pretty fingers. She entered this world with a mixture of joy and incredible sorrow—and a loud cry. A few minutes later, a little boy was born; however, he was silent. The umbilical cord was wrapped tightly around his tiny neck. The doctor and nurses worked frantically on the baby for what seemed like an eternity. Finally, they stopped; they had gone well over the normal procedures because this was the child of Dr. Larson.

When Joyce woke up in the recovery room, her sister gave her the news. She had a beautiful healthy daughter; however, Emily's twin brother had not survived. Joyce wept for her dead son and refused to hold her newborn daughter. She was well aware that Dr. Larson wanted a son. He had already informed her that their baby boy would be named Joshua after his wealthy grandfather.

By the time Dr. Larson arrived, Joyce was heavily sedated and resting in the nicest room in the hospital. When Dr. Larson learned about the births, he asked if his daughter was physically okay. When he was assured that the baby was fine, he simply nodded. It never occurred to him to stop at the nursery to see his new daughter.

When the attending physician came into Joyce's room to talk to him, he shoved him up against the wall and stomped out of the room. He slammed every door on his way out to the parking lot. He was shocked that his daughter survived, while his son had been taken from him. Filled with uncontrollable rage, he did not let anyone comfort him. He mourned for his dead son, who would never receive his proper place in the family. In some twisted way, he blamed his son's death on his newborn daughter. The doctors tried to explain that this was not the case, but it made no difference to him. He knew that he would have little to do with the daughter.

Joyce told him that she did not intend to become pregnant again. Dr. Larson fumed with outrage, knowing that he would never have a son to carry on his family name.

Emily Catherine Larson was baptized at Bethlehem Lutheran Church on New Year's Day in a church filled with friends and relatives. She was given the very proper name of Joyce's grandmother and the middle name of her great-grandmother. After the church service, there was an elaborate party held at the Larsons' beautiful home. From the windows of the house, Lake Alice sparkled with fresh white snow and a perfect blue sky as children skated to music. All the important people in town made a mandatory appearance at the baptism party. There were mounds of expensive gifts displayed in the formal dining room.

Tiny Emily made her appearance in a white silk and lace christening gown imported from France. As she was paraded around the room by her nanny, all the guests had a chance to comment on what a beautiful little girl she was with her big blue eyes and delicate features.

Isabel quickly took Emily upstairs, just as she had been instructed to do. Isabel was an eighteen-year-old girl from Norway and Emily's full-time nanny. She had a small room off Emily's spacious bedroom. She had prepared everything needed for the babies. She was excited about Emily's arrival into the big cold house. Joyce was pleased that Isabel spoke proper English. She immediately informed her that she was to never use any form of baby talk or speak Norwegian around Emily. Isabel was required to be available to care for Emily at any hour of any day. Because of the tragedy of the death of the other child, Joyce told Isabel that she would need more rest and quiet. Isabel quickly removed all evidence of the twin that did not come home. She was told not to bother Joyce with the baby. When and if Joyce wanted to be with Emily, she would simply inform Isabel to bring the child to her.

As the party continued, their guests all commented on how quickly Joyce had regained her hourglass figure. Although she looked beautiful in a deep red, formfitting dress from Claire's Dress Shop, her face showed no expression of happiness or sadness. Dr. Larson spent his time impressing his guests with expensive liquor, cigars, and humorous stories about their travels to Europe. He laughed as he told his guests that Emily needed to learn early on that children were to be seen and not heard.

Emily grew into a quiet, petite girl. Her long, blonde hair, blue eyes, pale complexion, and dainty appearance often made her look frail. She had sensed from a very early age that she was not loved by her distant parents. With a soft voice, she only spoke when someone asked her a question. Her shy and timid manners made her appear to be sad most of the time.

Her closest attachment was with Isabel, whom she adored. Isabel taught her how to ride a tricycle and then a big bike. However, she was never allowed to ride anywhere except around tiny Lake Alice. There was no swing set because Joyce feared that Emily might be hurt and thought it caused too much noise. Playtime was always quiet, learning how to draw and do her alphabet. Her life was a protected cocoon, away from any danger that might happen her way.

When she was five years old, a piano teacher arrived to teach her how to play. Whatever task she was asked to perform, she excelled at it. By the time she was seven, she held her first piano recital. She played "Amazing Grace" and a selection from Chopin. Having conquered the piano, it was decided that Emily should begin private voice lessons. The following year, she sang her first solo at the Christmas Eve children's service at Bethlehem Church.

Everyone who met her commented on her beauty, grace, talent, and manners. She was bright, polite, and talented. Her pale little face and big blue eyes rarely showed any emotion. People thought she was just like her parents. They did not see that she was painfully shy and always afraid of not being perfect.

Emily's parents continued to be remote and disconnected from her. Dr. Larson became the leading force to develop Fergus Falls' first golf course and country club. He served as the chief of staff at the hospital, and the Chamber of Commerce often sought his advice. His new, private clinic was overwhelmingly successful. He recruited three doctors into his practice so that he could work less. Although no one truly liked him or his wife, most people knew that they needed their generous donations and power to get things done around town.

Dr. Larson continued to have little inclination to spend any time with Emily. He agreed with his wife that there would be no more children. He surprised Joyce with expensive trips to Europe, beautiful clothes, and gala parties. Yet the only contact with Emily was when he came home for dinner one or two nights a week. At the dinner table, Emily would be asked to explain how she was doing in school and with her many lessons. She politely reported on her progress, awards, and grades. Her parents never asked her about friends or questioned if she was happy.

Joyce never fully recovered from the death of her son. She had failed to give her husband the son she knew he wanted. Instead, she became the unofficial social hostess of Fergus Falls. She organized many of the fundraisers for the hospital, church, and schools. She hosted events at the newly built country club at the golf course. Their large, five-bedroom home was decorated both inside and out to show her elaborate taste. Her closet overflowed with designer clothes and all the accessories to match. She was the only lady in town who had three fur coats.

Joyce also seemed to take a real fondness to expensive Scotch, which she drank daily. She had it delivered by the case from a shop in Minneapolis. Many times after an important charity event, she would go to bed for days at a time with the claim of a terrible headache. No one outside their home ever saw Joyce without her perfectly styled hair and makeup and wearing a high fashion, coordinated outfit.

She remained disinterested in Emily. The most time and attention she gave her was when she selected Emily's new wardrobes three times a year. Before she left for the shopping trip, Isabel would measure Emily so that the new clothes fit just right. This was done right down to the width of her shoes. Then Joyce would fly to New York and on the way home spend a few days in Minneapolis to finish the project. Never was Emily asked what she wanted, what her favorite color was, or if she wanted to accompany her mother on the buying trips.

Joyce demanded that Isabel take great care in Emily's appearance. She would throw a fit if there was a speck of dirt on Emily's clothing or a hair out of place. She sent Isabel to a beauty salon, where she learned how to style and braid Emily's long, blonde, silky hair.

It was always Isabel who attended Emily's recitals and school events. She would come home and report to the Larsons what a gifted daughter they had. Isabel became very emotionally attached to Emily. She knew she could never leave her to fend for herself in this loveless showcase of a house. She became Emily's protector. She was devoted to her; she loved her as much as if she were her own daughter.

By the time Emily was a teenager, there was no doubt that she knew exactly what was expected from her. She worked hard to be an A+ student, an excellent pianist, and a soloist. She was a well-mannered young woman and politely quiet until adults spoke to her. She grew to love Isabel and to hate all the phony social parties that took place in her home. Her refuge was her beautiful bedroom, which was in the back of the house overlooking a gracious weeping willow tree. In the spring, she would often take an old blanket and sit under the shelter of the tree while practicing her French lessons with Isabel. The two of them would sit there for hours talking about anything that came to mind. They would also sometimes sit there quietly, listening to the tree make gentle noises as its long branches swept across the ground.

Emily shared her dreams with Isabel under that tree. She cried with her about all the disappointments she had experienced. She once said to Isabel, "Why do my parents hate me so much? Why can't I get them to spend time with me like all the other kids' families do? I am trying so hard to be a good daughter, and it does not seem to get me anywhere with them. Isabel, promise me that you will never leave me. You are truly the only person on the face of this earth who cares about me."

Isabel taught Emily the facts of life and the rules of dating. She gave her lessons on how to flirt and laugh at silly jokes. Emily discovered the secret of how to be a charming young lady who all the boys would want to escort to the dances and special parties. Isabel convinced her that she was a wonderful young lady, whom she loved and admired.

When Emily was old enough to understand, Isabel explained the death of her twin brother. She told her it was not her fault. At the risk of being disloyal to the Larsons, she repeatedly told her that her parents were wrong for how they treated her. She said that someday they would regret not enjoying their special daughter and the wonderful times they could have had with her. Emily believed and trusted Isabel more than anyone else in her life. Isabel became her safety net.

From all outward appearances, people might think that Emily had a charmed life. By the time she was twelve, she had been to Europe six times. Her closet overflowed with beautiful designer clothes. Her bedroom would be the envy of most adults. Long before most families in Fergus Falls could afford to buy their first black and white television or record player, Emily had both of them in her room. However, what she longed for she did not have—the love and companionship of her parents.

She had no friends that she enjoyed. After-school evenings and weekends were always occupied with lessons to improve her skills in piano, singing, and French. There was no time to just be a girl. There were times when she would sit on the wicker furniture on the large front porch watching the neighborhood kids riding their bikes in the summer and ice-skating in the winter. She felt isolated and out of step with the world. She did not fit into her parents' lives nor did she fit into the lives of children her own age. Without Isabel, her life would have been an empty, hollow existence.

Emily was terrified when it came time to go to high school. For weeks before school started, she paced and worried about how she would get by. She knew when she walked into the school on her first day that she would be a misfit once again. Where other girls wore their new outfits from J. C. Penney, she would wear a designer sweater set and skirt from Villager of New York. Her schoolbag was made of the softest Italian leather. She knew that all of the other students had every right to think she was a spoiled snob. She simply did not know how to talk to them and convince them otherwise.

Therefore, she roamed the halls of Fergus Falls High School alone. Isabel would come and pick her up for lunch and again after school. Emily was amazed at how lonely she felt in the middle of hundreds of students. She continued to excel in all of her studies. Her only extracurricular activity was the choir. She loved being part of this group; singing became a wonderful way for her to find a little happiness.

Their teacher told them that they needed to decide on a name for their group. After much lively debate, they decided on SOLA, which stood for Sisterhood of Lake Alice. They were called the SOLA by many of their classmates from that day on. Emily, Grace, Lindy, and Rebecca had originally come together as freshman when they were asked to sing as a quartet for their Spring Music Festival at Fergus Falls High School. They instantly became friends.

The quartet was so well received that the music director decided to offer special tutoring to them to develop their talents. By the next fall, they entered the statewide contest and came in second place. When they came home from the competition, which was held in Mankato, the school welcomed them with a special student assembly. The following day, their picture holding the trophy was on the front page of the *Daily Journal*. From that point on, the girls were inseparable. They ate lunch together each day and shared their most important moments with each other. For the first time in Emily's life, she had friends.

The girls loved hanging out at Emily's house because they never had to worry about parents hovering over them. During the winter, they taught Emily how to ice-skate on Lake Alice. Then they ran across the street to her house for Isabel's special hot chocolate loaded with tiny melted marshmallows. During the spring and fall, they spent hours in Emily's bedroom, trying on her clothes and gossiping. Many hot summer days were spent sleeping under the cool and graceful weeping willow tree, where they drank ice-cold fresh lemonade.

One summer night, sitting under the tree, Lindy suggested and they all agreed that they would always be SOLA, the Sisterhood of Lake Alice. In many ways, they were closer to each other than their real sisters. They shared secrets that they knew would never be told to anyone else. Their honest and open conversations allowed them to understand the true meaning of acceptance, even at their early age. All of them believed that this was truly a special bond that very few girls ever would know.

They had long discussions about boys and decided who they should date. They talked about their periods, the constant changes in their bodies, and of course, their dreams of the perfect romance. Even their arguments were lively and fun. Emily and Rebecca normally took the logical side, while Lindy and Grace always seemed to take the opposing emotional viewpoint. Their disagreements never lasted long and were normally resolved with a sleepover and root-beer floats.

Emily celebrated most of her birthdays and events at her friends' homes. She loved the warmth of Grace O'Malley's house. She knew that when she walked in their front door, she would get a big hug from Mrs. O'Malley. Rebecca's tiny little home was always clean, quiet, and cozy. Her mother's cookie jar was always filled with the best homemade chocolate chip cookies in the world. Her grandmother loved to crochet doilies, and they were everywhere you looked—on the furniture, dressers, and tables. She made a special one for Emily for one of her birthdays. Lindy's home was the exact opposite. It was loud and entertaining. It was not unusual to find Lindy and her mother with rollers in their hair, singing along to the latest country-western song. Emily often returned home depressed, realizing how lonely her life was in the big beautiful house overlooking Lake Alice.

On her sixteenth birthday, Emily arrived home from school to find a bright red VW convertible parked in their driveway with a huge ribbon tied to the windshield. There was an unsigned happy birthday card lying on the front seat with the keys. Her parents had left two days before to vacation on St. Thomas in the Virgin Islands. Before they left, they had made all the arrangements for a fancy party at the country club. Invitations had been mailed to everyone in her class. The day her parents left, Emily cancelled the party, placing a homemade sign in the lunchroom for everyone to read. Isabel immediately taught her how to drive her fun new car. Within a month, Emily could be seen driving around the town. Her three best friends were always in her bright red car with the top down, laughing, regardless of how cold it was.

Emily was very generous with her things and her money. All of them borrowed her clothes. Isabel quickly became attached to all of the girls. She taught them how to put on makeup and fix their hair. Isabel was there to greet them when they arrived. She made up beds for the girls on their sleepovers. She kept them supplied with popcorn, ice-cold sodas, and the latest fashion magazines. Then she would disappear to her new room, which had been built in the attic. There she would smile, listening to the girls' laughter. She was so pleased that at last Emily had found friends and acceptance.

Emily never cared much if she dated. In fact, she was terrified of the experience. The boys started calling and asking her for a date when she was a freshman in high school. She used the excuse that her parents would not allow her to date until she was sixteen. After her sixteenth birthday, she no longer could use that excuse.

Warren Brooks had been Emily's next-door neighbor for many years. He was one grade ahead of her in school. They often walked to school together. Sometimes they just hung out on her front porch or went to Dairyland Drive-in for root-beer floats. Warren became her protector and friend.

When it was time for his junior prom, he knew that Emily was the only girl he wanted for his date. One evening in late April, he waited and watched out his front living-room window to see Emily come out and sit on her front porch swing. Quickly he combed his thick, curly hair and took a breath mint. He was shocked at how nervous he suddenly felt as he approached the front steps to the wide Victorian porch. He knew that he would lose his courage if he did not immediately ask Emily to be his date.

He sat down next to her, and for a few minutes, they sat in silence while they swayed on the large wooden swing. Softly he cleared his throat and said, "Emily, I am in desperate need of a date for the junior prom. Because I am on student council, there is no way that I cannot attend. Would you do me a gigantic favor and be my date for this lame dance?"

Emily smiled at Warren and quickly said, "Sure, no problem. How could I ever refuse my best big brother and friend?"

Warren smiled all the way home and for the next three weeks before the prom. His parents were thrilled with his choice, as they had grown to enjoy Emily over the years. As much as they liked Emily, however, they disliked her snobby parents.

The night of the prom, Warren appeared at Emily's door in his new tuxedo with a beautiful white orchid in a plastic box. Emily floated down the curved stairway dressed in a soft yellow, long, flowing dress, with her hair done up with curls. She took Warren's breath away. His first thought was that Emily looked like an angel coming to him. They stopped back at the Brooks house for pictures, and then they were off for Warren's dream date. For the first time, Emily realized that Warren was tall and handsome. Together they made a darling couple. They danced, laughed, and enjoyed the evening. The prom picture showed a couple who appeared to be having fun.

Their relationship changed from being good friends to becoming a couple. They would often go to the movies on Saturday night and then stop for hamburgers at the Viking Café. They enjoyed each other but always hesitated to become romantic. At the end of each date, Warren would gently give Emily a goodnight kiss, but nothing more than that. Emily was content to be with Warren. She continued to think of him as a good friend. The fact that they were now considered a couple meant that she did not have to deal with other boys asking her for a date.

Most important was that SOLA all approved of Warren as well. They could always count on him to take them someplace or bring them along with Emily. They often teased that Warren was the unofficial fifth member of the SOLA. He drove all of them to rehearsals in his father's large Cadillac, regardless of how far away it was. He was always in the front row, cheering them on at any competition they entered. He helped them celebrate their victories. Warren was just a nice guy.

Warren longed to tell Emily how much he cared about her. It seemed that every time he worked up enough courage, they were interrupted. It was after Warren's senior prom that he finally decided he could not hold back his feelings any longer. As they sat in his car after the dance, Warren turned to Emily and gave her a passionate kiss. He held her close and whispered in her ear, "Emily, I have loved you all of my life. There is no one else I can imagine being with. I hope someday when I am done with college that you will give me the honor of being my wife."

Tears came to Emily's eyes as Warren held her. She knew deep in her heart that Warren would always be a big brother and never a lover. She also knew that night that she was going to lose a good friend. Slowly she turned to Warren and said, "Warren, I love you, too, but only as a big brother. I am sorry. I have never meant to hurt you or lead you on. Please, can't we just keep being good friends?"

Slowly Warren released her. Then he turned away from her as he opened his car door. He took her to the porch, where they had spent so many hours together. Then, without a word, he turned and walked away as the tears rolled down his face. Emily stood watching him walk out of her life as her heart was breaking for both of them.

Emily was combing her hair in the mirror wondering how to wear it for her graduation when there was a knock on her bedroom door. As she opened it, Isabel rushed into her room and planted herself on Emily's bed.

"I can't believe it …" Isabel muttered and began sobbing into her hands. Emily put down her brush and went over to sit with Isabel on the bed. She put her arm around her caretaker, her helpmate, the only living creature that had ever listened to anything she had ever said.

"What's wrong?" Emily asked. "What has happened?"

"I can't believe …" Isabel moaned and sobbed again. Emily held her, stroking her hair.

"My parents … my father … he's dead." Saying it out loud caused Isabel to burst into a fresh round of tears. Emily stared in disbelief, tears welling into her own eyes.

"My mom, she's in a coma. There was an accident. I have to go see to her."

"Oh, God, Isabel …" Emily was crying too. "That's awful."

"I'm returning to Norway in the morning." Isabel turned to take Emily's hands. "I'm not sure if I'll ever be back."

It was now Emily's turn to bring comfort and support to Isabel. Within a day, all the arrangements were made for her flight to Norway. Dr. Larson drove Isabel and Emily to the airport in Minneapolis for Isabel's long journey home. Emily clung to Isabel and found it unbearable to watch as she boarded the airplane. On the way home, Emily cried uncontrollably.

Dr. Larson frowned as he told her that Isabel was simply an employee. He also informed her that he had given Isabel a large sum of money and told her it was not necessary for her to return. After all, Emily was now a grown woman and would be leaving for college in the fall. It was time that Emily stop being such a pampered child and grow up. She needed to know that much would be expected of her as the daughter of Dr. and Mrs. Larson.

For the next week, Emily spent all of her time alone in her princess palace, as they had named her bedroom. She had never felt so abandoned in her life. Isabel was truly the only person in her life who loved and understood her completely. The day Isabel left was a turning point in the life of Emily Catherine Larson. From that day on, she began to take control of her destiny with a determination that surprised her.

A few weeks later, Emily received a letter from Isabel, saying how much she missed Emily. She also said that it was the right decision to stay in Oslo, as Emily would be starting college in September. Her final paragraph in the letter read:

> In my life, I am sure that I will meet many people. Some of them, I will quickly forget. Some will leave lasting impressions on me. You, my dear Emily, have left your fingerprints on my soul. I will never be the same because of you. Remember that I love you. I will think of you always. Learn to love and value the wonderful woman that God has made you to be. I will pray each day for your happiness.
>
> Love always,
> Isabel

The arguments that Dr. Larson called "debates" started shortly after Isabel left. Emily came home from school one day to find a large envelope from Sarah Lawrence College sitting on her bed. The college was located in New York State and had an excellent reputation as being one of the top women's colleges in the United States. The school offered a unique array of classes that prepared rich, young women on such courses as literature and fine arts; however, there were also classes on fashion, interior decorating, social graces, and fundraising and communication skills. The quaint New England campus had charming English Tudor-styled buildings.

Emily's mother had always dreamed of Emily attending this college. She was thrilled that all the arrangements had been made and that her Emily would be a "Sarah Lady." There had been no discussion about enrolling Emily in any other school. As Emily read the material enclosed, which included a shopping list of both appropriate clothing as well as school supplies, she began to cry. Once again, her life decisions were taken away from her with no regard for what she wanted to do.

Emily stared out her window at the graceful weeping willow as the tears rolled down her face. She was just like the tree—always swaying and bending to someone else's demands on who she was going to become. Tonight, she was going to stand up for herself for the first time. She knew that she did not have Isabel to support her. It was now up to her to make her thoughts and dreams known to her parents.

After the usual quiet dinner, Emily reached for the two large envelopes that she had set on the china cabinet. The one from Sarah Lawrence College had a large red X drawn across it. As her parents looked at her in surprise, Emily cleared her throat and began to speak. "I am aware that you took it upon yourselves to enroll me in a college that I have no desire to attend. Seeing that I am now close to becoming an adult, I assumed that I would at least have the courtesy of a discussion before you made commitments regarding my future. If you had been thoughtful enough to ask me where I wanted to attend college, I could have saved you a great deal of time and money. I do not intend to become a 'Sarah Lady.' I want more out of life than becoming a socially acceptable woman. I want to make a difference and to use my God-given talents. With that in mind, I have applied and been accepted at the University of Wisconsin in Madison. Here is the packet of information that you can both look over. If there are any further questions, I will be in my room." With her knees shaking, she stood up straight and proud, leaving her two shocked parents staring at the envelopes on the dining table.

She waited for them to come to her room to discuss the situation. Instead, after about an hour, she heard the car pull out of the garage. They had left her again. Emily felt alone and angry that night.

There were many debates, threats of not paying for college, arguments, and long periods of silence over the matter. Joyce explained that UW-Madison had a reputation for radical viewpoints. She did not think it was a place for a refined lady such as her daughter. Emily's father, who had graduated from UW-Madison, had less to say. He did tell her that the campus was huge, with miles of walking between classes. He told her he feared that she would simply become a number because of the thousands of students who attended the school.

It was not until the evening of graduation that Dr. Larson announced to their friends at the country club that Emily was going to attend UW-Madison. He boasted about her wanting to follow in his footsteps, as their friends looked on in shock. Emily sat there quietly as she watched her mother go from embarrassment to anger. Joyce had been talking about her Emily going to Sarah Lawrence College since she was a toddler. She often made snide remarks about those uncivilized public colleges. Once again, Emily had failed her. Well, at least with Emily away at school, Joyce could travel and visit her friends in Europe, leaving dreary Fergus Falls behind.

Chapter Two

Grace O'Malley

The O'Malleys had been married for one year when they moved into a little rented house across the street from and owned by Our Lady of Victory Catholic Church. Paul O'Malley had been hired as the custodian. He took loving care of the church, school, convent, and rectory buildings and grounds. His wife, Anna, was hired to cook and clean for the ten Franciscan Sisters who lived in the convent and ran the school. Anna had just given birth to a beautiful, curly-haired baby boy named Dennis Michael. The nuns allowed Anna to bring Dennis with her to the convent, where they loved to hold him while she cooked. He spent hours being rocked and sung to by all the nuns.

Within a short time, Anna announced that another O'Malley was on the way. The nuns were thrilled, knowing that there would be another baby for them to love. They assured Anna that she could continue to bring her children with her to the convent each day. The nuns gave prayers of thanksgiving. They immediately began to knit baby blankets, sweaters, hats, and booties. They were all convinced that God would bring them a little girl this time.

In the midst of a terrible snowstorm in December, Anna went into labor and realized that they would never make it to the hospital in time for the delivery. Paul ran across the street to fetch the nuns. On Sunday morning, a beautiful baby girl was ushered into the world by Sister Vincent and Sister Margaret Mary. She was born with a full head of bright, curly red hair and big blue eyes. As soon as everyone knew that baby and mother were fine, they gathered around the bed and said a prayer for the miracle of birth.

Paul asked Sister Vincent to name their tiny newborn daughter. Sister Vincent smiled, looking down at Anna and her healthy new daughter and said, "This child should be named Grace Marie because she has been born on Sunday morning just before Mass was to begin and during the time when the rosary was being prayed in church." With tears in her eyes, she hugged Paul and said, "You and Anna will never know all the joy that you have given to us. As nuns, we have given up the option of motherhood; yet through your wonderful family, we are given the chance to hold your children and love them in a very special way. You are all such a blessing to us."

So on that morning, little Grace Marie O'Malley entered the world, surrounded by love, blessings, and prayers of thanksgiving.

Grace was followed by two more sisters, Hope and Joy, and twin brothers, Luke and John. The O'Malley household was a busy swirl of activity filled with happy people. As soon as they were old enough, all of the children were given chores to do at home, church, and school. The nuns had a special place in their hearts for everyone in the family. They continued to knit sweaters, hats, mittens, and scarves each year for all the O'Malleys. Sister Ruth Ann taught all the children to play the piano. The nuns enjoyed tutoring each of the children as they went through school. Gifts the nuns received of food and money from families in the parish were often passed on to the O'Malleys.

Dennis became a skilled pianist by second grade. By the time he was in third grade, he was an altar boy, writing prayers and poems. The nuns adored him and often used his behavior as an example to others. Denny knew at a very early age that he was destined to become a priest.

Grace became the family's social butterfly. She loved to sing, dance, and entertain anyone she could capture. Her high-spirited, generous manner and contagious giggle made Grace easy to instantly like. Grace loved being the center of attention. She was fearless when it came to reciting verses or speaking before a crowd. She was often restless and the first to volunteer for anything that would get her away from her desk.

A globe was her favorite toy. She would sit and dream about all the adventures that were ahead of her. There was never a doubt in her mind that all of her dreams would come true. When she was in fifth grade, Grace wrote a play about a little girl who sneaks onto a ship and goes around the world meeting children her own age. Sister Francis was so impressed with it that she helped to produce the play, called *Grace around the World*, for the parents at the annual end-of-the-school-year party. All the classes selected a country. They learned about the country's customs and history. Grace smiled as her words became real that night.

The nuns adored Grace; however, they often found that she needed more discipline than the other children did. Grace became the topic of many of the nuns' conversations. They would laugh about her bold and brave love of life. Sister Margaret Mary had taken a special interest in her. She secretly prayed that someday Grace would become a nun. Sister Vincent also prayed for Grace; her prayer was that Grace would always keep her delightful love for adventures and that she would always be happy and fulfilled and bring joy to others.

On a steamy, hot day in July 1953, the normal life that the O'Malleys had known abruptly changed. It was just before noon, and Anna was packing a picnic lunch for their family afternoon outing to Pebble Lake. Suddenly Dennis came running into the kitchen. He had a panicked look on his face as he said, "There is something really wrong with Hope. She told me not to say something, but Mom, I am scared. She looks like she is very sick, and now her whole body is shaking. I know she doesn't want to ruin the day at the lake. Please just go look at her, and I will finish getting our things together."

Anna found Hope lying on the floor in the living room in the midst of a seizure. Denny immediately ran across the street to fetch his father at church. After he found him, he ran to the convent and asked Sister Margaret Mary to come home with him. Denny started to pray as he ran back to the house with Sister Margaret Mary right behind him.

Within minutes, Paul, Anna, and Hope were driving to Lake Regional Hospital. Anna held Hope tightly in her arms as she watched her daughter becoming weaker by the moment. It was after midnight when Paul and Anna returned home to find all the children and Sister Margaret Mary kneeling in their living room, praying the rosary. Paul cried as he told them the doctors advised them that Hope had spinal polio, a terrible disease that everyone feared. Although the doctors felt she was going to be okay, Hope was going to stay in the hospital for a few more days.

Within the next week, one by one, each of the O'Malley children came down with spinal polio. They were terrified as to who would be the next polio victim. Paul and Anna decided that it was best for one of them to be at the hospital while the other stayed at home with the children, who were now starting to recover. They felt completely helpless as they watched their children suffer with high fevers, constant muscle cramping, and extreme pain in all of their muscles and joints.

At the end of the day, Anna spent hours praying, begging God to be merciful and to heal her children. She cried herself to sleep night after night, convinced that they had done something horribly wrong to deserve this terrible plague that had come to them. When Paul was not working, he often found himself staring at the little faces of his innocent children. His prayer was always the same. He asked God to take him and leave his children alone. He became angrier with each trip he made to the hospital. He went from being a carefree guy to a man with a short temper.

He slammed his car door on a regular basis. He no longer had patience for anything. One day, in a fit of rage, he threw a screwdriver across a room, nearly hitting Sister Francis. Finally, Sister Vincent confronted Paul. She told him, "We all feel your pain. We have no way to truly understand all the emotions that you are faced with each day. However, we need you to keep your temper under control. The sisters are concerned but also a little frightened by your constant outbursts. How can we help you? We are praying for you, but it is obvious that you need more from us. Perhaps you need to stay home with your family for a while until you can cope with the pressures."

Paul now feared that he might lose his job on top of all the other chaos that was going on in his life. He promised Sister Vincent that he would continue to work. He went to the convent to apologize to the sisters for making them feel uncomfortable. So Paul learned to keep all his rage inside of himself and began to shut out the world, including Anna.

No one in the O'Malley house slept through the night. Paul or Anna were constantly checking on the children to make sure they were okay. Each of the children lay awake in bed, fearing that if they fell asleep, they would wake up paralyzed. As each child was released from the hospital, a new routine started. Vials of medicine took up one whole shelf in the refrigerator. Anna learned to inject their tiny bodies three times each day. The dining room table was turned into a place where steaming hot towels were wrapped around their arms and legs while hours of painful exercises were done.

Their happy home quickly became a quiet, sad place to live. There was a smell of sickness in the air as everyone struggled to get through the day. None of the children complained because they all knew their brothers and sisters were living with the same searing pain that ripped through every muscle in their bodies. In the still of the night, you could hear the whispers of prayers, the clicking of rosary beads, and tears, each of them praying for a better tomorrow.

Each new case of polio was more serious than the previous one. Grace had been in the hospital for two days when she pleaded with her parents to take her home. The entire time she was in the hospital, she was determined that she would not sleep. She had seen too many kids in her ward wake up in the morning and be told that they were paralyzed. She was not going to allow this to happen to her. For hours at a time, she lay in her bed constantly moving her legs and feet. She vowed that this polio would not bring her down. She knew she needed to be strong.

The same day she came home from the hospital, an ambulance arrived to take her baby brother John late that night. Grace sat on Denny's bed, crying and asking him why God was being so cruel to them. Denny simply put his arms around Grace and told her that they needed to pray for John. They spent the night praying and looking out the window, waiting for their parents to come home.

At about three o'clock in the morning, Denny started to cough. He did not seem to be able to catch his breath and was suddenly burning up with fever. His arms and legs began shaking uncontrollably. Grace brought him a glass of water and held his hand, as he seemed to become sicker within minutes. She remembered how wonderful the cold washcloths in the hospital felt as she laid one on his forehead. She kept running back and forth, trying to keep Denny cool.

An hour later, the exhausted O'Malleys pulled into their driveway. Sister Ruth Ann was asleep in Paul's chair in the living room. The back door opened as Grace came running to them, shouting to them to come quickly. Denny was now sicker than any of them had been.

Once again, the ambulance pulled up in front of the O'Malleys' house. The nuns ran over to see what they could do to help and watched Denny being carried down the front stairs on a stretcher. Grace walked next to him, determined to stay with her big brother. She asked him if there was anything she could do for him. He looked at her and asked her to go to his room and bring his favorite statue of Jesus, which he kept on his nightstand. In pain, she ran back in the house to retrieve the statue. As she gently placed it in Denny's hand, for the first time in her life, she told him that she loved him. She cried as she told Denny to keep moving his feet and that he would be okay. As the ambulance pulled away, Grace sat on the front porch sobbing.

Despite the health warnings, the nuns took turns staying with the O'Malley children. They prepared their meals, read to them, and prayed with them while Paul and Anna stayed at the hospital. Everyone else was terrified to enter the house with the large, bright orange quarantine sign on the front and back doors.

It was dinnertime when the O'Malleys pulled into their driveway. Except this time, neither Paul nor Anna got out of the car. Instead, they sat in the front seat hugging each other. Finally, they came into the house. Before they could say a word, Grace knew that Denny had died. She felt the loss deep inside of her weak little body. Paul sat in his chair by the fireplace and wept uncontrollably. Anna sat in her chair next to him and simply stared down at her hands. The children were very quiet as they waited for their parents to talk to them.

After what seemed like hours but was just a few minutes, Anna raised her head and gathered the children around her. She spoke in a whisper as she told them that Denny had gone to heaven to be with Jesus and the angels. She told them to go get their rosaries. Once they had come together again, they marched across the street in silence and into the dark church. Each of them lit a candle and then proceeded to go to the front of the empty, dark church. Kneeling side by side, they began to recite their prayers. Their sobs mingled as their prayers echoed through the church. Silently, the nuns came into the church and knelt beside the O'Malleys. They joined them in prayers as their tears also flowed.

The health department called Paul O'Malley to inform him that none of the children were allowed to attend Denny's funeral services because of the quarantine restrictions. Any violation of the quarantine would result in a $500 fine and possible quarantine of others who were exposed to them during the service. He also mentioned that the health department was aware of the nuns entering their house. Unless he wanted to see the convent quarantined, this was to cease immediately. Paul wondered how much more any of them could take without breaking down completely. However, he knew that he needed to comply.

With great pain, he told his children that they would not be attending Denny's funeral. After that, he went to the convent and told the nuns that they were no longer able to visit his home. Sister Vincent was outraged and said, "Nothing will keep me from being with your family. We are called by God to aid the sick, and I, for one, will continue to visit. I cannot in good conscience stay away from them when I know how much suffering is going on in your house right now. I will accept whatever punishment the health department doles out. I will inform them that this is my decision and no one else's."

Paul told her that if she did come into their house, it was possible that their entire convent would be placed in quarantine. If that happened, the school would not be allowed to open in September. He could not bear that guilt. And so, all the nuns promised to obey his wishes. They told him that every evening at six o'clock, they would hold a one-hour prayer vigil for the O'Malleys. No one could stop them from doing that.

No one knew what to say to the O'Malleys or how to comfort them. Their kitchen overflowed with food that was left on their front porch. The family sat at the kitchen table hugging each other in silence, looking at Denny's empty chair. Each one of them felt that it should have been them, not Denny, to have died. He was the "good" one. He was the one who did everything the right way and for the right reasons. He was their protector. He was the older brother that they all looked up to and admired.

Each of them in their own silent way became angry with God. They all questioned the injustice of Denny's death, but none of them were brave enough to say it. Each one of them tried to heal themselves and be strong for the others. Deep, throbbing pain ripped through everyone and every room of the little house. None of them could think that they would ever find happiness or laughter again. The O'Malleys were locked into a soul-wrenching sorrow.

It was as though all of the joy had been sucked out of the O'Malleys' once-cheerful home. Paul walked around in a daze. He would sit for hours in his chair in the living room staring at nothing. Anyone who looked at him instantly knew that this was a broken man. Anna clung to her children and cried herself to sleep most nights. All of the children were afraid to be happy or to have any fun, fearing that it was disrespectful to Denny's memory. The once noisy, busy house was now still.

Finally, Grace felt the strong need to bring some happiness back to all of them. She started writing songs and poems; some of them were about Denny. They knew that they were all in quarantine until at least the middle of October. Grace started to play the piano again. At first, she sang old church hymns; but after a while, she started singing more upbeat songs that she had heard on the radio. Slowly, her brothers and sisters started to join her in the living room to sing and play the piano. Paul was the only one who simply could not bring himself back from his deep grief. When the singing began, he would quietly leave and sit on the back porch, always alone.

School assignments for each of the children were put in their mailbox on the front porch each day. Before bed each evening, their completed lessons were returned to the mailbox, where they were picked up by one of the nuns. The children often sat on the front porch watching the kids come and go to school. They watched sadly as the students poured onto the playground for recess. Each of them wondered if life would ever be normal for them again.

The first week in October, the health department truck pulled up in front of their house. Four men wearing gloves, masks, and white coveralls walked up to the front porch and told the children to go in the house. Mrs. O'Malley had been expecting them. She held the front door open, knowing that what was going to happen would be another painful experience for her children.

The men carried large boxes with the same ugly, orange quarantine label on the sides of each box. Without a word, they moved from room to room taking all the drapes, bedding, towels, and children's toys. At last, they came back into the living room, where the children were all huddled together on the sofa. The bigger man asked them to move from the sofa. He then ripped off all of the slipcovers that Anna had spent hours making last year. The last thing they took was all the living room drapes. The children watched in sheer terror from the window as the men quickly left the front porch, ripping the bright orange quarantine signs from the front and back doors of the house. They threw the signs, gloves, and masks into the large boxes as they walked back to their truck.

Their home felt cold and violated. Anna gathered the children as she tried to comfort them. She explained that this was the only way that it could be done. She told them that everything that had been taken was going to be burned so that the bad germs would never hurt them or anyone else again. When Paul came home that night, he found them still sitting together on the sofa, holding each other as they sobbed. He, too, was heartbroken once again. He felt he was a failure, unable to protect his family from all the pain they were going through.

Anna called to confirm that her family could now go about their everyday life. The nuns arrived with boxes of linens, towels, and material for Anna to use for new drapes. They had also brought a small stuffed animal for each of the children, knowing that it could never make up for their loss but hoping it might help ease their pain.

All of them celebrated the next evening with a big bowl of popcorn and ice-cold root beer. That evening after everyone was asleep, Grace quietly tiptoed out of bed. She got the flashlight from her desk and opened the small door behind her bed. There, in a little crawl space, she had made a pretend house for her dolls with a child-size table with two chairs and her favorite tea set. She sat at the table, which was too small for her, and cried. The next morning, she took her two sisters to the secret playroom. They vowed to never tell anyone about this special room or the four dolls that had survived the men in white. It would be their secret forever.

The following Monday morning, the O'Malley children were dressed and ready to leave for school almost an hour early. Grace, Hope, and Joy wore their uniforms, while Luke wore new navy blue pants and a white shirt. John was still too sick to go to school and required daily physical therapy. They raced across the street as soon as they saw their friends. All of them were met with looks of terror. Their old friends turned and ran away from them.

Anna and Johnny sat on the front porch watching the painful reentry. Anna knew that there would be more pain on the way. It did not take long for all the O'Malley kids to realize that no one was going to play with them. By lunchtime, they were back home crying and asking why people were being so mean to them. It took almost a year before the children were able to reconnect with a few friends.

Grace decided that she was simply not going to let a few stupid people get in her way. She was determined to be happy. Convinced that Denny was now her personal angel, she felt strong and nothing was going to stop her! At the tender age of eight, she had learned life lessons that gave her a wisdom that few girls at her age could understand. She felt his presence as she prayed every day for patience and the ability to forgive all the hateful girls in her class.

Sister Vincent's heart ached for her. The two of them spent hours talking about Grace's fears and dreams. Grace took up Sister Rose's generous offer for private voice lessons. Within a short time, Sister Rose realized that Grace had a beautiful alto voice. She encouraged Grace to sing often. Grace found that singing brought some happiness back into the O'Malleys' quiet house.

Grace realized that she not only enjoyed singing, but that she really liked being in front of a crowd of people. She was faithful in practicing each day, and within a short time had a large variety of songs that she knew by heart. She sang religious songs for weddings and funerals, as well as popular songs that she heard on the radio. Grace brought the entire audience to tears as she dedicated her eighth-grade graduation song to her brother Denny and then sang "You'll Never Walk Alone." She received her first standing ovation that evening. In her heart, she knew she had found something that would make her feel special. She was starting to feel healed finally; she was finding joy again.

The following year, she went to Fergus Falls High School and felt overwhelmed at the size of the school. She studied hard and received good grades, but never really felt as though she belonged there. Grace longed for Our Lady of Victory with its small classes and all the nuns who loved her. Just before Christmas vacation, the choir director asked her if she was interested in joining a quartet with three other freshman girls. She quickly jumped at the chance to do what she loved most. Quickly, she discovered that the girls not only sang well together but also enjoyed each other.

SOLA became their nickname. They went on to win competitions and had so many trophies and awards that the school put up a special display case just for them. The girls sang at all the concerts and school plays. Grace loved every minute of it.

Grace became very close to Emily, officially her best friend. She loved to sit in Emily's designer bedroom, dreaming of being a star on Broadway. The girls went to the Fergus Theater almost every Saturday afternoon. They saw *Singing in the Rain* six times. As they walked home, Grace started singing and dancing on and off the street curb. She knew Debbie Reynolds's part by heart, convinced that it would be her first acting role on Broadway. She even had her hair cut and styled to look more like Miss Reynolds. With her curly auburn hair, big blue eyes, and freckles, she grew cuter each day. Her perky manners endeared her to everyone she met. She soon discovered that she was truly enjoying life again and knew that Denny would be happy for her. Life was now full of possibilities.

During her high school graduation ceremony, Grace once again brought tears to everyone's eyes as she sang "To Dream the Impossible Dream." Graduation was a bittersweet event for Grace. She knew that her family had no money for her to go to college. In fact, they were counting on her to keep her job at Claire's Dress Shop to help pay some of their bills.

Right after graduation, Emily was leaving for a month of touring Europe. Both Lindy and Rebecca were heading off to college in late August. Her parents had told Grace that it was foolish to be a dreamer. Now, she needed to accept the realities of life. Her life was not like her fancy friends'; her life was going to be one of hard work. If she worked hard, she could save a little money for some nice things; however, she would probably never be able to afford the clothes and lifestyle that Emily Larson enjoyed.

One night her mother sat with her at the kitchen table and told her that perhaps it was best that the girls were all leaving. Now she could start accepting her lot in life and find some ordinary happiness. Grace knew in her heart that she would never settle for ordinary. She was determined to hold onto her dreams. Ordinary was simply not an option for Grace O'Malley.

Chapter Three

Lindy Pulaski

Lindy arrived in this world full of noise, surrounded by a family that knew from the start that she was special. Loretta and Lenny Pulaski had been happily married for twenty-five years. As Loretta told everyone, this baby was her change-of-life surprise. Lindy was warmly welcomed by big brother, Lenny Jr., who was seventeen and graduating from high school the next year. He planned to join the air force the day after graduation. Also in the bedroom was a very mature twelve-year-old Lana, named after the movie star Lana Turner. Next to Lana stood Grandma Flo, who lived with them. She did all the cooking for the family.

Everyone seemed to be talking at once. All of them were thinking about how life would be changing because of the tiny baby girl with a full head of black hair. Dr. Beal filled out all the paperwork and returned to the bedroom asking the baby's name. Loretta and Lenny both said at the same time, "Lindy," as they started to laugh. They told Dr. Beal that the Lindy dance was their favorite dance and they had decided to use the name whether it was a boy or a girl.

The Pulaski family owned and ran the Fresh Daisy Dry Cleaners and Laundry. The business occupied the first floor. They lived in the apartment upstairs. Everyone in the family worked in the business. Lenny Sr. was up each morning at four o'clock cleaning the laundry and starting up the presses. Loretta and the kids were up by five o'clock helping to get the dry cleaning ready for the customers. By seven o'clock, they all came back upstairs for Grandma's morning breakfast before the kids went off to school.

It was a simple and good life. There was enough money for the basics, though not much left over for anything else. The one thing they all had in common was they were all "big size" people, as Loretta liked to say. Rather than trying to hide her 250 pounds, Loretta chose to advertise it with brightly colored clothes that always seemed to sparkle. Everything about Loretta was big—her coal-black hair, her earrings and jewelry, and her laugh. She told anyone who stopped to listen that she was a big lady with a big love of life. In Fergus Falls, some people called her a character. Almost everyone grew to love the family.

Within a few days after her birth, Lindy arrived in the laundry, sleeping in a wicker wash basket with Grandma Flo's homemade quilt wrapped around her. Loretta set her on the counter for everyone to see. She already had her tiny ears pierced and was dressed in a frilly pink outfit. All day, the customers came to pick up their clothes and coo over the pretty baby girl. Grandma Flo even made some of her special cookies to celebrate the arrival of Lindy.

One day turned into another, always the same routine. Grandma Flo grew older and slower. Lenny Jr. enlisted in the air force and was stationed in Biloxi, Mississippi. He came home twice a year, which always meant big parties and lots of food. Lana was now a senior in high school and planning on going to beauty school in Fargo, North Dakota, in September with her two best friends.

Grandma Flo often got Lindy dressed up and would take her shopping downtown. She showed Lindy off to anyone she could stop. Grandma Flo adored her spirited granddaughter. She spoiled her with ribbons, bows, and special clothes that she sewed just for her. Grandma would cuddle with Lindy after her bath, sprinkling her with special lavender talcum powder. She would lie on Lindy's bed and tell her stories about the old country. By the time Lindy was four years old, she was singing songs in Polish. Grandma and Lindy often danced to folk songs from the old country, laughing as they spun around in circles. On Lindy's fifth birthday, Grandma Flo had a stroke and never came home from the hospital.

A few weeks after the funeral, Lindy came home from kindergarten to find a bright pink bedroom that was now hers. At first, she jumped with joy. Then she felt guilty about being happy to have Grandma's old room. Lindy decided that she would share the room with Grandma's spirit. Many nights, Lindy lay in bed talking to Grandma about her day.

She always felt the warm presence of her loving Grandma in that room. It was her secret.

By the time Lindy was in grade school, she knew the words to many of the popular country-western songs that she heard on the radio. The radio was turned on from early morning to late at night. It was funny to see this seven-year-old girl with long, curly black hair singing as though she was on the stage of the Grand Ole Opry. She entertained the customers on a daily basis. It never crossed her mind to worry about being shy or embarrassed. She loved to sing more than anything else. She had already developed her own style in clothes, which was just as bright and sparkling as her mom's wardrobe. The customers were truly impressed with her talents and told her so on a regular basis. Soon, the customers started requesting a favorite song while they waited for their clothes. Lindy felt loved and totally accepted at Fresh Daisy Dry Cleaners and Laundry.

Before too long, Loretta was making western style costumes for her daughter. They even saved enough money to purchase bright red cowgirl boots for her. Lindy began to sing at summer concerts. She entered the contest at the state fair when she was eight years old, coming in third place. From then on, each year she won first place as she worked on perfecting her style. She was a mini version of Dolly Parton, except her hair was black instead of blonde. Lindy was a talented and fiery little girl. Each year her hair got bigger and more rhinestones appeared on her outfits.

By the time she entered high school, everyone knew Lindy, her talents and her wacky personality. It did not come as a surprise when the choral director asked her to join a girl's quartet. What did surprise Lindy was the lecture she received on being a team player. It was made very clear to her that this quartet would be a place where all the girls would showcase their talents. It took Lindy a little while to adjust to not being the star of the show.

She quickly discovered that the friendships of Emily, Grace, and Rebecca were far more important than the spotlight. It was the first time she had close girlfriends, and she enjoyed every minute of it. On their sleepovers at Emily's house, Lindy would bring her bags filled with makeup and hair supplies. By the end of the night, all four girls had Lindy's big hair, bright blue eye shadow, and rings on every finger. They would dance around Emily's bedroom, singing and laughing.

The girls of SOLA had grown to be such good friends that when they started dating, they promised to get an okay from the other girls before going out. They all agreed that Friday night was their sleepover girls' night and Saturday was date night. They often would go out with their dates as a group. Most Sunday afternoons, they talked about their dates while they studied and practiced their songs.

Lindy told the girls all about the facts of life. She gave them graphic details about her dates, which sent them all into fits of giggles. Lindy dated a few boys but found that most of them were too afraid of her wild style to ask her out. She preferred to have many good friends that were boys instead of boyfriends. Anyway, she knew that she was destined for fame and did not want to be attached to anyone that she might have to leave behind.

Lindy surprised everyone by being an A+ student. She excelled in math and science classes. She knew that money was always tight around the laundry and had given up any hopes of going to college. Just before Thanksgiving of her senior year, the principal called her to his office. When she arrived, Loretta and Lenny were already there. At first, she thought something had happened to her brother. However, when she saw her mom wink at her, Lindy knew it was good news.

The principal stood up, shook Lindy's hand, and informed her that she had received a full scholarship to Mankato State University. The Pulaskis beamed with pride as they hugged each other. Lindy would be the first Pulaski to go to college. They knew that she would succeed at whatever she put her mind to. Lindy was excited about the promise of a new adventure. There would be no stopping her now. Mankato be warned, Lindy was on the way!

Chapter Four

Rebecca DuPree

People often described Monica DuPree as quiet, hard working, and a good student. She had a contagious laugh, gentle smile, and easygoing nature. She lived at home with her mother, Ruby, who had been widowed for many years.

Tim Meyer came from one of the most influential families in Fergus Falls. They owned most of the apartment buildings in town and had recently built a large apartment complex for senior citizens. Tim was the star quarterback on the Otters' football team. Monica and Tim had been a couple for more than a year. They had become inseparable. During their senior prom, they had sex for the first and only time. Monica considered herself a "good girl" with high morals. However, after a few drinks of rum and cola, they gave into their strong desires for each other. They truly believed that they were in love. Monica knew that Tim would soon be going away to school. She was going to Fergus Falls Junior College for two years. Then she hoped to join Tim in Minneapolis at the university.

Two months later, on Monica's eighteenth birthday, the family doctor confirmed what she already knew. She was pregnant. Tim had left for early enrollment at the University of Minnesota, where he had a full scholarship for football. He left without knowing about the baby. After weeks of torment, Monica finally broke down and told her mom her secret. Monica was quickly sent to Fargo to live with her Aunt Trudy until the baby was born. Plans were made to give the baby up for adoption.

In a few short months, Monica's calm world was turned upside down. Her plans for college and to become a teacher were gone. Her boyfriend, whom she thought she loved, had just sent her a letter telling her that he would probably not be back home all year and wishing her well in her future pursuits. She was alone and terrified. As she grew larger with the baby, she started to love this little person growing inside her. By the time Monica went into labor, she knew that she would be keeping the baby. She was determined to love and provide a good life for her child.

Rebecca was born six weeks early. Her first few days were touch and go. The doctors did not offer much hope because of the baby's serious heart and lung problems. Monica's mother, Ruby, and Aunt Trudy both tried to tell Monica that it might be best if the baby did not survive. Monica could then resume her life, and no one would ever know about the disgrace to the family name.

Monica prayed for her tiny daughter to fight and live. She promised God that she would dedicate herself to this child if she survived. Each day, the baby grew stronger. Her cheeks grew a little pinker every day. Finally, after three weeks, a nurse asked Monica what the baby's name was so they could put it on her tiny crib. Without a second thought, Monica named her daughter Rebecca Ann DuPree. She wanted her daughter to have a strong, noble name. She was convinced that Rebecca would survive. She also knew that God would make her keep her promise to become a caring mother to this fragile child.

After several emotionally charged arguments, Monica and her mother took Rebecca home to Fergus Falls. At first, Ruby insisted that they make up a story about Monica marrying a boy just before he left for Vietnam. After a proper period of time, they would tell everyone that her husband had been killed in the war; however, Monica refused to lie. She decided that the truth would just have to be good enough. If people were going to judge her, she would accept their harsh remarks and move on. Ruby, Monica, and Rebecca settled into their new life in the tiny little house on Bancroft Street.

The day they came home, the neighbors surprised Monica with a baby shower. Once the gifts were opened and the cake and coffee served, Monica knew in her heart that she had made the right decision. That evening after everyone was in bed, she wrote a letter to Tim. She told him about the baby and how much she loved her. She enclosed a photo of herself and Rebecca in the hospital. Monica told Tim that he was under no obligation to them, but that she hoped he would come and visit soon.

Two weeks later, she received a large envelope from a lawyer's office in Minneapolis. The letter stated that they represented Mr. Timothy Meyer. There was an offer for a payment of $40,000 if the enclosed papers were signed, which would release all parental rights of Mr. Meyers to the child named Rebecca DuPree. It further stated that if Monica agreed to this payment, there would be no future contact with Mr. Meyer under any circumstances. As Monica read the documents, it was apparent that she should take the money and sign the papers. Rebecca's life would be far better off with the two women who had grown to adore her.

The next day, she mailed back the signed papers and put copies in her little metal box for safekeeping. A few weeks later, the cashier's check arrived. Monica took the check to the bank and opened two accounts. Half the money went for an educational account so Rebecca would be able to go to college. The other half would take care of them until Monica could find a job to support the DuPree women. As she walked home, she knew that life was going to be okay.

Life turned into a simple kind of happiness for the DuPree women. Their neighbors, the Newtons, adored little Rebecca and spoiled her with surprise gifts and lots of attention. She was the little girl they never had. Rebecca grew into a younger version of Monica, with long, pale blonde hair and dark green eyes. She was often sick. By the age of five, she had been hospitalized several times with severe asthma attacks. Because of her health problems, she spent most of her time in the house. She was not able to keep up playing with the neighborhood kids. She could not ride a bike or run any distance without becoming winded and needing to rest.

During one of her hospital stays, a nurse suggested to Monica that when Rebecca started having an asthma attack, she should take her into the bathroom and turn on a hot shower to produce steam, and then start singing songs that Rebecca knew. Many times, this could get the child's mind off the breathing struggles and get her back into a stable breathing pattern.

Monica took the nurse's advice. Much to her surprise, it worked. Soon the Newtons listened as Monica and Rebecca sang at the top of their voices. Rebecca connected singing with feeling better. For Rebecca's seventh birthday, Lee and Sylvia Newton gave her singing lessons with the choir director from their church. Once a week, little Rebecca went for her lesson and enjoyed every minute of it. It was the one thing she discovered that she did well.

By the time she was ready for high school, she was singing in two choirs and was often the soloist at several of the local churches. People were always amazed at the strong and beautiful voice that came out of the tiny little girl with the soulful green eyes. Although Rebecca was comfortable singing in front of anyone, she was terribly shy when it came to any other kind of social situation. She did well in school, but never raised her hand. She often had to stay in during recess, which meant that she never made friends.

At home, from the time she could remember, Rebecca was treated more like an adult than a child. Her grandmother, Ruby, often remarked that she was an old spirit trapped in a little girl's body. She was mature beyond her years. Each year she became more shy and reserved. She even dressed different from the other girls in her class. Instead of the latest fashions, she often wore her mother's sweaters, which were many sizes too big for her, and long skirts that sometimes touched the floor. Her dull colored clothes made it seem as though she simply was not even there—invisible and a loner.

Rebecca dreaded going to Fergus Falls High School. She had been happy to sit in her classes at Adams Grade School, where she could fade into the corner, unnoticed by the world. She knew that would be more difficult in high school. She was so nervous about going to high school that she had a serious asthma attack. Monica rushed her to the hospital for breathing treatments. The attack was so serious that Rebecca missed her entire first week of school. To make matters worse, because she had missed school orientation, she always seemed to be lost and was often late to class. She was miserable.

Monica finally had a heart-to-heart talk with Rebecca. She encouraged Rebecca to audition for the school choral group and told her that it was time for her to make some friends. Rebecca was quickly welcomed into the choral group. At last, she felt as though she had found a place where she could belong. Every day, she came out of her shell of shyness a little more. Within a month, the choral director invited Rebecca to consider joining the girls' quartet that was being formed. That was the turning point—the day life changed for Rebecca.

For the first time in her life, Rebecca had girlfriends—friends who taught her how to laugh at herself, how to be silly, how to have fun, and how to share. The girls of SOLA bonded together in song. Quickly they became each other's best friends. Rebecca shared her secrets with Lindy, Emily, and Grace. She became the closest to Grace. She loved going over to Grace's house, which was filled with people and noise. Grace and Rebecca often slept over at Emily's house, in a bedroom that looked as though it was decorated from a magazine. Often, when they walked home the next morning, Grace and Rebecca compared their own tiny bedrooms with the beauty of Emily's and Lindy's.

Rebecca never felt poor, just not rich. Grace would often complain about her father and his constant bouts with depression. Rebecca would tell her that she often fantasized about what her father looked like. She dreamed that some day he would come to see her. He would shower her with gifts and take her on expensive vacations, while constantly apologizing for being such a jerk to her and her mother.

Emily passed her clothes on to Rebecca after she had outgrown them. They all teased Rebecca about her tiny size 4 clothes and the little shoes that she wore. Rebecca sang her heart out with the girls. She had finally found some happiness. Both her mother and grandmother felt relieved that Rebecca had learned how to laugh and be silly. Her grades were great, her singing grew stronger, and they were optimistic for Rebecca.

There had been no conversations regarding Rebecca's dad. Monica had been honest with her. On Rebecca's sixteenth birthday, she asked her mother once more about her father. Monica went and brought back the metal box. She handed it to Rebecca and allowed her to read all of the papers. When she was done, Rebecca simply closed the box and handed it back to Monica.

The box contained photographs of the two of them dressed up for the prom. There were a few cards and notes that Tim had sent to Monica. All the legal documents and the request that she never contact Tim were also there. Rebecca read them all through her tears. She stared at the prom photo for a long time before placing it back in the metal box. Rebecca turned to her mother and gave her a hug. She told her that now she knew what a cold and heartless father she had. She promised herself that she would never give him another moment of thought.

During her senior year, she received a full scholarship to the Music Conservancy at St. Catherine College. Grandma Ruby and Monica were so incredibly proud of all that Rebecca had achieved. They knew that God had truly blessed Monica's decision to keep the fragile baby girl eighteen years before.

Tim Meyer stood in the back of the auditorium. Married for almost ten years and the father of two very spoiled sons, he rarely came to Fergus Falls. He had made his fortune the same way as his father—in real estate. He had never felt any desire to get in touch with the daughter he had never met. His mother's funeral was the only reason he was in town. He had read in the *Daily Journal* about the graduation. There was a photograph and a small article about Rebecca DuPree. It announced her full scholarship. He felt that he just needed to see what she looked like.

So there he stood in the back of the auditorium, watching his only daughter receive her diploma. She received applause from people who clearly adored her. She had her mother's beautiful, long, silky hair and smile. Tim was shocked as the tears started to run down his cheeks. He quickly turned to leave when he saw Monica sitting with her mother. She turned looking for someone, and for a brief moment, their eyes met. She looked at him as a stranger, and then turned to wave at a friend. Tim walked away slowly, leaving the daughter he had chosen never to know.

Turning in her seat, Monica's heart was beating fast. She had immediately recognized Tim. All of the past surfaced as she sat there trying to reclaim her composure. *Why was he here? What did he want? Why did it still ache to see his face after all these years?*

Tim left town the next day. However, before he left, he drove slowly down Bancroft Street past the little yellow house where he knew Monica had raised their daughter. They were standing out in the backyard talking with the neighbors as he drove past. He knew that he had no right to stop. He also knew that because he had finally seen his daughter, he would never be the same. The guilt that he thought he had erased was now back in full force. He would never know her, see her smile, or hear her laugh. He realized that this was the price he paid for his selfish decision as a self-centered young man so many years ago.

Chapter Five

Going Away

Shortly after graduation, Emily was whisked off to Europe, much to her chagrin. All she really wanted to do was stay home. She longed to enjoy her last summer in Fergus Falls with her three best friends. She wanted to lie on the beach at Pebble Lake, where the girls would spend hours gossiping about their classmates, dreaming about the men that would capture their hearts, and making plans to travel together after college. Instead, she was going to spend time in London, Paris, and Oslo. Going to visit Isabel for one week while her parents went on a yacht with some friends was the only thing she looked forward to doing.

The vacation proved to be a total bore for Emily. She often stayed with strangers while her parents partied. She felt out of place, lonely, and unwanted. She begged her father to allow her to go back home, where she could start to prepare for college. She was told that her clothes had been purchased and arrangements had been made to have everything she needed delivered to her dorm room in time for her arrival. Quietly Emily passed each day away, dreaming of the freedom and friends she would develop at the University of Wisconsin in Madison. She was anxious for her new life to begin without the constant interference of her parents. She counted the days until she would go to visit Isabel, knowing that after her visit she would be flying home. She had two weeks at home before leaving for Madison and her new beginning.

Emily was greeted at the airport with homemade signs and a small group of strangers. In the front of the group stood Isabel, who quickly ran to Emily. Both of them felt the immediate connection to their past together. Isabel proudly introduced Emily to her brother, his family, and a good-looking man named Rolf. It was obvious that Isabel and Rolf had already become a couple.

The week was a whirlwind of sightseeing, eating, and laughing. Emily went to bed each evening exhausted. She was happier than she had been in a long time. From the mountains to the fjords, Norway was incredibly beautiful. Everywhere she went, Emily found the people were warm and welcoming. She quickly fell in love with their simple lifestyle and their small, colorful houses. The week flew by much too quickly. Before she knew it, she was back at the airport leaving for her flight back to the United States.

Isabel and Emily cried as they hugged each other. Isabel spoke softly. "Oh my sweet Emily, it is so hard to leave you again. However, now I know that you are a strong and wonderful woman. I know we will be miles apart, but remember you can always call me. I am so grateful that you have discovered yourself and your many talents. Now it is time for you to go have fun, learn new exciting things, and treasure who you are. My dear child, you deserve happiness. Go find it and enjoy the life you have been given. Hopefully, every once in a while, you will write me and let me know how life is treating you."

Both of them knew that this time, they would be parting for good. Each of them was headed to a new life, miles and miles apart. The only difference was that now Emily knew that Isabel was happy. She was exactly where she should be. Emily asked Isabel, "Promise me that you will also find happiness and that you will invite me to your wedding, whenever that takes place."

On the flight home, Emily knew that she had just closed a chapter in her life. Isabel would never be a part of it again. However, she had no regrets. She would be forever grateful for all the love, care, and time Isabel had given to her. Now it was time to grow up and move on to college.

After a long flight, followed by a two-hour limo ride from Minneapolis to Fergus Falls, Emily stepped out of the car and into the arms of Grace, Lindy, and Rebecca. The girls planned to spend the last two weeks of the summer together. They slept over in Emily's room every night and were inseparable. They laughed, giggled, and teased each other. Occasionally, they started crying at the thought of how much they were going to miss each other. It was difficult to imagine a day without the four of them being together. Sharing their life secrets had become an important part of their friendship. In many ways, they were closer to each other than sisters were.

Emily, Lindy, and Rebecca went shopping for the last few things on their school list, while Grace tagged along in silence. Grace had taken the time off work so she could spend the time with them. However, she was shocked at how painful it was for her. Each night when they went to bed, she cried herself to sleep. Life without the Sisterhood was going to be impossible.

Lindy and Rebecca also had mixed feelings about leaving behind the comforts and love of their homes. Rebecca had her first argument with her mother when she announced, instead of asking, that she was staying at Emily's house the last two weeks before leaving for school. Both her mother and grandmother were hurt. Rather than making a scene, they told themselves that it was time they get used to not having Rebecca around. Lindy's parents had already gone through leaving-the-nest behavior with their two older children. They tried to understand that Lindy needed to be with her friends, but they also felt hurt. Lindy had always been the center of their attention. She had given them both so much joy. They were going to miss her loud music and singing at all hours of the day and night.

Before they knew it, the two weeks had gone by and they were spending their last night together. They had spent days at Pebble Lake getting great tans. They partied at Ottertail Lake with their other classmates and drank their first beers. Their last evening together was bittersweet. Emily had ordered a special meal from the Chinese restaurant. She chilled two bottles of wine for them to celebrate. They all decided to dress up for the evening in their prom dresses. As each of them entered the dining room, lit by candlelight, Emily greeted each of them with a long-stemmed yellow rose, a symbol of friendship. Gently she placed a small tiara made of rhinestones on each of their heads.

They sat at the table in silence for a few moments. Then, Lindy gave each of the girls a framed photo of them singing at their last state competition, where they received first place. The bright, gaudy stones and ribbons surrounding the picture made them all laugh. Rebecca had made a small scrapbook for each of them with special photos and funny stories. Grace gave each of them a heart-shaped locket with a tiny photo of them inside. On the back was engraved, "The Sisterhood of Lake Alice."

After dinner, Emily led them outside to the weeping willow tree in the backyard. There was an old quilt spread out under the tree and eight beautifully wrapped gifts, candles, and more wine. Each girl had two gifts with her name on them. As they all took their regular spots in the circle, they seemed lost in the memories of all they had shared under this tree. They had learned the facts of life from Lindy under this tree. They had held Rebecca as she told them about her heartless father. They had comforted Emily after Isabel had left. They had listened to Grace talk about the love for her brother, Denny, while she questioned why she had been spared.

Finally, Emily told them to open their good-bye gifts. Inside the first package was a stunning handmade quilt of bright colors and expensive squares of silk and satin. Each quilt was different. In the middle of the quilt, their names were embroidered. Enclosed was a personal letter from Isabel congratulating them on their graduation and sharing some of her special memories and a wish for a happy future. They clung to their quilts and cried as they read Isabel's sentimental letter. The second package was a gift from Emily. Each of them had a Norwegian sweater; all of them were the same except their initials, which were embroidered on the right pocket. Even though it was a hot, humid evening, all four girls put on the heavy sweaters and toasted each other. They toasted each other that all of their dreams would come true.

That night, they all slept cuddled in their new, special quilts. They dreamed about what the future held for them. In the morning, before they left for their homes, they made a solemn vow to always stay connected to each other. They promised to write once a month with news of their new lives. Then, as though it had been planned, they joined hands and sang "You'll Never Walk Alone," with tears streaming down their faces. It was time to leave and begin their new beginnings.

Chapter Six

Emily

Emily's parents arrived home a few hours after the girls had left. Her mother immediately went to their bedroom, claiming to be ill with a severe headache. Emily was packing the last of her things when her father came into her room. He sat on her bed and told her, "Your mother continues to be extremely upset with your choice of college. I have decided that it is best not to upset her any more than necessary. Therefore, I think that you should drive yourself to Madison. Here is a packet with a map and directions from AAA and an envelope with $500. Your private dorm room at Chadbourne Hall is waiting for you. I opened a bank account for you, and there will be money deposited each month for your expenses. If you find that it is not enough, just call me and I will increase the amount."

After her father left, Emily sat on her window seat, looking at the weeping willow tree. Her father would never know that all she ever needed from him was just a little love and acceptance. She knew in her heart that when she left the next day, her life was going to take a dramatic turn. She also knew with certainty that whatever her new life was to be, her parents would not be a part of it. She was done feeling rejected for no reason other than she had survived while her twin brother had not.

She wrote a letter to her parents telling them how miserable she had been in this beautiful, sterile house. She told them that she did not intend to return to see them. Now they could consider themselves free of her. She vowed to leave all the pain behind tomorrow in the house that overlooked Lake Alice and start fresh. Hello, new world—Emily Larson is on the way!

It was a five-hour drive to Madison, Wisconsin. As she crossed the Mississippi River, which divides Minnesota and Wisconsin, she took a deep breath. For some strange reason, she began to smile. She was on her way in her bright red VW convertible to a new life.

Madison was a beautiful college town with two large lakes right in the middle of the campus. More than 30,000 students were on the campus, which was spread over acres of rolling hills. There were quaint old buildings on Beacon Hill surrounded by new, sleek, high-rise dorms. It was a campus of contrast and excitement. As Emily parked her car at Chadbourne Hall, she looked around at a sea of strangers. She watched as the other girls and their parents wheeled large carts of their belongings into the dorm. She watched all the laughter, love, and tears that were on display by both parents and their daughters. She seemed to be the only person with no one to share the excitement of her first day of college.

Emily quickly found her room on the first floor and moved in the few things that she had brought with her. She had a private room and bath, which was usually reserved for the dorm's housemothers. Emily had no idea how her parents had arranged it, but she knew that she would probably be embarrassed if she found out. The room had been stripped of the normal dorm furniture and replaced with a new oak bed, dresser, desk, TV, stereo, and loveseat. She had a small refrigerator stocked with her favorite drinks and a closet full of new clothes. There were plants on the windowsill, silk drapes on the windows, and a large, expensive Persian rug on the floor. The room looked more like a plush hotel room than a freshman's first dorm room. She vowed it was the last time this was going to happen.

Emily sat alone, listening to all the commotion that filled the hallways. Soon, it was replaced with giggles and the sound of doors opening and closing. She suddenly felt the need to get outside and go for a walk. As she opened her door, she ran into a group of girls standing outside her room. It was obvious that they were talking about her. Emily smiled and introduced herself. Next, she apologized for her overprotective and indulgent parents.

A pixie-looking girl named Maxie laughed and invited her to come with them to the welcome party. By the time dinner was over, Emily felt part of a new circle of friends. She invited them back into her room, which they had all been dying to see. It was quickly decided that this would become the official gathering place for the #1 girls who lived on the first floor of this all-girls dorm.

Maxie turned out to be a "wild child," as she had officially named herself. She talked the girls into escaping after curfew by crawling out their windows. She quickly introduced them to smoking and drinking. Within a few weeks, Emily was hanging out at a house on Mifflin Street. The large, unkempt house was home to more than twenty odd characters. The unofficial commune for wayward hippies was a place with no rules, lots of drinking, drugs, and wild parties that seemed to go on all day and all night.

At first, Emily was shocked at the open atmosphere. She stood out from everyone else with her plaid skirts and matching sweater sets. Maxie finally took her shopping on State Street for new clothes. Emily went from prim and proper to sloppy and relaxed. She wore long gauze skirts, baggy men's shirts, and sandals. She stopped shaving her legs and armpits. Instead of setting her hair in rollers each night, she had hundreds of tiny braids all over her head. She changed her diamond stud earrings for long, dangling beads.

Her old SOLA friends would have never recognized her. She thrived on the freedom of her newfound friends. Maxie and Emily often skipped classes, spending the days drinking at the Mifflin house. Instead of As, she settled for Cs with little effort at studying. She was not completely happy; however, she did enjoy the escape from her past overly protected life. The only thing that gave her any worry was how often her new friends asked her for money. She never denied a request; however, at times she was beginning to feel as though they were using her. She still was not completely comfortable with the drugs or sex. Nevertheless, she had learned to go with the flow.

She began to sneak out of the house when things got too wild. She would go back to the quiet of her dorm room, where she still felt safe. Her parents sent her an occasional letter from their latest vacation spot but never talked about coming for a visit.

During her second semester at UW, the Mifflin gang decided it would be fun to become activists. After a lively discussion, they decided that their cause would be protesting the Vietnam War. It started with small rallies held on Beacon Hill and in the nearby parks. After several months of carrying banners and homemade posters, they decided it was time to get more serious. They had all come to enjoy the attention they received at rallies.

A local man named Danny Driscoll was invited to the house to speak to the group. As Emily sat on the floor listening to his passionate speech, she was intrigued. He was handsome in a rugged, unkempt way, with curly red hair and deep blue eyes. Throughout his talk, his eyes often drifted toward Emily. Even with her new style, she still stood out from the crowd. There were moments when he seemed to be talking only to her. In that instant, she became his follower. She had fallen under the spell of a radical man with a radical way of life.

Within weeks, Emily and Danny became a couple. They spent hours sitting on the front porch discussing all the injustice of the world. They talked about how they had the power to change things. At the large rallies, Emily always stood at Danny's side. She was proud to be there. She added her voice to his many causes. He introduced her to sex, drugs, and the life of a radical. He told her how important she could be in leading a women's group. Danny talked her into selling her TV, stereo, and eventually most of her furniture and expensive clothes to support the latest cause. Emily was now spending all of her money to support the Mifflin gang. She had earned the respect of others because of her relationship with Danny. She had even led some successful sit-ins on her own. With Danny's coaching, she was also becoming a powerful leader. She vowed to be fearless. She dedicated herself to causes that Danny told her were important.

With strong encouragement from Danny, Emily became a spokesperson for their women's group. She boldly stood in the front of a picket line at a local coffee shop that had refused them service because of their wild behavior. When a police officer confronted the group, without thinking, Emily picked up a chair and threw it, breaking the large plate-glass window. She was immediately arrested. After three days, she was released and paid the $1,000 fine plus damages. Her story quickly spread throughout the campus. Emily became a celebrity. She had a reputation for being a woman who was not afraid of anything. Danny enjoyed her newfound status. He continued to teach her how to get a crowd worked up and how to get them to follow her every wish. Emily became very comfortable with the power she felt.

She wrote a few letters to her parents, but they had no idea how Emily had transformed. When she wrote to tell them that she felt it was time for her to leave the noisy dorm life for a more suitable small apartment, her father agreed. She also told them that she had enrolled in summer classes and would not be coming home. The letters from her Fergus Falls girlfriends sat unopened. She had moved on.

In August, she received a letter from her father telling her that due to her mother's poor health, they had purchased a home in Scottsdale, Arizona. They would be living there during the winter months, and he hoped that she would come for a visit sometime. He closed by telling her that he was proud of how hard she was studying; he knew she would continue to do well. He also informed her that he had deposited another $15,000 into her bank account, which she could use for her upcoming school expenses and new clothes. For some strange reason, Emily decided that she did not want anyone to read the letter. She burned it in the ladies room at Memorial Library and then flushed the ashes down the toilet.

Emily had planned on surprising Danny by renting a small apartment near campus for the two of them. She dreamed about fixing it up to be a cozy place for them. When she finally shared her idea with Danny, he was outraged. He called her a selfish little princess. He told her that her money was needed at the Mifflin house. All they needed was a small bedroom, which would also serve as their headquarters for organizing the demonstrations.

At last, Danny agreed that they could move into a bigger bedroom in the back of the house. The room had a mattress on the floor and a small metal desk and lawn chair in the corner where Emily could study. She soon discovered that she had a strong desire to become a journalist. Studying became impossible in the house, so she spent hours at the library. Danny was often gone on trips to help organize other college campuses. He was always welcomed home with a hero's greeting from the others.

Maxie had moved into the house as well. She kept Emily company while Danny was out solving the problems of the world. She was Emily's only true friend. Maxie warned her to watch out for some of the people that stayed in the house. She often told Emily not to come home until late because of the wild parties, drugs, and trouble.

Nothing changed for the next three years, except that the parties became more out of control. The demonstrations had several times turned violent. The police were always driving past the house, keeping their eyes open for any trouble. Almost everyone in the house had been arrested a few times for everything from illegal trespassing to drug possession.

The house was in a constant state of turmoil, filth, and people. Emily went from being repelled by all of it to feeling like a powerful leader. Her emotions ranged from a high when she was recognized, to complete depression when she did not sleep or study for days because of the partying. Her only refuge was the Memorial Library, which was always beautiful, clean, and quiet.

Danny and Emily remained a couple. When he was there, she never left his side. Danny continued to teach her how to work the crowd and often wrote her speeches. Emily enjoyed being a passionate speaker. It was always Danny who picked the issues. They had been arrested six times. With each arrest, they wore their probations like a badge of courage. Emily was known as fearless—willing to take a strong stance on any issue. She had stood in front of buses that she accused of polluting the lungs of innocent children and cut her hair off as a symbol of protest in front of a drugstore that sold *Playboy* magazine. She sprayed red paint on the sidewalk in front of the dean of students' office after he refused to let her speak about women's rights.

Yet, back in the shabby little bedroom, Emily was weak, disconnected, and longed to be cared for by Danny. She knew she had become his puppet. She was willing to accept Danny's terms for whatever love meant to him. She had nowhere to go. Whatever Danny wanted from Emily, she gave to him.

In the beginning of her senior year, she took some of her secret money to start an underground newspaper called *One Voice*. The paper was quickly noticed by school officials, who banned it on campus. The action drew the attention of the media, and soon there were stories on television and radio stations through the state. Danny immediately jumped in front of the cameras, claiming the paper was his idea. He swore to bring a lawsuit for violation of his constitutional rights. The press kept the story going for months. It made Danny Driscoll a spokesperson for the radical community.

Emily was outraged that Danny had taken credit for her paper. Yet at the same time, she was relieved that her picture had not appeared in any of the articles. It was the first time that she realized she no longer trusted Danny. She became withdrawn and depressed. All the others in the house believed that *One Voice* was Danny's.

Day by day, Emily became angrier. Finally, she confronted him and demanded an explanation. He just patted her on the top of head, telling her that she was once again behaving like the little rich Minnesota princess. He warned her to mellow out. If she continued to be such a drag, he might decide it was time to move on.

Emily stomped out of the house carrying her box of precious possessions—her quilt, which was still wrapped in the gift paper, her sweater, photo, locket, and a notebook filled with poems and short stories. She walked for blocks, tears streaming down her dirty face. Finally, she found herself standing in front of the stately Edgewater Hotel. As the desk clerk looked at her with disdain, she pulled out her credit card and took an expensive room overlooking Lake Mendota.

At the exact moment she walked into her clean hotel room, she had a revelation. She knew that she must stop smoking, drinking, and using drugs. She knew that never again would she allow herself to be demeaned and compromised. After a much-needed nap, she walked down State Street to buy new, clean clothes.

She stayed in the plush hotel room for two weeks, enjoying the peace. She bought lavender-scented bubble bath and honey shampoo. She soaked in hot baths. She ate delicious meals, which she ordered from room service. She studied for her finals. To her complete surprise, she passed all of her required exams with a 4.0. She felt better than she had in four years.

Alone, she walked to the graduation ceremony. Held in Randall Stadium to accommodate the thousands who were graduating with their families and friends cheering them, it was overwhelming to her. Some of the graduates decorated their caps so their family could find them in the massive crowd. Emily did not have to worry about anyone looking for her as she marched up to the large stage. There was no one there to cheer when they called her name. It surprised her how good it felt to hold her diploma in her hands. She clutched it close to her as she left the stage.

Emily came to the realization that she had just stumbled onto another turning point in her life's journey. She was leaving this life with nothing more than a small box of special things and her red VW. She had no idea where the thousands of dollars had gone that her parents had given her. Her current bank account balance was $500. However, she knew deep in her soul that she was ready to finally grow up. She was ready for the challenge to face the world, not as a crazed radical but as a woman with intelligence and value. She was determined to replace her freestyle life with a life of dignity.

That afternoon, she made an appointment with the doctor, who would tell her what she already knew.

Chapter Seven

Grace O'Malley

The day that Emily left for Madison was Grace's day off. She sat on her front porch waiting for Emily to make one last stop to say good-bye. After she sat there for several hours, Grace's mom came out to sit next to her. She told her, "It is time to get over the pity party. You need to accept your life as it is and move on. There is going to be little sympathy from anyone around here. You should be counting your many blessings. Be thankful for food on the table, a roof over your head, and a good job to go to each day."

Each day as she walked to and from the dress shop, she dreamed of the adventures that she would never have. She often took the route home that went past Emily's house on Lake Alice. The beautiful Victorian house now looked abandoned and uncared for. It broke her heart, especially when she remembered all the wonderful times she had in that house. She tried hard to accept her life without her friends. However, she could not seem to let go of her dreams. For the first time in her life, she felt poor. She hated herself when she finally acknowledged that she was jealous of Emily, Lindy, and Rebecca for their ability to go off to new adventures. She felt angry some days, but most days she was just plain lonely.

Her mother told her she was a foolish dreamer. She told her that she would never find a man if she kept that depressed look on her face. Her father spent most of his free time sleeping in front of the TV, never really talking to anyone in the family. She enrolled in Fergus Falls Junior College, which was in the new addition of the high school. She took business courses, working during the day while attending classes in the evening.

She was thankful that she kept busy. She hoped to get her two-year degree, save some money, then leave for a big city and finish her college education.

As the leaves turned shades of red and gold, Grace's mood became a little more lighthearted. She was surprised at how much she enjoyed her classes. She was learning more about the business world each day. Claire Klopetek, who owned Claire's Dress Shop, had taken her to Minneapolis for a buyers' convention. Grace was amazed by the large crowds attending the show and the miles of exhibits. She loved the experience and promised Claire that she was dedicating herself to her job from that day forward. Claire began to give Grace more office duties, carefully explaining the importance of each task. She even helped Grace with her homework.

In spite of their age difference of almost thirty years, they became close friends. Grace loved her job and most days looked forward to going to work. Claire worked with Grace to develop her own style in clothes and appearance. She gave Grace one outfit a month, making her promise that she would only wear clothes from the shop to work. Grace bloomed into a young woman with interesting fashion flair.

At school, Grace quickly made friends with the others who had graduated with her. They started to call themselves the LBG Club for *left behind gang*. Although there was no one who could replace the Sisterhood of Lake Alice, she made a few friends and went out on an occasional date to the movies and Dairyland Drive-in for ice cream. What surprised her most was that some of her classmates from high school, whom she had never given the time of day to, were actually very nice and lots of fun.

Grace received letters on a regular basis from Lindy and Rebecca. They told her about getting lost on campus, new roommates, boyfriends, parties, and their classes. They invited her to come for a weekend visit. Lindy came home twice the first semester, and it was wonderful to see her. It was also obvious that their connection had changed in just the few months away from each other. Rebecca wrote that she would be home for Christmas break, asking Grace to be their social director and to arrange as many get-togethers as possible. Grace smiled as she read each letter over and over again. It shocked her that Emily had not written or responded to the many letters and silly cards that she had sent to her. It was so unlike Emily.

One day as she passed the movie theater, she noticed an announcement for tryouts for a city theater group in Fargo, North Dakota. She quickly wrote down the address and the next day mailed a letter explaining who she was and her achievements and enclosed copies of some of the articles about them that had appeared in the Fergus Falls *Daily Journal*. Two days before Christmas, she received a response. The letter stated that auditions were being held in Fargo in mid-January for a new musical production of *Seven Brides for Seven Brothers*.

Grace's spirit seemed to perk up at the thought of singing again. When it was quiet in the store, she sang; in the evening at home, she sang; she sang walking home, and she sang in church each Sunday. She dreamed of singing on stage to an audience of adoring fans. She called and set up an appointment for her first audition.

When Rebecca and Lindy arrived home for the holidays, they all met at Skogmo, the local coffee shop, which was right down the street from Claire's Dress Shop. They smiled as each of them walked in the café wearing the sweater that Emily had given them with the locket from Grace hanging around their necks. They spent hours laughing, talking about their new lives and how much they missed each other. All of them were concerned about Emily. No one had heard from her except for a Christmas card, which said she would not be home for the holidays.

Too soon, Grace waved to her friends as they left to go back to their new lives. Lindy went back to nursing school at Mankato State and Rebecca to the Music Conservancy in Minneapolis. Grace was thrilled that she had the auditions to look forward to in a few weeks.

She was anxious but also confident and prepared as she hopped on the bus for a one-hour ride to Fargo. The city theater auditions were held at the movie theater on Main Street. There was a large group of people waiting their turns to show off their many different talents. Grace signed up, was handed a number, and found a seat in the back row of the darkened theater. She watched as people sang and danced to their chosen music. It suddenly hit her that she did not have a chance of being selected for any role.

Although she sang better than any of those she had heard, she had no dancing ability at all. The most dancing she did was at the VFW Post for their Friday night dances. Knowing that her number was going to be announced shortly, she quietly got up to leave the theater. Just as she reached the door, they called her name and number. For a brief moment, she wanted to run as fast as she could; but instead, she slowly turned around to walk down the aisle.

Grace had chosen the song "Singing in the Rain." As she walked to the stage, she closed her eyes and tried to remember how Gene Kelly had danced down the street in the movie, which she had seen so many times. As she began to sing, her feet started to mimic the funny dance that she had come to love. By the time her song ended, she felt she had a chance to get the part that she had almost thrown away because of her fear of rejection. A week later, she received a letter with an offer for the part of one of the brides.

She went to rehearsals every Wednesday evening and Sunday afternoons. Two months later, the play opened to rave reviews. Grace's beautiful voice was mentioned in several articles. She had fallen in love with being on stage. After six weekends, the play was over, but her love for drama was deeply embedded in her soul. She was convinced that she needed to bring plays to Fergus Falls. Grace had finally found a passion that she knew would bring her happiness.

With a newfound confidence in herself, Grace made an appointment with the dean of students, Mr. Sorenson, at Fergus Falls Junior College to present him with a proposal. She had spent a week carefully creating the plan and making sure the proposal was perfect. The proposal was to start a theater group at the college. She offered to work without pay. One of the directors from the city theater group had volunteered to assist in organizing the program.

Grace was willing to do whatever it took to produce their first musical. She had already convinced Claire that it was a wise investment to use some clothes from the shop as wardrobe. In return, she was to become an honored patron and receive a free ad in the play's program. Warren Rovang from Rovang's Men's Clothing Store matched the offer and agreed to take care of dressing the men in the play. The City Café agreed to pay for the printing of the program in exchange for an ad. Victor Lundeen's bookstore had already committed to the largest ad on the back cover.

Mr. Sorenson was so impressed with all of Grace's preparation that he knew he could not refuse her proposal. Therefore, the Fergus Falls Theater Group became a reality. Grace now had her job, the theater group, and school to keep her happy and fulfilled.

The first production of the Fergus Falls Theater Group was in the fall. The group had twenty-two performers and a six-piece band. Another group of fifteen volunteers made the scenery and props. More than sixty people of all ages were involved and dedicated to the group. *Brigadoon*, the first play, turned out to be far more complicated than anyone had originally thought. However, opening night and the next three weekends, they played to a sellout crowd. Grace played the starring role of Fiona. Nightly, the audience gave Grace and her leading man, Roy Kastelle, with his strong tenor voice, standing ovations. They loved their characters of Fiona and Tommy.

People came from Dalton, Detroit Lakes, and Fargo. Great reviews were written from as far away as Minneapolis. Grace's family came to every performance, cheering her on. Her father often sat there with tears in his eyes, while her mother smiled brightly. As an added surprise, Grace realized that she had feelings for Roy. They began to date, spending hours talking about their dreams for the future.

When the play ended, the group immediately started planning for the spring musical production of the roaring '20s play called *Flapper*. There were parts for all ages. Grace put an article in the *Daily Journal* for auditions. More than a hundred people of assorted ages from as young as six to as old as eighty tried out for the various parts. The play called for thirty-two actors. Those who were not chosen eagerly signed up for the production crew. Sets were created and clothes collected from those that still had their old raccoon coats, ukuleles, and flapper dresses.

Grace took a smaller part this time. Once again, the play was a huge success. This time people came from as far away as Alexandria and Breckenridge. The Fergus Falls Theater Group was now in great demand. They came together every Tuesday evening. When they were not rehearsing for a play, they practiced their singing, dancing, and acting skills.

This lighthearted group truly enjoyed their time together. Grace and Roy became a couple, with dates on Saturday evenings. They both knew that they would always be good friends. When Roy left to go to Mankato State College the next year, once again Grace cried and felt abandoned. However, she had so much to be grateful for this time. She loved her job at Claire's, liked taking some classes at the junior college, and never missed a Tuesday night with the theater group.

The two years of junior college passed by quickly. Each summer, she spent some time with Lindy and Rebecca when they came home. It became more obvious that they were changing and growing in different directions. The close bonds of high school were disappearing. They never heard from Emily. After many discussions, they all decided that Emily had replaced them with new friends in Madison and no longer cared about them.

When Grace graduated with a two-year degree in business, she knew she had to face the decision about what to do next. She had been saving her money and now had enough to go away to school. She applied and was accepted at Mankato State, St. Catherine's College in Minneapolis, and Duluth State College. All of them had strong programs in business and a drama department. Grace had all the college information spread out on the dining room table one evening, when her sister Faith came running into the room. She gathered the family together around the table for important news. She had just become engaged to her high school sweetheart, Rodney. Everyone hugged and congratulated her.

Faith immediately started making plans for a June wedding. She wanted a large wedding with all the fancy fixings. Anna and Paul sat silently listening to all of her plans, knowing there was no money that would allow her dream wedding to come true. It seemed to be a simple decision for Grace. She offered to loan Faith her college money for her wedding. Therefore, Faith had the wedding of her dreams and Grace remained at home.

The same thing happened when Hope needed money for her wedding. It seemed that every time one loan was repaid, there was another O'Malley in need. Grace was always happy to help. She often thought that perhaps this was a sign from God that she needed to stay in Fergus Falls. Much to her surprise, she did not mind. She had found friends, purpose, and a good life in Fergus Falls. After awhile, she could not think of anywhere else she would rather be. Most days, as she curled up in the special quilt from Isabel, she felt content and at peace.

Chapter Eight

Lindy

Lindy graduated with top honors from high school. She worked hard all summer helping her parents and training her replacement at the dry cleaners. She went on shopping trips with her mother, but in the end, Mom made most of Lindy's college wardrobe. It seemed that every one of her outfits had something that either sparkled or glittered.

The last week of August, she left for Mankato. In a borrowed pickup truck, Papa, Mama, and Lindy squeezed into the front seat, with the back loaded with all of Lindy's possessions. Mankato State College was a small campus with less than two thousand students. It was growing in popularity each year and was in a constant state of expansion. The two steep hills in town were located on campus. The campus buildings were divided into the lower campus at the bottom of the hill, which was close to downtown. Most of these buildings were older buildings with lots of character. The upper campus sat at the top of the hill with the newer buildings. Lindy loved the feel of the old buildings. She was happy when she found out that more than half of her classes would be held in the lower campus.

As the family toured the campus, her parents could not hide their pride. Lindy would be the first person on both sides of her family to go to college. They were optimistic for her. Just before her parents left to return to Fergus Falls, they took Lindy out for dinner. Her dad handed her an envelope with ten $10 bills. Lindy hugged them both, knowing how hard they had worked for that money. She promised to make them proud of her. She already had a part-time job at a local restaurant as a waitress. She was excited about her new life and all the adventures that were ahead.

When Lindy arrived on campus, she quickly discovered that she seemed to stand out wherever she went. At a size 22, she towered over all of the petite girls who ran around campus in their miniskirts. Her dark, thick, black hair added several more inches to her height. Her wild, colorful clothes and makeup caused many to turn their heads. Lindy decided to just be herself. There would be no changing into a preppy college coed for her. Her style was her statement, and she wore it with flair and no apologies.

Shortly after her parents left, her new roommate arrived. It turned out that her roommate, Catherine, was the worst possible match. Lindy was full of energy, while Catherine was quiet and loved to sleep. Lindy was a night owl, while Catherine was up at dawn. Lindy hated exercise of any type, while Catherine worked out daily. They never really quarreled; they just ignored each other. When forced to, they would tolerate each other's presence. Lindy just figured that it was yet another of life's little jokes. Catherine, on the other hand, did not find any of the situation amusing.

Lindy had known for years that she wanted to be a nurse. She felt her talent for brightening up any place she went would be very useful as a nurse. She was especially fond of the elderly. All of her special times with her grandma had made her very comfortable in relating to them. For some strange reason, the older folks accepted her bigger-than-life style more than people of her own age, who thought she was just plain weird. On the outside, Lindy looked brave, bold, and ready to take on the world. Inside, she was often hurt and carried much insecurity. Instead of an active social life, Lindy studied hard, taking twenty credits each semester. Her goal was to graduate in three years.

In addition to a heavy class schedule, Lindy worked long hours at a restaurant and bar called Molly's. It was the kind of place where all the college kids loved to hang out. Every Thursday evening, the bar offered beers for $1 and sponsored a talent show. The winner received dinner for two and a cheap plastic trophy. Lindy sang almost every week in the talent show; she also won almost every week. The crowd grew to love her big bold country-western style.

After six months, Molly offered Lindy a job singing on the weekends. The standing-room-only crowds would cheer her on as she sang her heart out every Friday and Saturday night. Lindy had never been happier. She knew she was going to love being a nurse. However, she loved singing on her little stage at Molly's in her homemade fancy western outfits. It was a place where everyone accepted her just as she was. For those few hours each week, Lindy forgot all her insecurities.

By the end of her first year, she was making enough money that she could afford to stay on for summer school. Just before school started in September, she found a furnished one-room apartment where she no longer had to worry about roommates. Lindy had only been home for one week during the summer. Although her parents missed her, they understood that Lindy needed to get on with life.

Her parents came to visit her over Labor Day weekend. They were anxious to see her little apartment and go to Molly's. They were overwhelmed with pride as they listened to Lindy singing. They were truly touched when they experienced firsthand how much everyone adored their little Lindy. They watched her light up the tiny stage. She made the room come alive with the special way she moved with each of the songs. By the time they left, they knew that Lindy was going to become a star and probably would never come back to Fergus Falls.

Just as she had planned, Lindy graduated from nursing school in three years with honors. She immediately had several excellent job offers. The most exciting one was at the famous Mayo Clinic in Rochester, Minnesota. She was getting ready to accept the offer when a friend from Molly's called her with an interesting idea.

Carol Ignace had become a close friend of Lindy's during college. She was the one person that Lindy knew she could go to whenever she needed a shoulder to cry on or an opinion on anything. Carol was the exact opposite of Lindy. Where Lindy was bold, brave, and full of energy, Carol was quiet, thoughtful, and conservative. The two of them quickly discovered that they balanced each other very nicely. They laughed, cried, and celebrated on a regular basis.

Carol was also graduating and had accepted an internship with a large brokerage firm on Wall Street in New York City. She was shocked by the salary she had been offered working as an actuary. Carol and Lindy had many conversations about how different their everyday life was going to be once college was behind them. Carol was extremely nervous about moving to New York. Being born and raised in Minneapolis, New York still seemed huge and far too cosmopolitan for a girl from Minnesota. Finally, she worked up her courage to ask Lindy if she wanted to move with her. At first, Lindy was going to refuse because the Mayo Clinic was a wonderful opportunity. Then she started to think about the magic of New York City. The Broadway shows, the energy, the excitement would be within her daily reach.

Within ten minutes, Lindy went from a safe bet at the Mayo Clinic to an exciting new adventure in New York City. Look out, world—Lindy is on her way!

Chapter Nine

Rebecca

When Rebecca's father, Tim, returned home to Minneapolis, he immediately arranged for three very profitable apartment buildings in Fergus Falls, which he owned, to be transferred to Miss Rebecca DuPree. All rental income from that date on was to be deposited into an account at Lincoln Bank in Fergus Falls. He instructed his attorney to notify her in writing, with an additional note stating that neither Rebecca nor Monica were to attempt to have any contact with him. He promised himself that his family would never know about the graceful young woman that he watched crossing the stage at graduation.

Tim had convinced himself that doing this would remove the guilt that stained his soul. It did not. His wife saw a changed man when he returned from his mother's funeral. She assumed that the death had somehow been more traumatic than he had acknowledged. Whatever had happened, Tim had a deep, empty look in his eyes that she had never seen before.

Rebecca's mother received the certified letter from Tim's attorney. For several weeks, she thought about how she was going to tell Rebecca that her father thought money was a substitute for a relationship with his daughter. She almost felt sorry for him. He had missed knowing a truly exceptional young woman.

Ever since graduation, Monica was haunted by the look on Tim's face. His expensive clothes could not mask the empty man who wore them.

In July, Monica was shocked when she received the first bank statement from Lincoln Bank showing deposits of more than $5,000. Monica would tell Rebecca that weekend. She decided to get the weekly wash going before starting the emotional conversation.

As Monica was carrying the clothes into the basement, she was daydreaming about the money when she lost her balance. She fell down the flight of stairs, landing on the hard, concrete basement floor. She cried for help for almost an hour before Ruby heard her. By the time the ambulance arrived, Monica knew that she had broken both her left leg and arm.

Rebecca received the call at Emily's house, where she had spent the night. Grandma Ruby was so excited that she had been difficult to understand. Rebecca had no idea what to expect as she rushed to the hospital. She found her mother being prepared for surgery to set both her arm and leg. As she was being wheeled into surgery, Monica looked at the two people she loved most in this world and simply asked them to pray for her.

The following day, Rebecca came to visit Monica with fresh-cut roses from their garden. Monica smiled as she told Rebecca that she needed to share some news with her. She told Rebecca about the transfer of the properties and the joint account that now held $5,000, with more to come each month.

Rebecca was startled by the news. She had worried for a long time about the financial burden for college, which was placed solely on her mother's shoulders. Even with a full scholarship, there were still many extra expenses. Now with her mother out of work, the news seemed to be a small miracle for them. Instead of being hurt by her father thinking money made up for his absence, she was convinced that this was a gift from God to help them. She took it as a sign to do well at college and to be assured that her mother and grandmother would be okay financially.

Monica simply hugged her positive-thinking daughter and once again said a prayer of thanks to God for her wonderful gift named Rebecca.

By the end of August, Monica was beginning to heal. She still wore her arm in a sling and a cast on her leg. However, she was now able to move around their little house with ease. Grandma Ruby had taken over some of the household chores, which she seemed to enjoy more these days. It looked as though everyone was going to survive.

After much discussion, the decision was made to take a small amount of the money out of the bank each month for daily living expenses for Monica and Ruby. They traded in their old car, which broke down on a regular basis, for a newer model. Rebecca would receive a monthly allowance so she would not have to work during school. Monica decided to go from full-time to part-time at her job, which would give her more time to spend with Ruby. She also hoped to do some volunteer work at the hospital.

Because they were fearful of driving in the big city, Rebecca boarded the Greyhound bus to Minneapolis. She was confident that all would be well at home. She was ready to begin her new life at college.

Rebecca arrived at St. Catherine's in the heart of Minneapolis. For the first time in her life, she was in a big city alone. Her clothes, books, and dorm room things had been shipped in advance. St. Catherine's campus was a women's college with beautiful, old, red brick buildings that had ivy growing up the walls. There were hundreds of graceful elm and oak trees scattered throughout the small campus. Once you entered the campus gates and found your way to the center of the campus, you would never know that you were in the middle of the city. As she walked into her dorm for the first time, she was overwhelmed with thoughts of what lay ahead for her.

Rebecca's roommate, Katie, was already settled in and unpacked. As Rebecca unpacked her belongings, Katie sat on her bed and told her all about herself. She was from Wauwatosa, Wisconsin, and had six brothers and three sisters. She had received a full academic scholarship and was planning to teach biology. Katie laughed as she told her that she was grateful Rebecca had not arrived yesterday as the entire family had driven in three cars to make sure that Katie was settled in and comfortable. Her twin brother named Kevin was also on full scholarship at their all-male brother school, St. Thomas, just a few miles away. She had already made plans for Kevin to introduce her to some boys from his dorm.

Rebecca listened as Katie seemed to talk for hours without taking a break. At first, she felt intimidated by her bubbly personality. However, by dinnertime, she realized that Katie would become a friend and perhaps force her to get out of her self-conscious shell. She also discovered that Katie loved to sing.

Life quickly settled in for Rebecca. She found each class she took to be challenging and exciting. She saw a notice for auditions for the St. Catherine's international choral group. Both Katie and Rebecca were accepted on the first round of tryouts. Her days were filled with music and studies.

Within a few weeks, both girls had gotten into a comfortable routine of classes and studying hard. Every Saturday evening, they met Katie's brother Kevin and some of his friends. It was normally just an evening of pizza and laughs.

By Christmas break, Rebecca realized that she had changed. Both her mom and Grandma Ruby commented on her new self-confident personality. Rebecca carried herself with pride. She laughed more, talked more, and in general, looked happier.

By spring, both Rebecca and Katie had received invitations to go to Europe during the summer for a concert tour. Katie worked extra hours at the dorm cafeteria to raise the money, while Rebecca knew she would be able to tap into her newfound money. The tour to Germany and Austria was a huge success; the choir received rave reviews. Rebecca's name was mentioned in almost all of them.

She was overwhelmed by the beauty of Austria. She prayed and sang in cathedrals that were built before the United States existed. She loved how her voice sounded as it bounced off century-old walls and stained-glass windows. She made herself a promise that someday she would bring her mother and grandmother to see those incredible sights.

By their junior year, Katie and Rebecca had moved into a small one-bedroom apartment just off campus. They often had Kevin and a few friends over for dinner. Katie had proven to be a wonderful cook, and Rebecca loved to bake elaborate desserts. Jeff Winkler, a tall, handsome, blond-haired guy, had become Kevin's roommate. One night after dinner while he was helping Rebecca clean up, he turned to her and asked her if she would ever consider dating someone like him. She simply blushed and said yes.

From that night on, they became a couple. Saturday evening was their date night, and almost every evening they would study together. The relationship was comfortable and convenient. There was seldom an argument and always a few good laughs. There was lots of cuddling but never any sex, which seemed to suit both of them just fine.

Rebecca invited Jeff to come to Fergus Falls during spring break of their senior year. He quickly agreed. She called to tell her mom that she was bringing Jeff home. Monica sounded excited about the prospect of finally meeting her special guy. As they drove home, Rebecca tried to warn him about her humble little house on Bancroft Street. Jeff simply smiled and told her not to worry about it. Although he came from a wealthy family, his parents had a bitter divorce four years before. He went on to explain that he would much rather live in a small, happy home than a big house filled with anger.

After that week in Fergus Falls, everyone including Rebecca assumed that Jeff would be proposing any day. The day before Rebecca, Katie, Kevin, and Jeff were graduating, the girls prepared a special dinner for the four of them. Katie had just broken up with Larry, whom she had been casually dating for about a year, and she needed a little cheering up. The boys arrived on time with a bottle of champagne and four beautiful champagne flutes. Katie and Kevin were moving back to Milwaukee. Rebecca was keeping the apartment and had just accepted a teaching position at Holy Angels Academy, where she would be teaching English and music. Jeff was leaving in a week for California, where he had accepted an internship at Universal Studios.

Rebecca was convinced that tonight Jeff would propose, and she was ready to say yes. She already had a shoebox filled with clippings of wedding dresses, flowers, and articles on the perfect wedding. It was after midnight when Jeff suggested that they go for one last walk on St. Catherine's campus. As they left, Katie winked at Rebecca and pointed to her ring finger. They walked in contented silence through the quiet parklike campus. When they finally reached their favorite bench, they sat down and stared at the full moon and abundance of stars.

Suddenly and without warning, Jeff broke down. He was sobbing so hard that Rebecca could not understand what he was saying. Finally, he took a deep breath and slowly started to explain that he was leaving and would never be back. He explained that he had been dishonest with her. He felt like the lowest scum of the earth, but he knew that he had to finally be honest. He was a fraud, and she deserved better than he was ever able to give her.

Rebecca reached for him and tried to comfort him. She said, "Jeff, I love you with all my heart. You are the best thing that has ever happened to me. I love you for who you are, not who you think you need to be. You have given me so much happiness and love. Nothing is so bad that it cannot be fixed or forgiven. Together, we can make a good life."

Without a word of response, Jeff stood up and ran into the darkness, leaving Rebecca alone and confused. He did not return to the apartment that night.

Rebecca went through the motions of graduation because her mom and Grandma Ruby had come for the ceremony. Monica asked her why Jeff was not joining them. Finally, the tears came while Rebecca told her about what had happened. Both Katie and her mom assured Rebecca that Jeff was probably nervous about his upcoming internship and not to worry. Men just had more problems dealing with stress and change than women did.

The next day, Rebecca helped Katie and Kevin pack up their car and U-Haul trailer for their journey back to Wisconsin. She promised to call them as soon as she heard from Jeff. The next two days were the longest days of her life. With no school or work, she had nothing to do but worry about Jeff. Her mind went from thoughts of there being another woman to Jeff having a serious health problem. She paced the floors morning to night. She spent hours walking, but nothing eased her worries.

It was almost eleven o'clock on the second evening when she heard a soft knock on her door. She opened it to find Jeff still wearing the same clothes he had on three days before. His normally neat and clean appearance was replaced with the looks of a crazed street man. His eyes were red and swollen. He leaned against the doorframe as he softly asked if he could speak to her for just a few minutes. They sat in complete silence for a few minutes. Finally, Jeff cleared his throat and started to speak.

"Rebecca, I want you to know that I have loved you from the first moment I met you. You are the woman I have always dreamed of being with forever. Your compassion and kindness are virtues that are so rare today. I never wanted to hurt you. All I ever wanted to do was to protect you. I have believed that I could make a good future for us. A few months ago, I was forced to face the ugly truth about what a fraud I am. I know now that I cannot hide from the truth any longer. I also know that I am going to hurt you. For that, I am incredibly sorry.

"The truth is that I am gay. I have always felt different from the other guys who boast about sexual conquests. I thought it was because I had not found the right girl. I have been seeing a therapist for the last year, thinking my problems were all because of my parents' terrible example and lack of love. Then one day, it just came to me that what the problem was had nothing to do with my parents. It had everything to do with me. I am living a lie. With the help of my therapist, I am able to accept who I am. Now I need to start to move forward.

"I would give anything not to have to hurt you. I know you have every right to think that it is time for us to get married. Please forgive me. You need to know that I will always care for you. I am leaving in two days for California. I plan to make that my career and my home. I hope that in time, you will understand." Without waiting for Rebecca to say anything, he got up and left. He never gave Rebecca a chance to discuss it with him.

She sat in stunned silence until early the next morning. Her emotions ran from anger to despair. In the morning, she called her mom. Rebecca packed her suitcase and headed to Fergus Falls for a few weeks of healing and loving comfort that only her mother and Grandma Ruby could give her. As Rebecca faced her future, she wondered if she would always be alone.

Chapter Ten

Emily

Emily graduated from college with a degree in journalism, a six-year-old VW convertible, and a small box of special things. When she went to the doctor, she already knew what she would hear. He confirmed that she was three months pregnant. She had no insurance, no job, and no one to love her.

After the initial shock wore off, Emily decided that she needed to inform Danny that he was going to be a father. It felt so strange to walk back into the house on Mifflin. She had only been gone for a few weeks. Yet it seemed as though she was seeing it for the first time. The house reeked from the smell of pot and body odor. There was litter everywhere. She did not know if it was morning sickness or the disgusting place where she had lived that made her go running to the bathroom to throw up. Emily finally composed herself, took a deep breath, and walked up the stairs leading to her old bedroom.

When she knocked on the door, Danny yelled to come in. She opened the door and found him sitting on the bed with two friends, smoking pot and drinking. Danny started laughing and said, "Well, you finally missed the big guy! Now that you are back, I hope you realize that you play the game by my rules and only my rules. Come join us, babe."

Emily stared at him, trying to remember what she had ever found so appealing about this jerk. She asked if they could be alone. The two friends made a snide remark, and one tapped her on the head as he passed by her. Emily stood by the door for another moment, then turned and walked away. Danny Driscoll was a lowlife who had no right to this child. Somehow, she would find a way to bring this baby into a safe and loving world. All she knew for sure was that Danny was not ever going to be a part of this child's life. She also knew that she now had a new center of focus, a reason to live and become a better person than she had been for the past four years. Today was the beginning of the new and improved Emily.

When Emily left Mifflin Street and returned to her car, she had no idea where to go. All she knew for sure was that Madison was not the place for her. She decided to head toward Milwaukee. She had heard it was a quiet city with gentle manners. It sounded like a good place to start over again.

Through one of her classes, Emily had gotten to know a woman named Marlene, who had opened a women's shelter in Waukesha, a suburb of Milwaukee. Marlene had been an older student, graduating when she was thirty-three years old after a bitter divorce. The two of them had worked on several projects together. Marlene had taken Emily aside to talk to her about her radical lifestyle several times. She spent hours trying to convince Emily that she could change the world for the better in a different way than she had chosen. She had invited her to come to the women's shelter near Milwaukee. She told her that she needed to value and believe in herself. They talked for hours about dignity and integrity. However, every time Emily was given a choice, she had always chosen Danny and his ways. Finally, Marlene had just given up on her.

About a month ago, Emily had read an article about the Women's Center, with a photo of Marlene. She knew that at least Marlene had found her calling.

It was almost six o'clock when she parked the car in front of a large, old, Victorian house, which was Marlene's Women's Center. In some ways, it reminded her of the house on Lake Alice in Fergus Falls. The biggest difference was that this house seemed to have a light on in every room.

As she walked in the front door, a young girl, perhaps sixteen and very pregnant, greeted her. Emily asked for Marlene and was told to wait in the hall for her. Within minutes, Marlene came running down the winding staircase. She gave Emily a big bear hug and then looked directly into her eyes. She said, "I see a lot of pain in these eyes, kiddo. What is going on? How can I help?"

Emily broke into tears. Through her sobs, she told her story. Finally, she took a deep breath. She finished by telling Marlene that she had no one and no place to go. She also had no idea why she was here. Somehow, she knew deep in her soul that this place held some answers for her.

Marlene told her she was welcome to stay. There were three basic requirements that she needed to commit to in order to stay at the center. The first was that she must help around the center wherever and whenever she could. The second was to stay free of all drugs and all other illegal substances. The third was that she needed to start her process of healing immediately by attending counseling and group sessions. Marlene knew that Emily had been living a life of drugs and abuse for several years. She also knew that Emily had all the ingredients to become a wonderful role model if she could leave her past behind and find happiness in a new life.

They hugged each other as they walked up the stairs to the tiny bedrooms. There were sixteen women and six children in the house; another ten women stayed at a secret location.

Emily's assigned small room held two sets of bunk beds that looked like rejects from a dorm room at Madison. She was given bed C, which was a lower bed with a few drawers underneath the mattress. The room was painted a strange shade of green, with hardwood floors and a small dresser under the window. Barren of any soft touches, it was clean and looked almost sad.

Marlene introduced her to her three roommates. Beth was a large woman with massive dyed, jet-black hair and tattoos of large flowers on both of her arms. Thirty-two years old and recently released from prison for embezzlement, she had been in the center for three weeks. She looked Emily up and down for a moment before extending her hand, saying, "Welcome to the Hilton of Waukesha. We keep our little paradise very tidy, so don't go messing up anything or you will be cleaning for all four of us."

Rita sat watching quietly. She was twenty-four and was so tiny that she almost disappeared into the far corner of her upper bunk bed. She had two black eyes and bruises around her neck. She softly said, "I just arrived three days ago, so now you're the new one in the group. I am sorry, but I guess I snore a lot. I will try to be quiet, but I can't seem to help it. We share the bathroom down the hall and keep an organized schedule. It is hanging behind the door if you want to read it. I am not feeling real good, so I sleep a lot."

Emily then turned to her third roommate. Rosa was from Mexico and spoke very little English. She simply nodded her head and said, "Hi." All three women were wearing similar sweat suits that were simple and clean. For some unknown reason, it made Emily feel safe. Rita slowly climbed down from her bunk and offered to show Emily around the house.

With that done, Marlene smiled and excused herself. She told Emily to grab a sandwich when Rita showed her the kitchen. She asked her to read the rules of the house, sign a few forms, and promised to see her in the morning for her first group session.

Within a few days, Emily had become comfortable in her new home. She worked hard each day, doing whatever she was asked to do. She cleaned; she cooked and watched the children while their moms had their counseling sessions. Both the group and private counseling sessions were painful. It seemed that she spent half her time crying. All of her old wounds were ripped wide open. She no longer repressed the memories of the cold and uncaring life with her parents. She talked about Danny and tried to figure out why she had become his puppet. Every day, she thought about this baby growing inside of her. Could she love it? How would she raise a child when she had never known real love? Was she capable of providing for her baby? The questions circled in her mind. Yet she found no answers.

Marlene came to her one day shortly after she arrived and asked her if she was interested in helping them put together a fundraising brochure for the center. Emily jumped at the chance to use her creative skills. After the brochure, she started on a monthly newsletter, helped organize the fundraiser event, and put together a press release. She laughed as she thought of how she was using the same skills that she had used when she was a radical demonstrator. Only now, it was for a noble cause. When a Waukesha newspaper reporter asked for an interview, both Marlene and Emily met with him.

After the article appeared in the *Waukesha Freeman*, a local radio station asked for an interview. The following month, the local television station asked if they could come out and film a two-minute segment on the center. Within a short time, local churches and organizations were requesting Emily to come and talk to their members. Marlene simply smiled as she watched Emily grow more confident each day.

A few months after Emily had arrived at the Women's Center, she knew that it would soon be time to leave. Other women needed her bed and needed to receive the care of the Women's Center. She rented a small one-bedroom apartment with Rita. They shopped at Goodwill for most of their furniture and laughed as they put together the two small twin beds. Emily was now about six months pregnant. She knew that she needed to make a decision about keeping the baby. Terrifying nightmares of losing the baby began to haunt her. She often woke up in the middle of the night, afraid of becoming a mother like her own mother.

Both Rita and Emily had gotten jobs working for an answering service called Spectrum Communications not far from the apartment. They were thrilled that the owners had hired Emily even in her condition. She promised that after the baby was born, she would continue to work at the company. Emily worked from 3:00 PM until midnight, while Rita worked midnight until 8:00 AM.

They shared an old car that they named Tula and put a variety of bumper stickers all over the car to cover the rusty holes. It seemed as though every day they were able to help someone in crisis, either at the answering service or in their volunteer time at the Women's Center. It felt good to give back to others who were in need.

One evening, Emily answered a call for a client called New Beginnings, an adoption agency. The woman who was calling had just lost a baby. It was her third miscarriage in four years. Her doctor had informed her that she was not capable of carrying a baby to full term. Although both she and her husband were grief stricken, they both felt it was time to adopt. They owned a little house with a swing set in the backyard and had lots of love that needed to be given to a child. As Emily was taking her message, she suddenly knew that her decision had just been made. She knew at that moment that she would give the baby up for adoption. Her child would have a life with two loving parents.

The next morning, she called New Beginnings. Within a few weeks, all the arrangements were made for an open adoption. She requested the couple who had left the message a few nights earlier. At last, she felt at peace. She knew without a doubt that this was the right decision. She prayed that the adoptive parents would give her baby all the love that she had dreamed of having in her life. She knew without a doubt that this baby would bring joy into the lives of two people who were waiting for her arrival.

December 1 started out as a frigid and windy day. Emily woke up at 2:00 AM to discover that her water had broken and her contractions begun. By 4:00 AM, Emily was admitted to Waukesha Memorial Hospital. Tiny Rebecca Grace Larson was born three hours later. The doctor teased Emily about her easy delivery and told her she was made to have babies.

Outside the delivery room, Maggie and Joe McMahon paced in the hallway as they waited to see their new baby girl. By the time Emily was wheeled into her room, all the papers had been prepared for the adoption. The McMahons came into the room and looked at Emily, fearing she would change her mind once she saw this beautiful, red-haired little girl. Emily simply smiled at them and asked for a pen. Within five minutes, all the documents were signed. Through her tears, Maggie told Emily that she would love, protect, and give Rebecca Grace a wonderful life. Joe stood silently with tears flowing down his face.

The next day, Emily returned to her little apartment feeling empty but proud. She had no doubt that she had made the right decision—a decision that required more love than she ever knew she was capable of having. Two weeks later, she was back to work at the answering service and volunteering at the Women's Center each weekend.

Emily chose to put all of her efforts into work. However, Rita became a social butterfly. She met John at a Catholic singles dance and fell madly in love with him. On a spring day in May, Rita and John were married in a little prayer chapel, with Emily and a friend of John's as witnesses.

Emily now had the little apartment to herself. She bought a bookcase and began to fill it with all the classic books she wanted to read. She was content and most days felt fulfilled. Her job at the answering service helped her keep a healthy perspective on the problems of others.

One day she received a call from Marlene asking her to meet for lunch. When she arrived the next day, she was introduced to a man who was to head a new county program for needy and displaced people. By the time lunch was over, Emily had accepted the position of executive director. She knew she would miss her days at the answering service, but felt she had just received her next gift in life.

One year slid into the next while Emily became a true pioneer in offering new opportunities for the people who came to her. She became an effective fundraiser. Local businesses supported her many programs. She started New Beginnings' Child Care Center, the Career Closet, a free community-sponsored health and dental clinic, a temporary help agency for women attempting to reenter the workforce, and a combined coffee shop with a bookstore called Beans & Books. Each year her staff, budget, and projects grew. She inspired everyone who came in touch with her.

Yet every night she went home alone. Although she was surrounded by many, Emily never let any one person into her private life. Yet she never thought of herself as being lonely. Her work fulfilled her and left little energy for relationships.

However, every year, she took off on December 1. She spent the day alone in her tiny one-bedroom apartment thinking about Rebecca Grace, the daughter she would never know. Sometimes she cried, while other times she tried to imagine what the little red-haired girl looked like. She wondered if she was bright, kind, and creative. For that one day each year, Emily felt empty. The next morning, she got up and started a new year. She never felt tempted to visit the McMahons. She knew deep in her soul that she had made the best decision she could. Her love was strong enough to ensure a loving home for her daughter.

Chapter Eleven

Grace

It did not take long for Fergus Falls to fall in love with Miss Grace O'Malley. The town appreciated her devotion to them. The women flocked into Claire's Dress Shop for her advice on the latest fashions and a special dress for a special event. She made sure that no woman in town was embarrassed by wearing the same outfit to the same party as someone else. Grace also had developed her own unique style, which was always up-to-date and well groomed, with some extra little something to make her stand out. She had her own large collection of pins, scarves, and jewelry that always helped her make a statement. Claire was working less, and Grace was working more. When Claire treated her to a dinner to celebrate her fifth anniversary with the store, she was amazed at how quickly time had passed.

Claire had become a devoted admirer of Grace. She enjoyed watching her grow into not only a stylish woman, but also a woman with a gentle heart. She taught Grace everything she knew about operating a retail business. Then one day, it became obvious to Claire that her student now had more knowledge and a better business sense than she had. Instead of becoming jealous, Claire was filled with the joy of knowing that she had a little something to do with this young woman's dynamic personality. With no family of her own, she started to plan for the shop to become Grace's one day.

Grace became involved with fundraising, not only for the theater club but also for the churches, Lake Regional Hospital, and any other good cause that needed her. She was laughingly nicknamed "Amazing Grace" by people in Fergus Falls. She was content in a way she never had dreamed possible.

Grace discovered that she loved going on buying trips. Twice a year, she left for Chicago to view the latest trends in fashion. She always made it a point to stop in Minneapolis and see what the big department stores were displaying in their windows and on their mannequins.

Rebecca and Grace always got together on those trips to Minneapolis. They would stay up all night, laughing and sharing their lives' twists and turns. When Rebecca's relationship with Jeff had fallen apart, she turned to Grace. Grace helped convince her that she needed to let go and move on with life.

Rebecca now lived in a quaint condominium, which she had purchased after graduation. She was constantly begging Grace to move to the big city. Grace always said that she would rather stay in Fergus Falls, where she truly enjoyed a good life.

The two of them valued their friendship. They were always honest with each other, and yet they respected each other as well.

The Fergus Falls Theater Group had also become a popular pastime for many of the residents. The group attracted people of all ages—from cute little five-year-old girls and boys to some lively senior citizens. No one was ever turned away from the group. A job was found for everyone— painting scenery, making costumes, acting, selling ads, and ushering. The Fergus Falls Theater Group belonged to the town.

When the announcement for the casting of the semiannual play was printed in the *Daily Journal*, it became the talk of the town. A steady buzz of gossip could be heard at the Viking Café as to who would be the stars for the latest offering. The newspaper had become a big supporter of the dramas. Cliff Petersen, the editor, was well aware of the number of subscriptions that had increased since they started running weekly articles about the theater club. If Grace did not perform, she was always involved in some way. No one knew that she was secretly writing a few plays of her own. Perhaps someday she would have the courage to present the plays as an option for one of their productions.

All of the other O'Malley children married and moved away. They scattered to Fargo and Minneapolis. Grace helped all of them with their weddings, from loaning them money to getting huge discounts on their wedding outfits. It became a family joke that Grace's bank was always open. None of them ever guessed what she had given up for them. All she ever asked was that the family be together for Christmas Day and July 4, which was Denny's birthday. She simply could not bear to be alone on either of those days.

Grace always found a date for any important event in town. She had dated Tom Wilson, who was the assistant manager at Lincoln Bank, for over a year. Although they enjoyed each other's company, there were never any real sparks in their relationship. When Tom told her about his transfer to a bank in Breckenridge, she was relieved. Six months later, she received a letter from Tom saying that he was engaged and hoped that she, too, would find happiness.

In some of her lonely days, she would laugh about trying to imagine how her love of fashion would mix with being a nun. Grace often talked to Sister Vincent, who had become her spiritual mentor. Sister Vincent often told her that God had a special plan for her, but she did not think being a nun was Grace's calling. She told her that when God's time was right, she would know what to do.

And so, life continued for Grace. She loved working at the dress shop. Each week, she changed the windows, put up new displays, and designed the ads for the *Daily Journal* on their sales and specials. She looked forward to the weekly theater club meetings and volunteered each Saturday at the hospital. Late into the night and during slow times in the store, she worked on writing her plays. She dated every now and then. Grace knew she had a good, steady life.

Her parents were getting older, and keeping up the church and school properties had become more difficult. During a winter storm,

Paul O'Malley was shoveling the walk to the convent when he felt the first stabbing pain. Within minutes, he was lying on the ground, struggling for each breath. Anna saw him fall and ran across the street. Sister Francis rushed to his side and then called for an ambulance. Paul had suffered a major heart attack, with severe heart damage. His days of hard labor were over.

After he spent more than two weeks in the hospital, it became obvious that the O'Malleys were in for another change. The day he came home from the hospital, Anna, Paul, and Grace sat at the kitchen table in a strained silence. Anna finally spoke. "We have decided to move into the senior citizen apartments next month. Your father is no longer able to keep up with the physical demands of his job and this house. We have been offered free rent for managing the apartments' front desk and organizing weekly activities for the residents. Both of us feel that this is another gift from God that we cannot refuse. Just to show you how the timing is right, Father McNulte has already found another couple to take over our duties. In many ways, they remind me of us so many years ago. There is a time to move on, and this is that time. We trust that you will understand and honor our decision."

Father McNulte had offered to let them stay in the house for six months or until they found somewhere to go. However, both Paul and Anna knew that the new caretaker's family needed the house. Nevertheless, they all felt the deep pain of leaving the home where there had been so many memories. They believed that their life needed to change; however, it did not change without a lot of sorrow for the O'Malleys.

Grace found a cozy and sunny apartment on Union Street. Because the O'Malleys' new apartment was so small, they divided the furniture between the two new apartments. They had a rummage sale, where strangers bartered for the excess furniture. After it was done, Anna handed all the money to Grace. She told her to buy herself some special dishes and something nice for her new place.

Grace moved first. Overwhelmed at the pain of leaving her tiny bedroom in her simple little house, she felt alone for the first time in her life. Her parents helped her move, put her things away, and made her bed. Anna made a pot of her special stew and a loaf of warm bread baked in her new stove. Anna told Grace that it was an Irish tradition that the first night in a new home, there must be a freshly baked loaf of bread in the oven. It was a symbol of good health, happiness, and new beginnings.

As Grace lay in her bed in her strange new surroundings, she began to feel a new sense of peace. Somewhere deep inside her, she knew that this was for the best. Another new chapter of her life was beginning to unfold.

Life was never quite the same after the O'Malleys moved. The big family dinners were no longer possible in their tiny apartment. Grace went over every Sunday for dinner, always leaving with leftovers for the week. The O'Malleys quickly adjusted to their new life. They ran the bingo games every Wednesday night, card night on Thursdays, and special trips for all the senior citizens who lived in the building. Within a short time, the residents all adored them. Anna and Paul felt welcomed and happy with their new life. Family Christmas now rotated between Minneapolis and Fargo.

However, the big problem was July 4. Grace was the only one who went to the cemetery. She would sit on a small bench, staring at Denny's simple headstone, and talk to Denny about all the events of their family for the past year. She would cry, laugh, and try to imagine what he would have looked like as a grown man. Grace decided that he would look like a mix of Josh Groban and Tom Hanks. She spent the day alone; and as the fireworks would begin to sound, she would cry for the brother whom she still loved and missed.

The next day, Grace would begin again. Life was kind to her in so many ways. She was truly grateful for the life that she had been given. Fergus Falls had proven to be a delightful place to live her life.

Chapter Twelve

Lindy

New York was overwhelming, even to brave, bold Lindy. She loved the sounds and hustle of the city but hated the constant stream of people pushing everywhere. She had become accustomed to a much quieter way of life in Minnesota. For some reason, people were always commenting on her cute accent. She was never quite sure if they were making fun of her or just making an observation. Lindy thought that all New Yorkers talked far too fast.

It did not take her long to see that her style made her stand out in any New York crowd. It seemed as though every person in New York owned the same tan raincoat and umbrella. When Lindy walked down Fifth Avenue in her bright red coat, boots, umbrella, and scarf, people actually stopped to stare. She simply smiled and kept on walking.

Lindy's graduation gift to herself was that she would not work for the first month in New York City. She planned on taking in all of the many things that New York had to offer. On her first day, she took the bus to Central Park. She sat in amazement at how big it was, spreading over many acres and right in the middle of the city. She quickly discovered the discount ticket booth, where she bought bargain tickets to some of the top Broadway shows. After an evening in the theater, she would take the bus to their apartment. She would fall asleep dreaming of being the star of the show.

Their loft apartment was located on the fringe of the popular Washington Heights district. Both Carol and Lindy laughed as they thought about their parents' reactions to their new home. Their apartment was a fifth-floor walk-up with only two windows and bugs everywhere. They felt lucky that the windows overlooked the street. Many of the lofts overlooked the next building, which was sometimes only a few feet away; they never received a ray of sunshine. The loft came furnished with the essentials but completely lacked color or style.

Lindy went shopping for anything that would bring life into their drab new home. Bright colored silk screens were used to separate the large room into a bedroom, living area, and kitchen. She covered the dull brown furniture with bold striped material. A variety of brightly colored pillows were scattered everywhere. Forty different-shaped wicker baskets were nailed on the walls in interesting patterns. By the end of the first week, their loft looked like a fun place to live, and Lindy felt at home.

Although Lindy put on a brave and bold face to the world, inside she was still frightened and crying for acceptance. As she looked around, all she saw were the women of fashion in New York City; she felt completely out of place. Depression began to overtake her. Her self-doubts began to multiply. During her alone times, Lindy questioned everything about her choices, from her appearance to her choice of a career. Yes, she did want to stand out in the crowd, but she could not bear to be thought of as a clown and laughed at. Lindy felt ashamed of who she was for the first time in her life. She told herself that it was time to get over the depression, so she kept up her happy façade while feeling empty inside. Lindy decided that no one was going to see the sad and weak side of her … no, never.

Lindy soon realized that it was time to find a good-paying job. Living in New York City was far more expensive than she had ever imagined. Her roommate, Carol, was already settled into her new job. She left early in the morning and often did not get home until after midnight. Their friendship became strained as they both realized that they had nothing in common.

For three weeks, Lindy went on interviews with both theater companies and nursing jobs. She decided that whichever job offer came first, it was a sign that it was fate. Lindy signed up with a nursing temporary help agency while waiting for her real job to come along.

Most of her nursing jobs were in busy doctors' offices, where she filled in for vacationing regular staff. After a few months, she started to become comfortable with hopping from job to job. She loved meeting new people in every office. Her bubbly personality won her new friends with each new job.

In November, she received a call from the nursing temporary help office asking her to consider taking an assignment as a personal nurse for a Parkinson's disease patient. Lindy knew she would work well with an older person and quickly accepted the assignment. To her surprise, the address was on Central Park Avenue, where there were many million-dollar condominiums overlooking Central Park. Lindy even asked Carol to help her dress for this very important interview. She had a gut feeling that this was the job that she had been waiting for so patiently.

When Lindy stepped out of the taxi at 25 Central Park Avenue West, she was both impressed and nervous. The uniformed door attendant held the huge brass doors open for her, while another man in the same uniform asked her whom she was here to visit. She told him that she had an appointment with Lawrence St. George. He nodded while he checked a sheet and then escorted her to the elevator. He held the door for her while sliding a security card into a slot on the wall and then pressed the 25 button. Lindy smiled, thinking that she had never been in a building with its own name. The Century even had its own little security force.

When the elevator door opened, there was a stern-looking woman waiting for her in a small marble hallway with two double doors that led into the apartment. The penthouse apartment occupied the entire twenty-fifth floor. The woman introduced herself as Maxine Harris, Mr. St. George's personal assistant. As the doors opened, it took Lindy's breath away. The massive living room and dining room had sun flooding into the floor-to-ceiling windows. Beyond the windows were balconies that overlooked Central Park's boat pond. Everything was decorated in various shades of blue, from sky blue to deep navy, with the exception of the white grand piano. She followed Ms. Harris down a marble hallway that had niches with incredible sculptures in each one. Lindy kept smiling to herself, saying this was really the cat's meow. If only Grandma Flo could see her now!

Lindy was sitting in a wood-paneled library, with bookcases up to the ten-foot ceilings and old, worn, leather furniture. The windows in this room overlooked the back of the building, which had a beautiful, landscaped courtyard. This place was majestic and magical. After a few minutes, there was a soft knock on the door, and a man in an electric wheelchair came into the room. He paused for a moment and then extended his trembling hand to her. In a harsh voice he said, "I am sorry to have kept you waiting. My name is Lawrence St. George, and I am pleased to meet you. I assume that you have been told about the conditions of employment and are prepared to accept the position."

Lindy nodded but told him that she had received very little information regarding the position. Mr. St. George advised her that she had already been cleared on the security background check. All that was needed was for her to agree to sign a privacy of information statement. After that was done, she would become his private nurse. He required care around the clock. A small apartment, which was located off the kitchen, was provided for her. She would have one day off per week; however, she would be required to travel with him. The salary was more than she ever dreamed possible, and he was willing to sign an annual contract with her.

Within two weeks, Lindy had paid Carol her part of the rent for the next four months and had moved into the penthouse on Central Park Avenue. When she arrived with her few belongings, she was led to a charming one-bedroom apartment. The windows in each room overlooked the peaceful courtyard. There were fresh flowers on her kitchen table and a note welcoming her to the staff of Mr. St. George. Lindy could not wait to take photos and send them home to her mom and dad. What a hoot they would get out of their little Lindy's new digs!

Maxine quickly became her new friend, taking her under her wing. She told her that Mr. St. George was a famous author and playwright. The apartment had once belonged to Ethel Merman, the Broadway star of the fifties. The white piano had been too much of a chore to move, so Mr. St. George had kept it. Until her death several years ago, Ms. Merman would often come to visit, along with many of the other Broadway stars. As the Parkinson's continued to worsen, there were fewer parties, and now just small dinner groups were invited.

Although the disease made him look much older, Mr. St. George was only fifty-two. He was a kind and gentle man with a creative mind. Lindy's job was to assist him each day in physical therapy. She also administered his medications and breathing treatments. Many evenings, she would spend time massaging his back, legs, and arms. After spending hours with him each day, she soon became very attached to this wonderful man.

Mr. St. George enjoyed Lindy from the first moment he met her. He immediately saw that her bright, cheerful personality could light up any room she entered. He knew that was just what he needed to keep him positive and motivated. As Lindy massaged his trembling limbs, he would run by a new idea for a show, song, or book. He respected her viewpoints and loved her quirky little suggestions. She finally agreed to start calling him Larry, which no one had ever done. He loved how comfortable he felt when he was with her.

After Lindy had been with Larry for a year, he asked her if she would like to go on a Caribbean cruise with him. She jumped at the chance. She had seen commercials for Carnival Cruises and always dreamed about going on a ship. Two weeks later, they flew in a private jet from New York to Ft. Lauderdale. There was a limo waiting for them as she wheeled Larry down the ramp from the plane. Quickly they were driven to the causeway, where the biggest private boat Lindy had ever seen was waiting for them. It was 125 feet long, with a staff of six to meet their every need. A special stateroom had been prepared to take care of all of Larry's special needs. At 6:00 PM, the yacht left the harbor, just in time to view an incredible sunset. Lindy felt like a princess in a dream as she stood on the deck watching the cityscape fade away.

For two weeks, they sailed to Nassau, St. Thomas, St. Maarten, Puerto Rico, and several small islands. They laughed together, ate together, played cards in the sunshine, and drank wine in the moonlight. It seemed as though they always had something to discuss. There were also comfortable quiet times. Several times after Larry had gotten comfortable in the big chaise lounge, he invited Lindy to come join him. The first time he quietly held her in his arms, Lindy instantly knew that this was where she was meant to be.

The evening before they were due back into Ft. Lauderdale, Larry arranged for a special dinner of lobster and champagne, which was served on the deck of the yacht. There were fresh flowers from the islands, candles everywhere, soft music, and a gentle breeze. After dinner, he moved his wheelchair around to her side of the table and said, "If I were capable of getting down on my knees at this moment, I assure you that I would. I guess you will just have to settle for me as I am. Lindy, you have brought rays of sunshine into my weary, tired body. I love you in a way I never dreamed possible. I realize that the package I can offer you is very flawed. I probably only have a few years of life left. I am sure that they might be challenging years. However, I know that I never want to spend another day without you. I love you with all I am. Will you marry me and help me celebrate each day that I have left?"

Lindy sat still for a moment; never before had she been without words. Larry had surprised her with a joy that she had only dreamed of having in her life. Finally, she pushed back Larry's chair and fell to her knees as she softly whispered, "Yes, Larry St. George. I am overwhelmed with all the possibilities that we will share together as husband and wife. You had better be ready to stick around for a long time because I plan to make you understand that this is the best decision you have ever made, big boy! I have no idea what you see in this girl from Minnesota, but I am ready and willing to start our marriage as soon as we can arrange it." With that said, she leaned forward and tenderly kissed him as she climbed into his lap.

The next day, when the yacht docked, she had another surprise waiting for her. Larry had hoped that Lindy's answer would be yes, and he took it upon himself to make some arrangements that he hoped would make Lindy happy. The entire Pulaski family was waiting for them on the dock. There was also Maxine Harris, a minister, and a stylish woman holding a large garment bag. Three hours later, Lindy walked out onto the deck in a beautiful white gown, her hair in soft curls, with both of her parents at her side. The wedding ceremony was short and meaningful.

The next morning, as they flew back to New York, Lindy slept cuddled in the arms of her new husband. When she awoke, she stared at the large diamond ring on her finger and knew she was not dreaming. She knew that she would love being Mrs. Lindy St. George. God had given her a very special gift to cherish. Now she just needed a lifetime to show Larry that he had made the right choice.

One year flowed into the next for the St. Georges. Both of them were amazed at how deep their love for each other had grown. They could finish each other's sentences, knew when the other needed a laugh or a hug, and most important, they learned to simply enjoy each day that was given to them. Larry often held Lindy's hand as she walked beside him in his electric wheelchair. Of course, Lindy had a special wheelchair fabric designed that looked like a beautiful abstract painting and painted the wheels fire-engine red.

The St. Georges became one of the most popular couples in New York City. They entertained small dinner parties and attended charity functions. After several years of just having fun, Larry asked Lindy to assist him in writing his final play. The project gave them both a newfound purpose. It took two years to complete, and in the end, Larry decided to produce the play himself. The Broadway musical sounded very much like their life story. The opening night of the play *Thanks for the Loving* took place on their wedding anniversary and was a smashing success.

Now Larry was on oxygen all the time. It took days of bed rest before and after opening night for him to get enough energy to attend. He was constantly having more difficulty swallowing and breathing. Finally, he accepted that a feeding tube needed to be permanently installed. Both Lindy and Larry were well aware that the signs were not good.

Slowly, their daily routine began to change. Larry spent more time in bed sleeping. There were fewer visitors and no more outings. They decided together after a long, difficult night of breathing problems that Larry needed to be admitted to the hospital. Lindy never left his side except when some painful treatment was being administered that she could not bear to watch. Together, they had made the decision that no extreme measures to keep him alive would be taken. All they wanted was that Larry would be pain-free for as long as possible.

Lindy slept on a couch in his hospital room. Many nights she would climb into his hospital bed, cuddling close to him. One morning as she woke up next to him, Larry slowly opened his eyes, looked at her, and softly whispered, "My sunshine, thanks for the loving, kiddo." He took his last breath while holding her in his weak arms.

Lindy's life without Lawrence St. George was empty and barren. The beautiful penthouse no longer held any magic for her. Because of the complex multimillion-dollar estate, it took almost two years before all the legal work was done. Lindy donated millions of dollars to causes that she knew Larry wanted to support. She bought her parents a beautiful condominium in Naples, Florida, where they could escape the hard, cold Minnesota winters. She took art classes and tried each day to find a way to simply live until it was time to go to sleep. Vivid dreams in which she and Larry danced and sang in the moonlight aboard the yacht came to her. She woke one morning crying. The previous night in a dream that seemed so real, Larry held her gently as he softly told her it was time to let go and move on. She knew it was time to learn how to find happiness without Larry.

When she put the penthouse up for sale, she had no idea where she would go from there; all she knew was that this chapter in her life was finished. Larry was gone, but she was alive; she needed to find joy once again. Within a short time, the penthouse was sold with most of the furnishings to a couple from England. They were completely unaware of all the magic moments that had taken place within this beautiful home.

As Lindy packed her belongings, she came across a box marked SOLA. When she opened it, she found the sweater from Emily, Isabel's wonderful quilt, and the locket from Grace. She clutched all of them as she started to sob uncontrollably. Life had taken her to places that she had never dreamed of going. Only this time, she knew that she could survive anything. There would not be an experience more painful than losing Larry.

She slept in his chair in the den the last night in the penthouse, wrapped up in Isabel's special quilt. She smiled as she remembered the first time she had walked into this room. She thought of the wonderful memories she had been blessed to have. Tomorrow, the few personal things she had decided to keep would be taken to a storage company. She had arranged for a private jet to fly her to Florida, where she had just purchased a condominium sight unseen close to her parents. She knew they would have a special meal with Polish sausage and desserts waiting for her arrival. Lindy also knew that they would give her a hug and tell her that she was going to be okay. Then she would figure out what to do next with her life as a millionaire. Tomorrow, Lindy would begin again.

Chapter Thirteen

Rebecca

Rebecca's love of music became her link to happiness. She moved into her condominium in Minneapolis shortly after graduation. For the first time in her life, she decided it was time to spend some of the money that she had been receiving from the income properties. An interior decorator was hired, and she gave her a generous budget. Then Rebecca left to spend the summer with her mother and grandmother.

Summer back in Fergus Falls was just what she needed to heal her wounds. During those lazy days, Rebecca healed her soul and renewed her spirit. She enjoyed the time with her mother and grandmother. They took long drives into the country, passing well-tended farms and small, pretty lakes. They rented a cabin on Ottertail Lake, where they went fishing, took naps, and ate out every evening. Monica had the time to get to know Rebecca as an adult woman. She loved what she saw in this strong but very gentle young woman. Grandma Ruby and Rebecca spent hours sitting on the front porch talking about her heritage and Ruby's memories of the past.

What had started out as an escape for the pain of a broken heart turned into a blessing. All three women knew that this summer would always be remembered as a very special time, filled with laughter, good food, and lots of love. Fergus Falls had never looked prettier to Rebecca than it did that summer.

On a hot summer day in August, Rebecca was ready to return to Minneapolis. Her time at home had filled her up with a newfound courage and healed the pains of her past. Her spacious new condominium had been painted, furnished, and decorated. As she walked in the door, she gasped with amazement. The cold, sterile apartment had been magically transformed into the feel of a cozy English cottage. The soft colors seemed to shimmer on the walls. The furniture was overstuffed with colors of springtime flowers. Her bedroom was done in many different shades of pink, from a soft rose hue to bright raspberry. Even the balcony was decorated with two comfortable chairs, a small, beautiful mosaic table, and pots filled with roses.

Rebecca smiled as she looked at the soft beauty that surrounded her. To match the beauty of her new home, she went on a shopping spree for new clothes, which gave her the same soft quality. A new chapter was opening in her life, and she felt completely comfortable about what the future would hold for her.

Before leaving for Fergus Falls, Rebecca had accepted a teaching position at a private all-girls high school named Holy Angels Academy. It was a school steeped in old-fashioned and honored traditions. It held a high reputation in the academic community. Rebecca was going to be teaching freshman English literature and music.

The last week in August, Rebecca walked down the sparkling clean marble halls of the academy, ready to face the challenges of her new career. After a week of orientation conducted by a stern-faced Sister Mary Rosa, she felt prepared for her students. Sister Mary Rosa was a taskmaster who warned Rebecca that she would be keeping a very close eye on her and that she expected her to follow the rules of the academy at all times. As Rebecca watched the stream of giggling girls walk into their new school, she knew in her heart that Holy Angels was just where she needed to be.

After getting off to a rough start with Sister Mary Rosa, who kept true to her promise to constantly keep a watchful eye on her, Rebecca quickly found a comfortable routine. To her amazement, she enjoyed teaching English literature as much as she enjoyed all of her musical duties. Her students quickly became attached to Rebecca. She introduced many of them to poetry for the first time in their young lives. They laughed as she read a love poem.

Each year, she found a few new girls who needed her gentle mentoring, and she carefully took them under her protective wing. She worked with them on their self-esteem and helped them to develop their talents. Even Sister Mary Rosa sent a few troubled girls to her for her special kind of help. Before she knew it, her first class of freshmen girls were graduating.

When asked to be an escort for the senior choir to Ireland, Rebecca jumped at the opportunity. After a long flight, the group settled into a hotel in Dublin, sinking into their lumpy, soft beds for a good night's sleep. The next six days were a whirlwind of singing in old gothic cathedrals and sightseeing. Their tour guide was a delightful man in his early thirties named Connor Delaney. His bright blue eyes always seemed to have an extra little sparkle when he talked with Rebecca. It seemed that most evenings when they arrived in another small Irish town, the two of them would end up sitting next to each other for dinner.

With two days left of the tour, they had a free day in Waterford. Connor asked Rebecca if she would like to spend the day with him. He lived nearby in a small fishing village. Connor was going home to celebrate his grandfather Patty's eightieth birthday. Rebecca quickly agreed and was anxious to see the real life of these delightful and friendly people.

When they arrived in the village of Clonea, Rebecca was surprised by the beauty of Dungarvan Bay and its sandy beaches. As they walked through the small village, she felt as though she had been taken back in time to when life was simple. After walking for a while, Connor told her that they had arrived at the party. They stood in front of Muldoon's Pub, which looked as though it had been built centuries ago. In fact, it had been built by the Muldoons and Delaneys in the 1800s. After arguing about what to name the pub, they finally decided to flip a coin. Michael Muldoon won, and that was the name ever since.

As the pub doors opened, smoke billowed out the old wooden doors. Once inside, Rebecca found herself in the middle of a crowd of Irish folks who knew how to drink, dance, tell a joke, laugh, and smoke, all at the same time. They were all there to celebrate Patty Delaney's birthday. A long table was set against a wall with enough food piled high for twice as many people. There were people of all ages, from the elders of the clan to little babies in strollers. The day was filled with tall glasses of Guinness beer, singing, dancing, long-winded toasts, and storytelling. Patty quickly told Rebecca that she was the vision of an angel that God had given him for his birthday. They danced around the bar together laughing and talking as he spun her around and around.

As Connor and Rebecca were getting ready to leave, Patty announced to the crowd that he had one more toast to make for his special birthday wish. His sons quickly lifted him to stand atop a table. Patty lifted his glass and said, "The Lord has been good to this old fisherman. He has given me a good woman, my Mary, my sweetheart to this day, good sons, and many fat fish. Now, he has seen fit to give this bag of bones one more surprise. I say to you all, that this gift is an angel named Rebecca, who finally has put a twinkle into the eyes of my grandboy, Connor. May they be smart enough to know they need to marry and give me lots of hearty great-grandbabies!" The crowd all lifted their glasses to the toast and then turned to look at Connor and Rebecca as they stood there with shocked expressions on their faces.

On the drive back to Waterford, Connor kept apologizing for his grandpa's old-fashioned ways. Rebecca simply assured him that she had never had so much fun. They laughed and talked about how different their worlds were. For the last two days of the tour, they were always together. They talked about their past, how they grew up, and their dreams for the future. Connor asked if he could write to her, and Rebecca quickly said yes. By the time the group arrived back at Dublin's airport, both Connor and Rebecca knew they would miss each other's company.

They both returned to their ordinary worlds. Connor's world was a small fishing village filled with his family and boyhood friends. He continued to work for the tour company for a few months each year, but his real love was to work on the Delaneys' fishing boats with his brothers, Sean and Quincy. He dated a few of the local girls but never really found a burning desire for any of them.

Rebecca's world was busy. She also casually dated but never seemed to find Mr. Right. After the trip to Ireland, they both exchanged letters for a few months. Slowly Connor began to realize that he had nothing to offer Rebecca and decided to stop writing. Rebecca wrote several more times but eventually became discouraged and tore up her last letter. They both missed each other; however, they both knew their worlds just did not seem to blend together.

The following three years, the senior choir traveled to Spain, France, and Italy. Each trip, Rebecca thought of Connor and their time together. Then four years later, it was announced that they were returning to Ireland. Rebecca quickly contacted the tour agency and demanded that Connor Delaney be their tour guide. She wrote Connor to tell him about the upcoming tour but never received an answer.

Four months later, as the group walked through Dublin's airport, she saw him waiting for her with a bouquet of wildflowers. She ran to his arms as the girls all stood in shock. The next ten days, they never left each other's side. Connor had arranged for his cousin, Thomas, to be their tour guide. This gave him and Rebecca time to walk together through the beautiful gardens, stand on the cliffs overlooking the ocean, and watch as the emerald green hills rolled by their bus. They talked late into each evening and started again as soon as they came together for breakfast. By the end of the tour, Rebecca had agreed to come back for a visit during the summer. Connor had agreed to visit her home also so she could show him the beauty of Fergus Falls and Minneapolis.

On the long flight home, Rebecca thought perhaps Patty Delaney's birthday wish might actually come true. She wondered if this could possibly be true love in such a brief time together. As she fell asleep on the plane, she could have sworn she heard the soft Irish voice of Patty saying, "Yes, my darling girl, this is just what love feels like. Enjoy it, my sweet angel."

Two weeks after school was finished, Rebecca was back in Ireland. Connor met her at the Dublin airport. As they drove back to Clonea in an old pickup truck, they talked nonstop. The Delaney clan lived in a row of three-story identical townhouses two blocks away from the water and around the corner from Muldoon's Pub. Grandpa Patty and Mary Delaney lived in the corner unit, which was blessed with the most windows. Next door to Patty and Mary's, Connor lived with his mom, Kathleen, and pops, Timothy. Next to them lived Sean and Katie with their four children—Andrew, Michael, Brigit, and Nora. The last townhouse was home to Connor's brother Quincy, who was married to Patricia; their twins were named John and Sarah. Rebecca would be staying with Grandpa Patty and Maggie, as that was the only proper thing to do.

For two weeks, the Delaneys embraced Rebecca with their warm Irish hospitality. They proudly introduced her to everyone in the village. They ate, laughed, danced, told her story after story, drank, and toasted her arrival.

Then came Sunday, when everything changed. Every Sunday morning all of the Delaneys came out of their front doors at the same time to walk the three short blocks to St. Matthew's for Sunday Mass. When Rebecca calmly announced that she would not be able to attend the church because she was Lutheran, Grandpa Patty shook his head and left the room without saying a word. Sundays the Delaney clan had a tradition of nine o'clock Mass, followed by hot ham and rolls with coffee in the church basement. After that, everyone came back home, changed, and grabbed their hot dish or dessert. By noon, the clan had settled in at Muldoon's for an afternoon together.

Rebecca's missing the church service brought all of the closeness she had felt to a halt. She felt alone for the first time since she had arrived. At Muldoon's, there was another birthday party celebration. By mid-afternoon, Rebecca was having an asthma attack. Quietly she walked outside, sat on a bench, and used her inhaler. Half an hour later, she was still having problems breathing when Connor came out looking for her. He looked shocked when he saw how pale she was.

He told her to wait right there and he would bring the car to take her to Waterford. It was late that night when they walked into Grandpa Patty's door. Patty and Mary were sitting at the kitchen table waiting for them with worried expressions on their faces. For the next few days, Rebecca was treated like a china doll. They did not know how to deal with someone who was not hearty and healthy.

By Friday, Rebecca had changed her airline tickets. Connor and Rebecca hugged as they waited for her flight to be called for boarding. They both had mixed feelings of a longing to be together and a relief from the tension of the past few days. They talked about Connor coming to visit, but they knew it would be a long time before he could save the money for the trip.

Rebecca returned home confused and in love. Their letters overflowed with what was happening in their daily lives and their dreams to be together again. As the months went by, they both felt they needed to see each other. Rebecca had offered to give Connor a roundtrip ticket to

Minneapolis, which he immediately turned down as a matter of pride. In November, Rebecca bought the ticket as a Christmas gift for Connor to come for a visit for New Year's Eve. She needed to find out if they truly had any hope for a future together. One week later, Connor called and said he would be arriving on December 27 for two weeks.

Unlike their time in Clonea, there was no family to chaperone them in Minneapolis. It was Rebecca's turn to meet Connor as he walked off the plane. She saw him first, and she ran to him with her arms outstretched. When they walked into her apartment, Connor stood in shock at the size and beauty of it. He quickly turned to her and asked if she was rich. All this space for one person was amazing to him. Compared to Dublin, Minneapolis was only a little bigger but five times busier. Rebecca was his tour guide by day and his lover each night. It was an incredible two weeks of happiness and love. When he left, they both were talking about their future and wondering how they could make this work.

For the next few years, Connor and Rebecca took turns coming to visit each other. The only difference was that the first few days of Rebecca's visits to Ireland were spent in Dublin with each other. Rebecca made Connor promise that she would never have to be in Clonea on a Sunday, and he made sure it was always arranged. Their love continued to grow—as well as their frustration with being so far apart.

During his annual New Year's visit, Connor proposed and offered Rebecca a small antique diamond ring that had been his grandmother's engagement ring. Rebecca immediately accepted. They drove to Fergus Falls and made their announcement to Grandma Ruby and Monica. Everyone was thrilled. It was decided that they would have a small church wedding in August in Fergus Falls and another blessing of the marriage in Clonea the following week.

Connor agreed to apply for a visa. He would move to Minneapolis. He said he would try to become an American lad.

On June 10, Rebecca received a call at two o'clock in the morning from Connor. He was sobbing as he told her that Grandpa Patty had just passed away from a massive heart attack. Rebecca immediately made plans for the trip, and two days later she arrived in Dublin. She rented a small car and drove to Clonea. When she arrived, she found a large black ribbon draped over Patty and Mary Delaney's front door.

The next morning, the village of Clonea closed all the small shops and came to honor Patty at his funeral Mass. The church had standing room only. After Mass ended, there was a procession with Patty's casket to the cemetery at the outskirts of the village. Once again, prayers were said and people sobbed as one by one they took a small wildflower and placed it on his casket. Then the crowd turned around, and the procession walked through the narrow streets while singing hymns.

To Rebecca's surprise, the path went straight to Muldoon's, where Patty's wake was held. For the rest of the day, people drank and celebrated Patty's life by sharing stories about him, toasted some more, and laughed. The only difference between Patty's birthday and his wake was that there was no dancing. Patty was given a wonderful Irish send-off, and all agreed that he was now dancing with the angels while he shook St. Peter's hand at the pearly gates of heaven.

It was after 10:00 PM when the Delaney clan wandered back home. Ever since Patty's death, Connor had stayed with Grandma Mary. He tried to comfort her and give her the assistance she needed to make all the arrangements. As Mary crawled into bed that night, she was overwhelmed with the loss of Patty's bright spirit, but nonetheless amazed at the joy she had experienced when celebrating his life at the wake.

Rebecca left a few days later, promising to return during the next month for a large wedding shower that was being arranged for her and Connor. Unlike American showers, which were only for the women, an Irish wedding shower included both the bride and the groom. Once again, the village would gather at Muldoon's Pub for the celebration.

Two weeks later to the day, Monica called Rebecca to tell her that Grandma Ruby had died in her sleep. Rebecca now called Connor and arranged to have his airline tickets waiting for him the next day. It seemed like a nightmare to relive all the emotions of a few weeks ago, only this time it was Connor who drove himself from Fargo, North Dakota, to be with Rebecca in Fergus Falls. When he arrived, Monica greeted him with a soft hug and told him that Rebecca was taking Ruby's death very hard.

The funeral home visitation was that evening, with a funeral service the next day at Bethlehem Lutheran Church. The experience of the two funerals could not have been more opposite. The quiet funeral home, with people coming to talk softly to Monica and Rebecca, was scary to Connor. He finally had a chance to meet Grace O'Malley, whom he had heard so many good things about. He now understood why Rebecca considered Grace such a close friend. She was delightful and obviously cared a great deal about Rebecca.

The next day, with the church almost empty, the funeral service was brief, with the minister announcing at the end that all were invited to have lunch in the church hall, the food provided by the women of the church. The tables were set with fresh flowers. A lunch of ham, potato salad, fruit, homemade cake, and coffee was served to the few who attended the funeral. There was neither drinking nor toasts. There was no celebration or even going to the graveside. People sat politely discussing Ruby but also talking about the strange weather they were having.

Connor left the church hall feeling sad and confused. He was sad for Rebecca's loss of her grandmother and confused at the lack of celebration of the dear, sweet woman's life. A week later, he flew back to Ireland and was happy to be back with his people. He knew life in the United States was going to take a lot more adjustment than he had earlier thought.

Because of the funeral and staying with Monica for a while, Rebecca missed a fitting for her bridal gown, an appointment with the minister, and the deadline on ordering the special cake she had wanted for the wedding dinner. During her time in Fergus Falls, Rebecca often went to lunch with Grace. They talked about Connor and what a handsome man he was. Rebecca told Grace all about Clonea and the difference in their backgrounds.

The day before Rebecca was leaving to return to Minneapolis, she received a call from Pastor Meissner, asking her to stop by for a chat. When she arrived, the pastor immediately started discussing the preparations for the wedding, which was going to be held in the small prayer chapel in the back corner of the church. Without warning, Rebecca began to sob. Pastor Meissner tried his best to console her, but nothing seemed to help. Rebecca finally composed herself and told the pastor that the wedding would not be taking place as scheduled.

She went home and told her mother that the timing was just not right for the wedding. With two deaths of loved ones so close together, she felt that they needed to postpone the wedding for a respectable period of time. She called Grace and asked her to cancel her wedding dress and Grace's dress, which she had ordered as maid of honor. Five minutes later, Grace appeared at her front door and took her by the hand into the backyard. They talked for hours as all of Rebecca's fears for the marriage came tumbling out of her. They hugged, they cried, and Grace gave Rebecca the comfort and courage she needed to make the call to Connor.

The next morning, Rebecca sat in the dining room by the only phone in her mother's house and made the most difficult call she had ever made. She quietly explained to Connor that she felt the timing was wrong. Connor quickly agreed and told her that perhaps they both needed time to take care of their loved ones and mourn their losses. He would cancel his flight and call her in a few weeks.

Crying, they said their good-byes. When the call disconnected in Fergus Falls and in Clonea, there was a painful disconnect in their two lives. Although they had not spoken the words, they both knew that their futures would never blend. They had loved much and lost much; however, they had both learned much. Neither of them would ever be the same.

Chapter Fourteen

The Invitation

Grace was appointed chairperson for the Fergus Falls High School twentieth class reunion for their graduating class. She enjoyed designing the invitations and announcements that would appear in the *Daily Journal*. The reunion would take place in October, a perfect time to return to Fergus Falls. It was during the week of the Fall Festival, when all the trees would be at the height of their colors of gold, orange, and amber; the weather promised to be cool and fresh.

Grace had already reserved rooms at the Holiday Inn for her returning classmates who would not be staying with family. The Eagles Club, which looked like a ship in the middle of a field, had been reserved for the Friday evening get-together. The Elks Club, which had been remodeled, was the perfect place for the reunion dance and dinner on Saturday night. The weekend would finish with a breakfast in the church basement of Our Lady of Victory and a parade of cars that would make their way through the town and end at Dairyland, where Grace had arranged for the owner to make their favorite chocolate with chocolate chip ice cream. She knew that many of her high school classmates had not been home for many years and would be surprised by the changes in Fergus Falls these days.

The once busy downtown now had many vacant stores due to the new mall that was built right off the new highway exit. However, a few of the stores kept Lincoln Street alive. The Viking Restaurant and City Café still served wonderful food six days a week; they had both decided to stay closed on Sundays. Claire's Dress Shop remained the best place for miles to find or order that special outfit. Grace was now the full-time manager and buyer. She never missed her weekly lunch with Claire, who was retired. Grace kept her up-to-date with the latest styles and town gossip. Victor Lundeen's bookstore had expanded and had recently started selling some local artwork. The movie theater had been renovated and now hosted special concerts, plays, and recitals. Its new red velvet seats and matching red velvet stage curtain made it a very impressive place. Olsen's furniture store remained downtown; however, they had built a separate funeral home a few blocks away. The men continued to shop at St. Claire's for their church suits, as well as their flannel shirts and coveralls in the basement. J. C. Penney and Woolworth's had moved to the mall, leaving large, empty buildings for rent. Most of the folks had mixed feelings about the mall and considered it both a curse and a blessing.

Grace had every intention to track down her Sisterhood of Lake Alice girlfriends and persuade them to come home for the reunion. However, her days became busy with work and performing in the Fergus Falls Theater Group play of *Camelot*. The retired high school assistant principal, Mrs. Klein, took over the project of trying to track down the classmates and mailing out the invitations. The search for the students became her mission. She put ads in the *Daily Journal* asking for the whereabouts of the missing classmates. She was amazed that she found almost every graduate.

The invitation to the reunion was in the midst of piles of mail that had been stacked, wrapped in rubber bands, and saved for Lindy while she was on her trip. She had surprised her parents with a two-week trip to Poland. With no responsibilities back home in Florida, they decided to roam around the country.

Lindy hired a chauffeur named Walter, who took them anywhere they wanted to go. They saw the scars of World War II. In painful silence, they stood in a graveyard that had been lovingly cared for. It was the final resting place for the people of an entire small village, all of whom had been killed by the Nazis. The town now stood silent as a memorial to its brave citizens. They drove through areas where the beautiful green hills reminded them of Fergus Falls. They saw the industrial towns filled with large factories billowing thick, black smoke in the air. Every day brought a new emotion. What had been planned for two weeks quickly turned into a month. Finally, with extra-large suitcases packed full of all their treasures, they returned to Florida.

It took Lindy over a week to sort through all of her mail, magazines, and catalogs. She was sitting out on her veranda with her morning cup of coffee when she opened the invitation to the class reunion. As she looked out over the simmering waters of the Gulf of Mexico, her mind raced back to her bright pink bedroom above the Fresh Daisy Dry Cleaners and Laundry. Memories washed over her as she thought of her loving Grandma Flo. As she sat there, she could almost hear the machines as they tumbled clothes with their distinct rhythm.

She knew she would attend the reunion, if for no other reason than to revisit the Fresh Daisy Cleaners. It was the place where her life began. Now she lived in a million-dollar condominium, with furniture that cost more than the entire building where she had been raised. Her memories were good ones. She was looking forward to returning to her old stomping grounds.

Lindy immediately called her parents and invited them to make the trip with her. To her surprise, they quickly agreed. The only condition was that they could bring their new puppies along. The thought of seeing Fergus Falls in the fall was exciting to all of them. The following day, Lindy purchased a forty-foot RV loaded with all the comforts of home to take them back to Fergus Falls. It had a leather sofa and chairs, a kitchen, a bathroom, and a bedroom area for her parents. There was plenty of space for her to sleep on the sofa, which folded out into a bed. She hired a driver and told her that the trip would probably take a few weeks, with time to visit friends in Fergus and also some stops along the way. Lindy looked forward to sharing this adventure with her parents.

With the travel plans done, Lindy went to her dressmaker and ordered six special outfits for the reunion. She was a big woman, still a size 22, with the same love of sparkles that her mother had long ago. She enjoyed bright colors, unusual fabrics, and outlandish styles. Lindy had developed a dramatic style over the years; she looked like an overweight Dolly Parton with her high hair and glittery outfits.

As she mailed in her RSVP with her check, she began to think about the SOLA girls and hoped that they could all come back together for some good girlfriend time. Lastly, she called the Holiday Inn and reserved the biggest suite they had available, with adjoining rooms to each side of it. She wanted to make sure that there was enough room for at least one PJ party with the girls while she was home.

She smiled as she went to sleep, thinking about the dreams of the little girl who sang her heart out at the county fair. It was an interesting journey so far, and there was much more to come. Look out, Fergus Falls, Lindy is coming back to town!

Rebecca had heard all about the reunion from Grace on their many late-night telephone calls. She had agreed to help Grace in any way possible. However, the school year and all of its challenges quickly got in the way of her best intentions. As Rebecca opened the beautiful invitation, she was sure that Grace had designed it.

Rebecca could not help but think about the fact that twenty years had slipped away. As she sat on her sofa, she thought back to the days when Fergus Falls had been her universe. Life was so uncomplicated then. She smiled remembering Grandma Ruby's humming as she made lefse. Now Ruby was gone, but the memories remained. Monica still lived alone in her tidy little home on Bancroft Street. She worked long hours at the Pioneer Nursing Home as an aide. She had a special gift of working with the elderly and truly loved her job.

Rebecca thought about how different life had turned out for her. She had just assumed that she would get married and have two or three children. She would teach piano so that she could stay at home with the children. Instead, she had remained single, devoted to the girls in her English classes and choirs. She traveled each year with the senior choir as they toured Europe. Although she found great rewards in her profession, she always felt unfulfilled at the end of each year. Yet each September, when her classroom filled with a new group of girls who were eager to learn, she felt renewed.

Her health had been a constant problem. She was hospitalized three times in the past year with serious breathing problems. Nevertheless, she did not want her mom or friends to worry needlessly, so she kept the poor test results to herself. Just last week, her doctor had insisted that she see a cardiologist. He was very concerned with her declining health.

It seemed so ironic that today she held the reunion invitation in her hands. It was the same day that the cardiologist had reviewed the test results and called her for an immediate appointment. Rebecca already knew what Dr. Norton was going to tell her. However, she still was not prepared when she actually heard the words spoken. Congestive heart failure combined with poor pulmonary function was an incurable disease. Her health issues had already progressed to the point where serious treatment was required. The doctor had recommended that she be on oxygen and limit her daily activities. There was nothing to stop the disease from rapidly growing worse at this stage. Only a complex combination of medications would help keep her comfortable.

The doctor's final comments were startling: "Given your current poor physical condition, I would say that without a miracle, you have no longer than a year to live. If it were me, I would enjoy every day as much as I can. Try to live with as little stress as possible. In time, the medications will cease to be effective in your treatment. I am sorry to give this news; however, I believe it is always best to be honest with my patients."

Rebecca left his office with a fistful of prescriptions and a schedule for weekly breathing treatments. Upon her request, Dr. Norton had given her a lot of information that detailed how the disease would progress and what she could expect to have happen along the way.

As Rebecca left the medical building, she looked around at the busy streets of Minneapolis. She wondered why everyone was in such a hurry. Against the doctor's recommendation, she had decided to take one last student tour to Europe. She had reluctantly agreed to cut back her teaching schedule for the rest of the school year. Rebecca assisted in finding her replacement at Holy Angels Academy. The nuns were deeply saddened; however, they also understood. Rebecca knew that her life had just made a dramatic change of course. She also knew that her new priority was to make the best of each day she was given from now on.

She called Grace and left a message that she was coming to the reunion and that she was thinking about moving back to Fergus Falls. Then Rebecca went to bed. She cried all night for the life that she would never have, for the children she would never hold in her arms. Tears flowed for the husband she would never love. As the sunrise came up, she simply decided to live each day to the fullest. Rebecca knew that Fergus Falls was going to be her safe haven. The reunion was going to be very important.

The reunion invitation took almost three months before it finally reached Emily. After it was returned several times, Mrs. Klein was finally able to track down Dr. Larson in Scottsdale, Arizona. He was traveling with his new wife in Europe and was not expected back for several months. In his absence, his mail had been forwarded to his attorney's office. After another few weeks, the unopened envelope was finally mailed with several other documents to Emily's address in Waukesha, Wisconsin.

A cover letter from the firm of Kelly, Harris, and McGraw reminded Emily that she had inherited the Fergus Falls residence upon her mother's death six months ago. The house with all its furnishings was vacant and in need of immediate repair. If she wished the house to be sold, she needed to advise him. He would arrange for the repairs to be made and then contract with a local real estate agent to put the house up for sale.

As Emily read the legal wording, a chill ran through her body. She thought it was so fitting that this was how she discovered that she had any inheritance from her mother: just a cold, impersonal packet of legal documents. It seemed a very fitting way to end this part of her life. As much as Emily gave to others in need, there was still no one to care for her when she was in need.

Emily mourned for the wasted life her mother had lived. She had wasted her days always trying to impress people. Those same people simply did not care about her enough to attend her funeral. Emily had flown to Arizona after receiving the call from her father that Joyce had passed away suddenly. Although she was never told, Emily assumed the years of drinking had finally taken their toll on her mother.

It had been almost eight years since she had seen either of her parents. She stayed at the Hyatt in Scottsdale for her brief two-day stay. There was a simple memorial service, with no minister or religious service. Joyce Larson had left this world with an elegant ending; however, there was not a tear shed for her.

While she sat reading the boring legal forms, she found another envelope. She opened it and found an engraved invitation to her twentieth class reunion. Emily sat in amazement. How was it possible that twenty years had already passed? Then she smiled. She thought that perhaps the two pieces of information coming together was a sign. It could be that it was time to return to Fergus Falls. It would be the last time she would walk through the house that was never a home except for when she was there with Isabelle, Grace, Rebecca, and Lindy. Yes, it was time to return for one last visit.

Emily smiled as she remembered the beauty of Fergus Falls in autumn. She filled out the reservation card and mailed it with a check the next day.

✧

As Grace made her to-do list for the reunion, she wrote down that her first task was to find the girls of SOLA. Convincing them to come home for this special reunion was her top priority. After she had accomplished that, she would try to talk them into performing once for their classmates. Rebecca had already agreed to the plan. She told Grace that she would help in any way she could. They both knew the challenge was going to be to find Emily and Lindy. In her heart, she knew that somehow they would all be together again.

Grace was also in the midst of a major expansion of Claire's shop. After she leased the empty space next door, which had been vacant for several years, the work began. She had just made the last payment to Claire, and Grace was now the sole owner of Claire's Dress Shop. It was time for her to take a little risk. An idea came to her that Claire's should carry clothes for everyone from babies to women in their eighties. She bought everything from baptismal gowns to dresses with Velcro closures instead of buttons. She found a new high-energy level that she had not felt for years. Soon she had drawn up new floor plans for the shop. The racks of clothing, new special display windows, and an outdoor sign were scheduled to arrive within six weeks. She had spent all of her savings, as well as taken out her first business loan, to pay for all the new improvements.

Grace spent every night and all Sunday working on the new shop's look. She discovered how to paint murals on the walls by using a projector and outlining the figures. The shop was divided into six very different areas.

In the infant area, she painted angels and pixies on the walls in soft shades of pink and lavender. She draped a soft gauze fabric on the ceiling to soften the lights and create an interesting effect. She had a corner for the little girls to play with a giant dollhouse and stuffed animals. She finished the area with two hand-painted benches with soft cushions.

Candice was in charge of the infants, toddlers and small children's area of the shop. She often brought her three-year-old daughter named Taylor and her son, T. J., with her to work. They dressed them both in the newly arrived outfits and took photos of them for their catalog. This way the grandmothers could see how darling their granddaughters and grandsons would look in the clothes. Taylor would spend hours playing with the dollhouse and often sleeping on top of the huge soft teddy bear, which was several inches taller than she was, while T. J. worked on his homework. She had officially become the shop's mascot.

Next to that was the preteen section. Here the walls were painted deep lavender and rose. On the walls, she painted a screen of girls on bicycles, ice-skating, and playing. The racks of clothes were sorted by color and then size, so if a girl had a favorite color, she could easily find it. She hung twinkling white lights to add a whimsical feeling to the area. There were wicker baskets filled with socks that matched each outfit and ribbons and hair accessories. On what looked like a tree, she hung little purses, hats, and belts. She painted the floor with patterns of hopscotch and tic-tac-toe.

Grace promoted Jodi to manager of the preteen and teen section of the shop. Jodi's teenage daughter, Adriana, quickly pointed out what was the latest fashion trend. She stopped at the shop at least one day each week to advise her mother on what to buy and how to display the latest fads. Adriana hoped that when she turned sixteen, she could work in the shop. Photos were taken with her in her favorite outfits for the catalog.

In the teen area, with its bright purple and raspberry swirls, there were beanbag chairs scattered around. Instead of display racks, Grace put together cubes that held the latest jeans and T-shirts. She decorated one wall by nailing up old 45 records and hung them from the ceiling as well. Right outside the dressing rooms, a platform was built to resemble a model's runway, with a huge three-way mirror at the end of it. The lighting around the mirrors gave the appearance of being on a stage. Jodi hung belts and accessories on a unique pulley system so her customers had to work a little to reach their favorite items. Since this area was in the far corner of the store, Grace installed a separate music system; however, Jodi had full control of the volume from her desk.

Grace painted the original section of the shop in soft shades of pink, green, and lavender with the same soft gauze for a special lighting effect. She purchased comfortable, overstuffed floral chairs and hand-painted an English garden scene on the brick wall. For the final touch, she created a small make-believe garden that appeared to extend out of the wall painting by arranging baskets of the same silk flowers. There was a casual clothing display area and another for better suits and dresses.

JoAnn had been with Grace and Claire for many years. She was in charge of assisting the senior women in their selections. She often would call one of the regulars to tell them about a new sweater or dress that would be just right for them. When a customer walked in the front door, JoAnn could greet them by name. She often had a dressing room reserved for her favorite ladies, with a selection of clothes waiting for them to try on. Each of the four dressing rooms was large enough for a three-way mirror and one comfortable chair.

In the back corner of the shop, there was a section with a counter holding many catalogs. This was the place where a woman would order a wedding and bridesmaid dresses, a formal, or a special outfit. Kelli was in charge of taking and tracking every special order. She also maintained all of the "regulars'" information, which included their current size, preference in colors, and styles. If a customer mentioned that she liked a certain outfit, Kelli quickly entered it into her computer.

Most of the men in Fergus knew that Kelli would help them pick out the perfect gift every time. There was a running joke in town that the first stop after a couple became engaged was to see Kelli at Claire's shop. She created a database for their birthdates and anniversaries as well. Kelli made sure to mail a postcard to the husband's or boyfriend's office, reminding them it was time to come in to purchase a special gift for their wife or girlfriend.

For the final welcoming touch, Grace put a small coffee and tea serving area with five little tables in front of the beautiful new display window. This was where the women could come to slowly sip cups of coffee. Each table had a linen tablecloth and a small vase with fresh flowers. Tea and coffee was always served in a china cup and saucer, accompanied with two small butter cookies. The shop had a wonderful, cozy, and inviting quality to it. When it was done, Grace knew it was now truly her shop.

At the grand opening ceremony, her new sign was undraped. It read *Claire's Shop for Girls of all ages* and underneath, *with Grace*. As the mayor cut the ribbon, unveiling the sign, the crowd that had gathered applauded. Claire gave a little speech about the joy of watching Grace grow into an elegant, stylish lady. She handed Grace a small envelope and told her to open it later when she had some quiet time. Then double purple doors swung open and the crowd rushed in to admire all that Grace had done. Grace had never felt more fulfilled.

That night, when she finally went back to her apartment, she opened Claire's envelope. The note read:

> My Dear Grace,
> I have come to love you as a daughter. I respect you as
> a very creative and gifted businesswoman. I want you
> to accept this gift for the love that it represents. Use it to

keep the shop as lovely as it is today. I feel honored and blessed to have been a part of your life. You have filled my life with your wonderful energy and creativity. You truly are my "Amazing Grace."
Love always,
Claire

As Grace unfolded the check, tears ran down her cheeks. The check was for $75,000, which was all of the money that Grace had paid to Claire for the purchase of the shop in the last four years. She knew that this was Claire's way of telling her to keep the shop of her dreams open and ready to serve the women of Fergus Falls for many years to come.

Two weeks later, Grace stopped over at the high school to apologize to Mrs. Klein for neglecting her duties in organizing the twentieth reunion. She was shocked to learn that more than 70 percent of her old classmates had already mailed their reservations in to her. As Grace looked down the list of those who had registered, she found the names of Lindy, Rebecca, and to her surprise, Emily. Grace took this as a sign of good times to come. The reunion was going to be a time to remember. She was anxious to share this time with her childhood friends.

Fergus Falls in the fall was the perfect place to renew their friendships. As Grace walked home that night, she thought to herself, "Life is good." Then she started singing "Singing in the Rain."

Chapter Fifteen

Coming Home

When the big red, white, and blue giant RV pulled up in front of Loretta and Lenny's condominium building, it created quite a scene. A special paint job made it look like a forty-foot flag on each side. Lindy went to escort her mom and dad to their new home on wheels for the few weeks. Lindy led Sammy and Nani, the Pulaskis' two dogs, to the RV while their driver helped Lenny carry their luggage. Loretta began giving all of her friends the tour of the RV. Lenny quickly began interrogating the driver. The RV was stocked with all their favorite foods, two doggie beds, and all of Loretta's favorite magazines. As they pulled away from the driveway, the small crowd stood waving good-bye as Loretta hung her head out the window, blowing them all kisses. It was quite a send-off.

Their route would take them to Atlanta and then on to Nashville, where Lindy would surprise them with front-row seats at the Grand Ole Opry and a special backstage party. The next stop was St. Louis for a few days. Then they would go to visit Milwaukee and see Lake Michigan. From there, they would spend some time in Minneapolis.

They planned to arrive in Fergus Falls a few days before the reunion, so that they could visit with the new owners of Fresh Daisy Dry Cleaners and Laundry and visit Grandma Flo's grave. Both Lenny Jr. and Lana were planning to surprise their parents in Fergus Falls for a family reunion. Lenny was a mechanic in Fargo, married to Marion, and had three boys—Larry, Leon, and Luke. Lana owned a tiny beauty shop called Curl Up & Dye in Alexandria, Minnesota. She was recently divorced, and she was bringing her twins, Lucy and Lucky, who had just turned nine. It was always interesting to see Lana with her latest style and hair color.

The trip went better than even Lindy could have imagined. Their days were filled with fun new adventures. All of them fell in love with the RV, now named *Old Glory*. Their driver, Sally, was immediately adopted into their family. Sally was sixty years old and had been a long-haul truck driver for many years. She thought driving the luxury RV was a real cakewalk. She was the perfect match for this family—loud and a real character. As they rolled down the highways, they sang songs and laughed. They listened as Sally would tell them about what they were about to see. She had studied all the places they were going to stop and see. She often filled in with spicy stories about her time on the road in a man's world. *Old Glory* arrived in Fergus Falls three days before the reunion. As the RV pulled into the Holiday Inn, Lenny, Lana, and all the grandchildren rushed out to greet them.

After screams of surprise and lots of hugs, they went inside for a special dinner that Lindy had arranged for them. During dinner, it seemed that everyone was talking at the same time. Lucky announced that when he was old enough to drive, he would take *Old Glory* out for a spin. At almost the exact same time, all the adults turned to him, saying, "No way!" Lana's daughter, Lucy, had become a mini-Lana. She had bright red hair, looking like her namesake, Lucille Ball. Lana was now a platinum blonde with long, flowing curls. Sally commented that all the beautiful women at the table sparkled and glittered in their outfits. Everyone laughed, thinking back to their days at Fresh Daisy with Grandma Flo upstairs, who with great love was always cooking and sewing new outfits for them.

After dinner, they all piled into the RV and took a ride around Fergus Falls. They noticed that downtown was quieter than they remembered. They drove past the fancy new library and the high school with its large new addition. Grotto Lake had not changed at all. When they drove around Lake Alice, Lindy was shocked at the Larsons' house. In the past, it had been the showcase of the town. Now it sat vacant, looking neglected and abandoned. Then they drove by the new junior college campus, which had once been a cornfield.

Their last stop was pulling into the parking lot of the Fresh Daisy Dry Cleaners and Laundry. A large banner hung on the front of the building, saying, "Under new ownership—open 24/7." Their entire family sat quietly for a moment, remembering the good life that they had in this funny-looking, long and narrow white building. As they filed out of the RV, they walked quietly inside. The walls were now painted army green. The floor was the same one that Lenny had installed more than thirty-five years before; it looked worn out and dirty. Two rows of washing machines were in the middle of the room, with the dryers on the outside walls. Their beautiful, handmade wood counter had been replaced with a Formica counter behind a small area that was walled off for the dry cleaners. The place looked unkempt and shabby.

Within minutes, Loretta and Lenny turned and walked out of the building. All the rest of the family followed in silence. As soon as they were all back in the RV, Lenny cleared his throat and said, "Well, sometimes it is better to leave well enough alone. Our life in that building has nothing to do with what it is today. As for me, I don't care to see it again. My memories are far too good to be spoiled by someone else's business. Let's get this buggy on the road and go get some ice cream."

Everyone agreed, and minutes later, they were at the Dairy Queen enjoying some root-beer floats and once again, all talking at the same time. The Pulaskis were a colorful and delightful family anywhere they happened to be.

Rebecca's last day of school at Holy Angels Academy had been bittersweet. She had decided that she did not want anyone at school to know about her diagnosis. So instead, she gave her reason for leaving that her mother needed her back in Fergus Falls. Everyone seemed to accept that without asking any further questions.

There had been a large going-away party with more than two hundred people. Her girls took turns singing her favorite songs and thanking her for her guidance. Rebecca's fellow teachers and the nuns each spoke of their admiration for her. As she sat in the chair normally reserved for the bishop at graduation, she wiped away the steady flow of tears, while at the same time laughing at some of the stories being told. The nuns had also arranged a private dinner party for her, where they gave her a watch, with diamonds that surrounded the face made of mother-of-pearl, as a token of their love for her. By the end of the night, Rebecca was exhausted.

For two months, she made her final arrangements for the move back to Fergus Falls. At first she thought of surprising her mother, but then decided that would not be smart. Rebecca called Monica and asked her if it would be all right for her to move back home for a while. She did not tell her about the health issues; she simply said, "I felt it was time for a change, and Fergus Falls seemed like the right place for me to be."

Monica was both surprised and excited to have Rebecca back with her. Her days were full with working at the nursing home. Nevertheless, her evenings remained lonely. She looked forward to sharing an evening meal with someone again. As a special surprise, Rebecca told her mother that she had arranged for a contractor to remodel the house. The back bedroom that had been hers was very tiny, as was the small bathroom. Rebecca knew that in time, she might be in a wheelchair and would need more space in both rooms. Therefore, she hired a builder to expand both rooms, making them handicapped accessible, as well as to put in a new kitchen and all new carpeting.

Rebecca asked Monica if there were any changes she wanted to make. After a slight pause, Monica told her that she had always dreamed of having the washer and dryer on the first floor. Rebecca quickly called Mr. Jensen and asked him to add that to the plans for the house. He advised Rebecca that the project would be started immediately, with a completion date set for October 1. Rebecca smiled as she thought the timing was just right. She would make it home in time for the reunion. Only this time, she was coming home for the last time.

Rebecca was shocked at how painful it was to give up her teaching career. She kept busy finalizing the arrangements to transfer some of the properties that she had received from her father to a private foundation. The balance of the properties would go to Monica. Rebecca sat each day sorting through all of her precious possessions. She had two china cabinets that displayed the many special things she had purchased during her European trips with the choirs and special gifts of gratitude that her girls had given her over the years. She had kept one large box of things that she could not bear to give away, so she decided she would take it home.

Finally, the last week of September, Mr. Jensen called to tell her that the remodeling was done. He also reported that Monica was very pleased with the new addition, including her new laundry room off the kitchen. She called the Women's Resource Center in St. Paul to come pick up her furniture, except for her bedroom set and television, which were being shipped to Fergus Falls. Rebecca spent her last evening in Minneapolis at the downtown Hyatt.

As she went to sleep that night, her mind was filled with memories of the past. She was surprised at how peaceful she felt. Her life had been meaningful and full. What more could anyone ask for? She had mixed feelings about her move back to Fergus Falls. On the one hand, she looked forward to being with her mother again, enjoying their everyday simple life. On the other hand, she wished that she did not have to cause her mother the sorrow that she knew was going to be in the future. All she could do was to live each day the best that she knew how. As she slipped into sleep, her thoughts were all about the upcoming reunion. She looked forward to seeing her old girlfriends and hopefully finding something to laugh about for a few days.

Emily was sitting in absolute shock. For the first time in her memory, she was speechless. She was sitting in a board meeting at the Women's Center. The state of Wisconsin had notified her that the budget committee had just voted to cut all of their support for the Women's Center. The unnamed person on the other end of the call coldly informed her that it was time for the center to stand on its own. The financial support would end within sixty days. This announcement meant the center would be losing more than $150,000 of support. Emily was so shocked, she never asked a question or made a plea for the committee to reconsider. She knew enough about politics to know that her request would only be ignored. While she was receiving the bad news, her board of directors were making plans to expand the day care center and possibly looking to purchase a small apartment building to be used as a halfway house.

When Emily walked back into the meeting room, all conversation stopped. Everyone seated around the conference table looked at Emily with concern for her. Her face was pale, her hands were shaking, and she appeared to be distressed. As she sat down, she remained silent for a few uncomfortable moments. Finally, Marlene asked her what was wrong. Emily took a deep breath and proceeded to inform the group of her conversation. Everyone sat in stunned silence, contemplating what this meant for the future of the center. They agreed to adjourn and reconvene the following week. In the meantime, Emily was instructed to contact the state and get a detailed report from them. They all promised to think about what they would do if this were, indeed, true.

The following week, Emily confirmed that they had lost all of their state funding. She presented the board of directors with copies of the current budget. The evening was a painful process for everyone involved. They immediately discarded all plans for expansion and improvements to the existing buildings and programs. Even after all of that was removed from the budget, they were still well over $80,000 short of the needs to keep the programs alive. As they adjourned the meeting that evening, they again committed to thinking of new ways to raise the money needed.

The Women's Center had served as a model for many other communities. Not only were the women and their families given refuge from violence, they received tools to reenter the world with new skills and some healthy self-esteem. Most important of all, they were given hope for a better tomorrow. From the shelter program, the day care center was born. It had the combined benefit of teaching women good parenting skills while providing safe day care. The day care center was available twenty-four hours a day, every day of the year. For those who found a third-shift job or worked on holidays to receive double pay, this day care center was a blessing. The donut shop helped give jobs to people who otherwise would have been unemployed. The counseling services were key to everything the center stood for. There was not a single program that they could cut.

Emily lost sleep night after night trying to think of a solution to this crisis. At the time, her salary was $40,000. She sat at her kitchen table trying to figure out the minimum she needed to survive. It still would not be enough. It was while she was struggling with this dilemma that she remembered the letter from her parents' attorney regarding the house in Fergus Falls. She finally knew in her heart that she had found the answer. Perhaps this was God's way of telling her that it would all work out.

The following week when the board of directors met, Emily opened the meeting by announcing that she had found a solution. She told them about the house she had inherited in Fergus Falls located on Lake Alice. She continued by saying that she was cutting her salary, effective immediately, to $25,000. After their big fundraiser dinner and auction in September, she was going to take a two-month leave of absence. Ann Conrad, who was her assistant, would fill in for her during her absence. She would go back to Fergus Falls, fix up the house, and sell it. The profit from the house would be enough to keep the center going for at least a few more years.

The board sat in silence, pondering all that Emily had offered to sacrifice for the Women's Center. Finally Pastor Paul spoke. "My dear Emily, we cannot allow you to donate your inheritance to the center. What if, after two years, we are still faced with the same issues? You will have lost your family's home, and we still might have to close. No, we must find a permanent solution to this matter. I know a consultant who deals with these types of situations. He has offered to donate his services to us. Because he recently retired, he can start tomorrow to do an audit of all of our programs. He will make recommendations on what we need to do to keep the center going. I believe this is a much better solution." The board of directors took a vote to approve hiring Gerald Willis to assist in deciding the future of the center.

Two days later, Mr. Willis appeared at Emily's office door. He wore an expensive suit, a white starched shirt, and a silk tie. His expression was very stern. Within an hour, Mr. Willis took over one of the counseling offices and was hard at work. He handed Emily a list of all the information he would need. Emily assured him that he would have complete access into their computer system and to all data. Returning to her office, she closed her door—and then she allowed the tears to flow.

As she was entering his access information, she knew that this man would never understand the heart of the Women's Center. She knew that he thought only in terms of dollars, spreadsheets, and bottom line. Emily was equally sure that he was the only person who might be able to save at least a portion of the programs that she had given most of her adult life to offer to those in need. Only someone without a heart could make the cuts that needed to be done. As much as she hated him for what he was about to do, she also respected him for having the courage to do this terrible task.

Her predictions were accurate. By mid-September, Mr. Willis asked to have the board of directors convene for a special meeting. Two days later, they gathered in their conference room. It was the first time that Emily had ever seen this devoted group of volunteers sit in complete silence, waiting for Mr. Willis to enter. All of them knew that the news would be extremely painful.

Mr. Willis arrived with a neat binder for each attendee. He immediately got to the task of discussing the future of the Women's Center. No one made a comment as he read his recommendations. They included selling the donut shop, as well as cutting the day care center staff in half and going to "normal" hours of operation from 7:30 AM to 6:00 PM. The fees for the day care would be increased 30 percent, with penalties for anyone picking a child up late. The Women's Center would let go three of their counselors and cut an additional 25 percent of their staff. No one would be allowed to stay in the center for longer than thirty days. Finally, he explained that all the residents of the center would be charged a daily fee based on their ability to pay.

Emily sat in stunned silence as she watched one program after another be ripped apart. It was obvious that Mr. Willis had no idea why the day care hours were important or that the residents, for the most part, had no ability to pay. She waited for others to start fighting for the programs; however, as she looked around the table, all she saw were people with their heads bowed down. She could not bear another moment of this insanity. She rose from her chair and for the next fifteen minutes proceeded to shoot down each of Mr. Willis's recommendations. When she was done, she again noticed that no one in the room stood to support her.

Then it hit her. This was not a debate; this was a done deal. She tried to compose herself, taking a few deep breaths, but it did not work. In his low monotone voice, Mr. Willis simply replied to her by saying, "The reason I was called into this task is because I have no attachments to any of the programs. My recommendations are based on the best possible outcome for this agency. You can put your head in the sand, Miss Larson, and be noble about all the services you offer. On the other hand, you can be realistic and attempt to save at least some of the programs. At least under my options, there will be something left to offer. By ignoring the severity of the matter, there will be no services left in a year. Which do you prefer?"

Again, there was an uncomfortable silence in the room. Emily finally stood up, took a deep breath, and said, "I cannot be a part of destroying programs that I truly believe are vital services in our community. Please accept my resignation. I will make myself available for a smooth transition to whomever you name as my replacement." With her legs shaking, she stood and walked out of the conference room. She went back to her office, got her purse, and left the building. It was not until she closed the door to her apartment that she allowed the agony to take over. Emily spent the weekend going between pain, anger, and despair. She felt as if she had just lost all meaning in life. She felt once again like the unloved little girl in the big uncaring house on Lake Alice.

On Sunday evening, she received a call from Mr. Willis informing her that she did not need to return to work. They had arranged for a temporary manager to work through the transition. He felt that it was best for her not to be involved in the process. The papers and her personal possessions would be delivered to her within two days, including a check for three months' salary. He thanked her for her years of service and very insincerely wished her well in her future pursuits.

Two days later as promised, a box of her belongings and a large envelope were delivered to her apartment. Emily had not showered or dressed for almost four days, nor had she left her apartment. As she looked through the box of special mementos, suddenly it all seemed so meaningless. She looked at the papers and signed wherever was indicated with an X. It was almost midnight when she walked up to the front door of the Women's Center, a place she had grown to love over the years. She slipped the thick envelope into the mail slot and walked away.

A week later, she had donated her furniture and packed up her car. Her last stop was the bank. She wrote two checks—one to herself for $2,000 and the balance of more than $10,000 to the Women's Center. She enclosed a handwritten note stating that this money was to be used only for keeping the day care center open twenty-four hours for as long as possible. She mailed the envelope and started her drive back to Fergus Falls.

For the eight hours as she drove toward Fergus Falls, she remembered how battered she felt when she had first arrived at the Women's Center. She remembered the beautiful baby girl who was never a part of her life. There was a flood of faces of the women she had helped to understand that they were women of honor and value. For miles, she drove through tears; but as she crossed over the Mississippi River, for some unknown reason, she started to smile. It felt as though Fergus Falls was calling to her, telling her it was time to come home. A peaceful calm come over Emily as she neared Fergus Falls. She believed that God had some new plans for her. She knew she had enough courage and faith to meet whatever new challenges God was ready to hand her. Emily knew deep in her soul that she was going to survive another day. There was some new purpose, and it was just a few miles away.

The summer passed by quickly for Grace. Claire's was filled with the latest in fall fashions by early August. This year, Grace had arranged to sell the girls' uniforms for Our Lady of Victory along with their approved sweaters and blazers. She sat behind the counter watching the little girls try on their new uniforms. She smiled as she remembered her happy days at Our Lady of Victory. As she sat there, she could almost smell the school on the first day, when the floors were all polished with a sweet-smelling wax, the blackboards were without a spark of chalk dust, and all of the desks were shining clean. Grace had come a long way from that little girl who ran across the street, eager for each new school year to begin.

The first sign that fall was truly here was when the baskets of free apples began to appear outside the stores along Lincoln Avenue. Everyone was welcome to grab a few to take home. With the kids back in school, the moms were free to get back to their volunteer work at the hospital, museum, and nursing homes. They often stopped by Claire's to meet for a cup of her special blended herb teas or coffee with peppermint sticks. Grace's shop continued to be a great success. Her staff enjoyed the world of high fashion, Fergus style.

During her last trip to Minneapolis, she had ordered some reunion gifts for all the attendees. Then she spent hours looking through catalogs until she found the perfect gift to give to Emily, Lindy, Rebecca, and herself. Each day she grew more excited about the reunion. She daydreamed about all the wonderful memories they would share while they were together. She truly hoped that she would be able to talk them into singing at the reunion dance.

Grace was anxious to have them visit her shop and see all that she had done to make it her own. There was also a bit of anxiety, wondering if the four of them had changed so much that they would not be able to recapture the sisterhood they had developed over their years together. Somehow, Grace knew that they would find a way to reconnect as women. Perhaps it would bring them a more meaningful friendship. Only time would tell.

Chapter Sixteen

Reconnecting

As usual, Grace was the first to arrive at her shop each morning and the last one to leave each evening. There was a *Welcome Back to the Fergus Falls High School Reunion* banner hanging in front of Claire's. The shop had been busy the past few weeks with the homecoming dance at Fergus Falls High School, the newly opened Fergus Falls Junior College celebrating their first homecoming, plus the twentieth class reunion. Kelli was frantic trying to process all the special orders for the formal gowns and special outfits. Jodi had been exhausted trying to keep peace and order in the dressing rooms as the teenage girls arrived at the same time to try on their gowns for the dances. The reunion was now only a few days away.

Grace had not been this excited about any event in a long time. She had even bought herself a few new outfits for the weekend. As she was getting down from the ladder in the storage room, she heard a laugh that could only come from one person. As she jumped off the ladder, she fell right into the arms of Lindy. As they both tried to catch their balance, they were hugging and laughing. Lindy said, "Lordy, Lordy, Fergus Falls has treated you well. Have you been stored away in bubble wrap, girl? You are prettier than ever, and not a wrinkle on that perky little face. How do you do it? I guess you can tell by my size and wrinkles that I have been living life to the fullest!"

Lindy was truly impressed as Grace showed her around the charming shop. Of course, she always had known that Grace would do well in whatever she decided to tackle. Grace made Lindy a cup of her special blend of peppermint tea. When she joined Lindy at the table, she laughed saying, "Will you look at that monster RV out there. It must be taking up five parking spaces. Can you believe the paint job on it!" As soon as she finished the sentence, she knew who the proud RV owner was.

Typical of Lindy, she simply laughed and said, "As soon as I saw it on the lot, I knew it had been created just for little ol' me. I guess even my vehicles have to make an entrance. My driver is out getting a rental car for me. If I drive that thing, I am sure to wipe out half of Fergus Falls. I must admit after living for years in New York and never driving, I seem to have a problem making turns these days."

Both of them wanted nothing more than to sit and catch up on their lives. However, it soon became obvious that the shop was getting busy and Grace needed to get back to work. They promised to meet for dinner that evening at the Mabel Murphy Restaurant. As Lindy was leaving, she turned around and gave Grace one more big hug. Then Lindy proceeded to stop all the traffic both ways on Lincoln Avenue as she finally moved the colorful RV out into the street. As Lindy pulled away, she started singing an old Patsy Cline song, and she was suddenly aware of how good it felt to be back in Fergus Falls. Somewhere deep inside her, a feeling came over her that made her giggle. Fergus Falls was a good place to come home to.

Rebecca arrived just as the movers were pulling in behind the house. When she got out of the car, she was pleasantly surprised at how nice the new addition looked. As an afterthought, she had had the entire house painted in a soft shade of yellow, which was Monica's favorite color.

As she walked from the alley to the house, she saw her old neighbors, the Newtons, running across their backyard to greet her. They proceeded to tell Rebecca that even though they were older and slower these days, they still went square dancing every Friday evening and sang in their church choir every Sunday. They were thrilled to know that Rebecca was moving back home. They invited Rebecca to join them at church on Sunday and become part of their choir once again. Monica came running out the back door, smiling from ear to ear. "Rebecca, I need you to come tell the movers how to arrange that beautiful new bedroom of yours."

Within a few hours, all of Rebecca's things were in place. She joined her mother in the kitchen for some homemade apple cider. Mom had made her favorite meal of Swedish meatballs, mashed potatoes, green beans, and of course, lefse with butter and sugar. The smells in the tiny home brought back years of good memories. That evening she was shocked at how much she ate for dinner. She had not felt this good in a long time. Rebecca knew that she would soon have to have a painful conversation with her mother about her failing health. However, today was not the day. She had planned on calling Grace and trying to get together with her after the shop closed. Instead, she fell sound asleep, feeling safe, loved, and at home.

Fergus Falls was a gentle place filled with good people and warm memories. In a few days, she would be going to the reunion. She looked forward to seeing all of her old friends. Rebecca wanted to just enjoy her friends and her life. She could wait until after the reunion to discuss her health crisis with her mom. There was no hurry.

The next morning, Monica woke Rebecca up to tell her that Grace had called to invite her to dinner. Grace would be picking her up around 7:00 PM. Rebecca was sitting on the front porch when Grace pulled up and honked her horn. As Rebecca walked down the stairs to the car, memories of the old days flashed before her of her girlfriends all piling into Emily's VW convertible for another evening of fun and laughter. Their nights often ended back at Emily's beautiful house overlooking Lake Alice. As she walked to the car, Rebecca gave a prayer of thanks for all the wonderful memories she had shared with her high school friends.

It was after midnight when Emily drove into Fergus Falls. At the truck stop she had bought enough food to last her for a day or two. As she slowly drove down Lincoln Avenue, she was shocked by the many changes that had taken place over the twenty years since she had last seen it. She drove past Claire's shop and wondered if Grace was still working there. As she passed Our Lady of Victory, she admired the beautiful new church and a school addition. It was just a short drive up the hill, and within minutes, she was pulling into her old driveway.

She was glad that she had thought ahead to arrange for the utilities to be turned on. Emily had called a man who worked for Adams Realty and offered Charlie Adams a generous bonus to get the house ready for her. For the favor, she promised to list the house with him when she was ready to sell. Charlie kept his promise and had all the utilities reconnected, the furnace checked and turned on, the lawn mowed, outside debris removed, and new locks installed. After he personally did the final check himself, he slipped the key under the back doormat, just where he had said.

By the time Emily unlocked the door, she was completely exhausted. She quickly put her few items in the old refrigerator. Walking through the once-elegant dining room, she saw that beautiful linen wallpaper hanging off the walls in strange patterns. In her father's den, the walls were lined with musty books and cobwebs. There still seemed to be the scent of his pipe tobacco lingering in the room. Finally, she lay down on her father's old leather couch. Within minutes, she was sound asleep, cuddled with her coat over her for warmth. That night her dreams were a mix of her childhood home, the Women's Center, and her cozy little apartment in Waukesha.

It was almost ten o'clock the next morning when she awoke to the doorbell. As she stumbled to the front door, she realized that the noise was coming from the back door. To her surprise, three little girls stood there staring at her. The oldest girl, who seemed to be the leader, glared at her.

"My name is Melissa. I am ten years old. This is Katherine." She indicated the child beside her. "She's eight, and Sarah just had her sixth birthday last week. Who are you?"

Emily stared in stunned silence at the children.

"Don't you know this house is haunted?" Melissa asked. "No one lives here. What is your name? We live next door with my dad, and he will call the police. Then you will be arrested! So, I think you had better run away fast. We also have a big dog named Harley, who will bite anyone that tries to hurt us."

Emily adored the little girl's spunky attitude. She told them that her name was Emily and that she owned the house. Many years ago, she had lived here. She had come home to fix it up and sell it. Then she told them that she hoped they could all be friends while she was living there.

Melissa told her that it did not make any sense. Why fix up a house and not stay to enjoy it?

Emily told them that when she was their age, a very nice boy had lived next door whose name was Warren Brooks. All three girls started laughing as they told her that was their daddy. They had moved back to Fergus Falls just before school had started.

Emily ran out the door grabbing the girls' hands as they all ran across the backyards. Within minutes, she stood in the kitchen looking at Warren bent over the sink, finishing the breakfast dishes. As he turned to tell the girls to calm down, he saw Emily. He stood there speechless, just staring at her. Finally, they embraced. Both of them started talking at the same time. Warren said, "Welcome back home, Emily. I never thought I would set eyes on you again. It has been a long time, girlfriend. Are you home for the reunion?"

Emily explained that it was time in her career life to do some reevaluation, and Fergus Falls seemed as good a place as any to do that.

Warren told her that they had just moved back to town a few months ago. His parents wanted to sell the home because it was just too much for them to keep up these days. Warren had been living in Dallas, Texas, when his wife was killed in a car accident more than a year ago. He could not bear the thought of anyone else living in the Brooks' house. It was also time for him to move on and leave the painful memories behind in Dallas. He bought the house from his parents and helped them move into the senior citizens' apartments. He told Emily that the girls loved Fergus Falls from the moment they arrived. They were going to Our Lady of Victory, where he was shocked to see that there were still nuns teaching. He had taken a job working for Lincoln Bank, where he was making $25,000 less than in Texas, but here he was finally happy and actually looked forward to walking to work each day. There was no stress in his life. He worked every weekend to restore the house to its original beauty and enjoyed every minute of the hard work. Moving back to Fergus Falls was one of the best decisions he had ever made.

After their second cup of coffee, Emily left to start getting her house in order. Charlie was waiting for her on the front porch swing. He had prepared a list of all the repairs and work that needed to be done in and around the house. He just assumed that just like for her parents, money was no problem. As Emily looked over the long list of repairs and the costs to fix everything, she was in shock. She finally turned to Charlie to tell him that she did not have this kind of money. They worked for hours dividing the list into things that she would do on her own versus things that required someone with the skills needed to do the repairs. By noon, Charlie was promising to try and get the contractors to sharpen their pencils and lower their estimates, providing cheaper options for redoing the kitchen and bathrooms. Finally, he agreed to come up with some less expensive places to purchase wallpaper, paint, and flooring.

Emily did not want to dwell on the challenge she was facing just to get the house repaired enough to sell. She decided to take a break from her worries and treat herself to a late lunch at the Viking Café. As she parked the car on Lincoln Avenue, she realized that she had not changed out of the clothes she had worn all day yesterday and slept in all night. She quickly brushed her hair, putting it into a ponytail, applied some lipstick, and decided that was just going to have to be good enough for now.

Grace was walking out of Viking's door when she bumped into a stranger. Emily nodded as she tried to move out of her way. At almost the exact same time, they both recognized each other. For a brief moment, they softly whispered each other's name. Neither of them could believe whom they were seeing. There were no hugs or laughs as there had been with Lindy's arrival. Instead, they stood simply staring at each other.

Emily spoke first. "I really never look as bad as I do right now. I just got into town last night." As she looked at Grace in a beautiful sky blue sweater with perfect makeup and hair, she felt like a bohemian. Grace smiled and simply welcomed Emily home. She told her how happy she was to see her and thrilled that she was coming to the reunion. After a few uncomfortable moments, Grace invited Emily to join her and Lindy for dinner at Mabel Murphy's that evening. Hoping that she could cancel out later, Emily agreed to meet them at 7:30 PM at the restaurant.

As Grace crossed the street to Claire's, she was surprised that Emily was planning to stay after the reunion. She took it as a good sign. It was hard to believe that all four of them were back in Fergus Falls for the first time in twenty years. Tonight, Grace would do her best to talk them into singing at the reunion. Yes, this was a good sign, a very good sign indeed!

Chapter Seventeen

Dinner

Grace and Rebecca pulled into the restaurant parking lot just as a big black Lincoln was parking at an odd angle. Lindy got out of the car, and then they ran together for the first group hug of the evening. It was almost eight o'clock when Emily finally arrived. They were all convinced that she would not come but had ordered a second round of drinks just in case.

Emily had spent most of the afternoon scrubbing down the kitchen and bathrooms in the house. When she finally came back into the kitchen for a cup of coffee, she realized that it was almost seven o'clock. At first, she decided that she would just not show up for the dinner; no one would really miss her anyway. It had been twenty years with no contact with Grace or Lindy. She would call Grace tomorrow and give her some lame excuse. However, just thinking about the girls of SOLA gave her a deep longing to be with her girlfriends once again.

Emily realized that she did want to see if it was possible to recapture even a tiny bit of the friendship that they had shared so many years ago. Besides, she was starving. Quickly taking a shower, she braided her long blonde hair and grabbed the warmest sweater she could find. As she drove out to the restaurant, she almost turned around several times. She had no idea what she feared, but in the end, she knew a dinner with old friends was not going to kill her, so why not go and eat. She figured that she would discover that they had absolutely nothing in common anymore. Life goes on, and people change. Although she had to admit that Grace appeared to be the same sweet, loving woman she was when she was in high school. Perhaps only Emily had grown into a very different person. Oh well, one dinner with old friends is no big deal, she thought. I will have a drink, eat quickly, and leave before dessert.

As Emily walked into the restaurant, she immediately heard Lindy's laugh coming from the corner of the dining room. She stood for a moment by the door just observing her three old friends. Grace was the picture of contentment and simple beauty. Rebecca looked smaller than she remembered and pale, but seemed to be enjoying Lindy's story. Lindy was dressed in a bright purple patterned blouse, with her massive black hair piled on top of her head. She was waving her hands as she told her story. Emily felt a little happiness sneak into her soul as she watched them enjoying each other's company.

Emily quietly walked over to the table and apologized for being so late. There was another brief moment of quiet before they all jumped up to give her a hug. They all began to talk at the same time. Emily laughed for the first time in a very long time. As she sat down at the table, she noticed that there was a bottle of Asti in a bucket. Grace had ordered it especially for their reunion dinner. They remembered their last evening together at Emily's house overlooking Lake Alice. They sat under the weeping willow with their gifts toasting each other with a glass of Asti. It seemed only natural that this was how they would begin their private reunion.

Lindy started the conversation by giving a short version of her life story. She told them about loving being a nurse and caring for people, and that God had given her Larry as a special gift. As she spoke about their romantic engagement, wedding, and life together, tears filled her eyes. There was not a word said until she finished by telling them that she was now worth millions of dollars but with no idea how to spend it all. She would much rather have Larry alive at her side living above Daisy Dry Cleaners than all this money and a fancy condominium. Life alone was for the birds! She ended by telling them about the mini family reunion she had pulled off over at the Holiday Inn. If nothing else, she could use the money to spoil her parents and have a little fun with them.

Grace went next and talked about Claire. She told them that she had truly grown to love the business. She felt blessed to have been able to buy the shop and by how close a relationship she still had with Claire. She talked about her drama debut in *Seven Brides for Seven Brothers.* They all laughed when she told them that she used "Singing in the Rain" as her song for the audition. Grace also told them about the theater club, which gave her lots of enjoyment. She finished by telling them that she adored her life in Fergus Falls, where she felt fulfilled and respected.

Rebecca followed the others' lead and told the girls all about Holy Angels Academy for Young Catholic Women of the World. She talked about her many trips to Europe and all of the honors that her choral groups had won throughout the years.

Emily was the only one who did not share her life story. They all realized that there was pain in her eyes and that she was not ready to discuss it with them. What they all knew for sure was that Emily was suffering, and they wanted to be there for her.

After a dinner of polite chitchat, Grace said she had an important question to ask all of them. She paused for a few moments and then asked if they would please consider singing together at the reunion dance. Grace told them that the band that had been booked for the dance had just cancelled yesterday. The best she was able to do was to rent a karaoke machine. A good friend and local radio announcer had volunteered to be the disc jockey if she could not find anyone else. She begged them to say yes, or a very special evening that she had planned for almost a year was going to be a terrible failure.

Lindy immediately said, "Well, little Gracie here is in a real pickle; and I, for one, am more than willing to help out. You know me, just get two people in a room, and I am ready to put on a show. Count me in, Gracie girl!"

Rebecca also happily agreed. She might even have some music that they could use for the evening.

All eyes turned to Emily, who was sitting there quietly trying to fade into the background. She finally said, "Ladies, I have not sung since we were all together in high school. I am afraid that my rusty voice will only ruin a perfectly wonderful trio. However, if you truly feel that I am needed, I will sing softly in the background. Nevertheless, I want it to be known that I have warned you all about my total lack of talent. So you have to accept me at your own risk."

Grace was so thankful to them. She told them that this was really going to be a wonderful evening for all of them. They agreed to meet at

Emily's house the next morning to select their songs and then practice using the karaoke machine.

Tonight, they had all been overly polite to each other. There was none of the usual bickering or teasing that had gone on in the past. As each of them had given a brief overview of their life for the past twenty years, they all had decided to eliminate the most painful parts of their stories. A stranger listening to their conversations would have thought that they were four successful happy women in town for a class reunion.

As they left Mabel Murphy's that evening, each of them felt that their special friendship was beginning to resurface. Yet at the same time, none of them felt comfortable enough to trust the others with the complete truth of how they had really lived their lives. They all had the same longing to be able to tell the others about their pain as well as their victories.

Tears welled up in Emily's eyes as she thought about her college years; all the mistakes she had made; Danny Driscoll; a tiny baby girl named Rebecca Grace, whom she never had a chance to love; and the Women's Center, where she failed to protect the women who had trusted her.

Lindy thought about Larry and the deep pain that his death still caused her every time she thought of him; the cloud of loneliness continued to hang over her.

Grace thought back to the feeling of being left behind and struggling to find her new place in Fergus Falls. She was always amazed that after all these years, the scar of polio and the loss of Denny was still an open wound. Even though she had given up on any dreams of having children, she still yearned to find a good man who would love her and allow her to love him. The older she had grown, the more she felt a deep sense of loneliness that working twelve-hour days could not cure.

Rebecca was thinking that whatever her past mistakes were, they were now so terribly unimportant. She grieved that her life held so little future. There were still so many things that she wanted a chance to experience. Yet she knew that she had no major regrets as to how she had lived her life. She trusted that God would be with her and lead her to whatever future she had left.

Yes, all four of the women went away from their dinner with false smiles on their faces and pain lingering in their souls. Each of them separately thought the same thing: *Maybe tomorrow when we meet at Emily's to practice some songs, I will have the courage to tell the truth. Maybe tomorrow I will find the sisterhood that I had as a young, innocent girl at Fergus Falls High School.*

Chapter Eighteen

Singing Again

Emily was wide-awake by six o'clock. Last night she had slept in her bedroom for the first time in twenty years. She curled up under the quilt and fell into a deep sleep. This morning she felt refreshed and ready to face the challenges of getting this old house fixed up. She was also ready to face her old friends.

Emily was astounded at how gracious Grace, Rebecca, and Lindy had been at dinner. They had every right to cut her out of their lives, just as she had done to them. They never asked for an explanation of her complete disappearance. She was so grateful to them for simply allowing her to enjoy an evening with old memories and a few good laughs.

Grace arrived at 9:00 AM, carrying the karaoke machine and a bag of warm donuts from the City Café and Bakery. As Emily opened the front door, they both had a rush of old memories. How many hundreds of times had this same scene been played out? There was rarely a time when Grace had not arrived with a bag full of their favorite donuts. Just as they had over twenty years ago, they immediately walked into the kitchen. They both automatically sat in "their" chair at the table.

Grace smiled and said, "Well, I guess some things never need to change. Eating our favorite donuts together before Rebecca and Lindy arrive was the way we started many mornings a long time ago. It feels so good to be here with you again. Even after all this time, I still feel a special bond with you. It's funny that it does not make any difference about what has happened to us in our lives; being in this kitchen feels right."

Emily simply nodded as the tears welled in her eyes. There was something so comforting about just sitting there with the sun shining on Grace's face. For a brief moment, Emily forgot about her pains and worries. It was good to enjoy this peaceful moment in time. She promised herself to let go of the past and simply enjoy today for what it was—a simple day with old friends.

Without bothering to ring the bell, Lindy walked in the back door with Rebecca. She gave Emily and Grace a hug and said, "Looks like once again, Rebecca and I have missed getting the two best donuts in the bag. Well, I still love girlfriends. I swear, if I arrived at 5:00 AM, you two would have been eating those donuts at 4:45! Now, hand over that bag, and who is in charge of getting some coffee going? I guess we are right back to where we left off—just a little older and a little wiser." In a matter of moments, they were back in their old familiar pattern. It felt right even if the once stately house was now in need of some tender loving care.

Grace set up the karaoke machine in the living room. Rebecca joined her with a large folder filled with music sheets that she had brought along to share with the girls. They all sat on the floor looking through the songs and humming. They had mutually decided that each of them would do a few solos, except Emily who refused. The rest of the songs they would sing together in their once-famous harmony. Lindy started because she was the most familiar with the machine, which she had used many years ago at Molly's in Mankato. She showed them how it worked; explaining there was a pedal where you could speed up or slow down the background music or tempo.

Finally, each of them had picked their solo songs. Lindy was going to sing her favorite Patsy Cline tunes, "Walking after Midnight" and "Half as Much." Together they decided to sing a melody of ABBA songs, which included "Dancing Queen," "Take a Chance on Me," and "Thank You for the Music." That would be followed by the disco songs of "Staying Alive," "Night Fever," "My Life," and "YMCA." After a break, Rebecca would accompany them with her guitar to sing some of their favorite songs by Emily Lou Harris, Linda Ronstadt, and Dolly Parton from the album called *Trio Two*. Rebecca picked "When We're Gone, Long Gone" for her solo. Grace would sing her signature song, "You'll Never Walk Alone." After several hours of practice, Emily finally agreed to sing "Feels Like Home" as her solo. They agreed to end their mini-performance by singing "You'll

Never Be the Sun, You Will Be the Light," which was their very favorite song from the *Trio Two* album.

When they started singing together again, they realized that their voices had changed over the years. However, to their delight, each of them now possessed a much richer tone and quality. They practiced into the afternoon, singing, laughing, and remembering the good old days. When they left to get ready for the welcome party at the Eagles, they were ready to give their former classmates a good show the next evening. Emily had invited them to come back to her house the following evening after the reunion for a sleepover, and they all quickly agreed.

The following days flew by, filled with laughter, warm memories, and the simple pleasures of reconnecting with their past. Classmate and Grace's old boyfriend, Roy Kastelle, proved to be a wonderful emcee for both evenings. His deep, rich voice, quick sense of humor, and storytelling skills made the reunion a memorable event. After dinner, Roy took the microphone to make some announcements and welcomed several of their teachers who had come to share the evening. Then came the slide show with photos from their high school days. He also told them that three of their classmates had died—one from cancer, one in a car accident, and one in Vietnam.

Finally, the tables were pushed to the sidewall to create a dance floor. As the lights were dimmed, Roy announced what he said was his best surprise of the evening. He introduced Grace, Emily, Lindy, and Rebecca, telling the crowd that they had agreed to perform some songs for them. As they walked onto the stage, the crowd began to cheer.

Lindy started the show, singing her Patsy Cline songs with more feeling than she had in years. After her solo, Grace, Emily, and Rebecca joined her. Their voices blended in perfect harmony. Instead of everyone getting up to dance, the crowd sat in awe of the beauty of their voices. The audience clapped and yelled for more when it was time for a break. As the girls left the stage for a fifteen-minute break, they were surrounded by all their classmates, and drinks were lined up at the bar, waiting for them.

When they came back for the second set, they received the same loving attention from the crowd. As Rebecca played the guitar, they sang their songs with tenderness. At the last minute, they all decided to sing "You'll Never Walk Alone" together. They stood holding each other's hands as they sang, with tears streaming down all of their faces. All four of them were swept away by the memories of the past and the experience of now. Halfway through the song, the entire room rose to their feet, reaching out to the person next to them as they swayed to the beautiful music. Almost on cue, the entire gathering sang the last verse of the song. When the song ended, for one brief moment there was complete silence. Then the applause began as everyone clapped while wiping the tears from their eyes.

Roy finished the evening by presenting each of them with a bouquet of roses and a kiss on the cheek. He said a closing prayer and wished them a safe trip home. The reunion had been a wonderful success and truly a night to remember for years to come.

Chapter Nineteen

Emily's Sleepover

Grace rode with Emily, and Lindy drove Rebecca back to Emily's house. As they came into the kitchen, the first thing they did together was to kick off their high heels. The second thing was to have a group hug without speaking a word. Within fifteen minutes, they changed into pajamas, their faces scrubbed clean and their hair brushed.

Emily had no idea how to prepare for this sleepover. She had offered to do it, thinking that they would probably all take a pass on her offer. She was surprised and anxious about having them stay for the night. After all, they were no longer high school girls but adult women. In the end, she made up beds in four different bedrooms on the second floor. The only room she refused to touch was her parents' bedroom. For whatever reason, she had still not gone into that room.

They gathered back in the kitchen, which was still the most comfortable room in the house. As they sat down at the old kitchen table, they found a tray with a towel over it. Each of them started trying to figure out what the surprise was. Finally, Emily lifted the towel to reveal two chilled bottles of Asti. Without asking, Lindy picked up the two bottles and said, "Well, girls, get your coats on, and let's see if we are still able to sit under that tree and get honest."

They each ran to their overnight bags, put on their coats, and within minutes were standing in the backyard. As they looked at each other, they realized that they had all had the exact same idea. They stood there holding the quilts they had received years ago. Emily had put an old tarp on the ground. Lindy lit the dozens of candles that Emily had found in the back hall. Grace opened the first bottle of Asti and poured some into plastic cups.

As all four of them huddled in their quilts on the cool October evening, they felt warm and secure. Rebecca was the first to comment on the various conditions of each of the quilts. She said, "I guess my quilt has had the most use from the looks of things. Emily, your quilt looks almost as new as the day you received it. Grace's looks as though you have taken great care of it. My dear Lindy, have you really added some rhinestones to that quilt? Why am I not surprised?"

They giggled as they each examined the others' quilts. They were enjoying some small talk about their lives when Grace announced that the Asti was now gone and that her butt had officially fallen asleep and she was cold. They quickly all agreed it was time to go in and warm up.

Emily started a fire in her father's den while Grace opened another bottle of Asti and carried in a bowl of Doritos. Instead of sitting on the furniture, they all sat on big pillows in front of the fireplace, again wrapped in the security of their quilts. For a few moments, they seemed to be lost in their own thoughts.

Lindy broke the silence by admitting that she was getting a little tipsy but that she had no intention of not drinking this wonderful Asti. In a soft voice, which she rarely used, she said, "Girlfriends, can I be honest with you? Maybe it's the wine talking, but I need you to know that my days have not all been the fairy tale that I have told you about." Rebecca was the first to tell Lindy that she would be honored to hear about all of her life since she left Fergus Falls. She promised that she would never judge her and that she had become a good listener over the years.

Lindy cleared her throat and said, "There was a time when I was living in New York City when I really hated myself. I would look at the perfect, size 10 New York women walking down the street in their stylish clothes, perfect makeup, and smart hairdos. They all seemed to have such an air of confidence. I felt like the biggest misfit on the planet, like a whale out of water. I felt ugly, unlovable, and totally out of place. There was one night when I had finally had enough of the critical stares and snide remarks. I did not know what to do anymore. It was a real turning point for me. I spent two days crying, praying, getting angry, and then crying some more.

"I got up at four o'clock in the morning and walked to St. Patrick's Cathedral. I didn't care if some crazy person killed me that night. In a way, I felt that if I were attacked, they would be doing me a favor by putting me out of my misery. Well, I wasn't mugged. However, I did discover that the church was locked up tight until seven o'clock. As I sat on the church stairs, I looked up at the sky, which by the way is hard to see in New York City. I did not realize that I was crying and loudly yelling at God until a cop came up to me. He asked me why I was on the church stairs and what drugs I was using. I told him my choice of drugs was chocolate cake with cream cheese frosting and Snickers candy bars. Just as he was getting ready to arrest me for being a smart aleck, the church doors flew open.

"An ancient old priest, who had to have been eighty years old, walked down the stairs to me. His name was Father O'Shea. He called the cop by name and told him that he would take care of me. Within minutes, I was inside the most beautiful church I had ever seen. Father asked if I would be okay while he prepared for the 7:30 Mass. He left me standing in front of a statue of a peaceful and kind-looking woman. I later found out that it was a statue of the Blessed Virgin Mary.

"Her face seemed to glow in the darkness of the church. I swear to you on a stack of Bibles that I heard her speak to me. She told me not to be afraid. She said that I was just fine, just the way I was. That God loved me for who I was on both the inside and outside. I remember talking back to her and telling her that I was not even Catholic. I was there because it was the only church that I knew how to find. I swear to you, she smiled at me and said that it didn't make any difference because I was a child of God. I finally knelt down and cried my eyes out.

"A little while later, the priest returned and again asked me if I was okay. He offered to call someone for me. I told him that for the first time in a long time, I really was okay. I don't know why, but I lit a candle, put twenty dollars into a slot for donations, and left. The woman that had sat on the church stairs crying had been transformed and finally had some peace in her heart.

"I went back to the apartment and took a long, hot shower. Just as I was drying myself, the phone rang, and my very own personal miracle happened. It was the temporary help agency telling me about the job for Mr. Lawrence St. George. I know in the depth of my being that Larry was truly God's gift to me. Because of Larry, I have known what complete love is. Because of that love, I was able to care for him. As I watched him die, I had the profound belief that God was ever so gently taking Larry from me to be with him. The pain of his death was softened by the knowledge that he was going to Jesus, who would take care of him from that point on. There are still evenings when I talk to Larry and ask him to help me get through the next day. I dream of him being healthy, running through fields of flowers, laughing, and telling me not to be sad because he is in paradise. Then I say a prayer of thanksgiving and sleep in peace.

"Well, girls, now I spilled my guts to you. It's okay if you think that I'm a little wacko. Nevertheless, boy, I have to admit, it feels good to share my story with someone else. I have never told anyone about that. I guess it is true: liquor does make for loose lips. Oh well, you all know that I have always been a few bricks short of a load."

The entire time she was sharing her story, she had stared into the burning logs; now she turned to look into the eyes of her old girlfriends. Rebecca was sitting next to her, reached over, and gently rubbed her back. Emily reached over and held Lindy's hand as she told her that she had always been the bravest of the group. It was nice to know that she had not changed. Grace thanked Lindy for sharing this very beautiful part of her life with them. She told her that she felt very blessed to have a friend like Lindy. All of them agreed as they again stared into the flames in front of them.

Grace sighed deeply, and then she began to speak. She said, "If Lindy can be so honest, I guess that I am called to be the same. After all of you left for college, I felt so abandoned. There was a time when I was very jealous of all of you; at another time, I was just plain angry. I was angry with my parents for not thinking about a future for me. They could have helped me get a college education, but they chose not to. I was angry that the three of you had this perfect life while I was stuck in Fergus Falls. I guess I was heading toward being a bitter young lady. I felt as though I was always going to be a loser.

"One day, I was steaming some new clothes that had just arrived at Claire's. There was a stunning, deep purple suit lined in a pale pink silk. It was one of the most expensive suits in the shop. I have no idea why I did it, but a few days later, I stole the suit. I justified it by saying that I would never get anything else that I deserved, so what was one suit? Well, a few weeks later, Claire went to find the suit to show a woman who was visiting town. She looked everywhere in the shop, then she went through the sales receipts for the past few days. I had never seen her so furious.

She was upset for several days and kept talking about calling the police to report it. Meanwhile, I had the suit hidden in the back of my tiny little closet. Every time I looked at it, I felt like throwing up. I finally hid it in a small crawl space where I had once hid our toys when the men came to take all of our stuff after we had polio.

"I was a thief, but worst of all, I had stolen something from Claire. She had always believed in me, cared for me, and had been my mentor. The suit became my torture. I could not look Claire in the face for weeks. I had nightmares for months about being arrested in the middle of the shop, then taken out into the middle of Lincoln Avenue with a sign around my neck saying, 'Beware: Grace is a thief and cannot be trusted.' After several months, I thought I was going to lose my mind.

"Finally, right after Christmas, I took the suit back to the shop. I asked Claire if I could see her in her office. When she walked in the door, I was clutching the suit to my chest. I confessed to her and begged her to forgive me. I knew that I had just lost the job that I had grown to love, all because of my stupid greed for an expensive suit. As I sat there sobbing, Claire simply sat looking at me. Finally, she told me to go home for the rest of the day while she thought about what had just happened. She told me to return to the shop the next day at ten o'clock. She felt that would give her enough time to think about the situation and come up with a solution.

"As I walked home that day, I have never felt so miserable and alone. I spent the rest of the day in my room terrified about what was going to happen to me. Yet I also felt as though a huge burden had been lifted from me. I was happy that I had finally told the truth. I was now completely willing to accept the consequences of my actions. I knew that whatever Claire decided to do would be fair. I did not know if she would have me arrested or if she would simply fire me.

"In the morning, I arrived at the shop just as I had promised. Garnet, one of the other saleswomen, told me that Claire was in her office. The first thing I saw was the suit hanging on the back of the door. Claire told me sit down and then she said, 'I want to tell you first of all that I admire the courage it took for you to tell the truth and return the suit. I have thought long and hard about what to do regarding this matter. I believe that you have suffered greatly because I know you have a strong conscience. It is obvious that this has been a burden for you. What you did was terribly wrong. I could call the police and have you arrested. However, I do not know what good that would do anyone. Therefore, here is what I have decided. You will not be able to work in the shop for one month, and you will not be able to purchase anything in the shop for three months. When you return to work, this matter will never be discussed again. I believe you when you say that you are sorry. I want to trust you again, but that will be up to you. You will have to earn your trust back, and I believe that you will be able to do that. At this moment, I feel betrayed, but I know that in time, this will pass. I strongly believe that we all learn some of the most valuable lessons of our lives from the mistakes we make. You can turn this incident into a success by learning from it. I am forgiving you in advance. Now go home, and I will see you in a month. That is when we will begin again to rebuild our relationship, and most importantly, our trust. We never need talk about this again.'

"As I walked home that day, I thanked God for giving me Claire. Through her wisdom and compassion, I had learned one of the most important lessons of my life. In time, I was able to rebuild the wonderful bond between us. I have used Claire as my example of how to live as an honorable woman. She did forgive me. Several times over the years, I tried to bring up the suit and once again apologize. Each time she would stop me, saying that it was forgiven and forgotten.

"Years later, after I had bought the shop from Claire, I was cleaning out the storage area. I found an old garment bag. When I opened it, I found the suit. I remember sitting down in the corner of the room, again clutching the suit to my chest. I said a special prayer that day for Claire's wisdom and forgiveness.

"I have no idea why I am telling you my dirty little secret except that it feels so good to finally get it out in the open. Even though we have been apart for all of these years, when I am here with you, I feel safe and protected. So now you know that Grace, little Goody Two-Shoes, is not so wonderful. I hope you will understand me a little better after hearing my story."

Rebecca was the first to move to Grace. She gave her a hug and whispered that she still was Amazing Grace in her eyes. Lindy told Grace that her daddy had told her so many times in the past, "Everyone makes mistakes; it's our chance to learn and grow. Make it again, and you are just flat out dumb!" Then Lindy added that the suit must have really been something to tempt Grace to do it. Lindy had once again broken the tension with her wonderful sense of humor.

As Grace, Lindy, and Rebecca were hugging, Emily sat staring into the fire. She seemed to be miles away from them. Lindy asked her if she was all right. Emily simply stood up, went out in the kitchen, and returned with the last bottle of Asti. When she had filled everyone's glasses, she finally spoke. "Well, I guess that it is my turn to shed my image and tell you about my life's major screw-ups. When I left here to go to college in Madison, I quickly connected with some real bad-news people. It was my first taste of freedom—drugs, sex, and becoming very self-centered. I guess I was rebelling against my parents. Do you know they never came to visit me in college, not once? However, all my rebellion just hurt me in the end. I was such a fool.

"After I graduated, I found myself alone, broke, and three months pregnant. I longed to call all of you. Even then, I was still too proud to ask you to help me. Well anyway, I had a beautiful baby girl, whom I named Rebecca Grace. Sorry, Lindy, I just could not fit in a third name. I only held her for fifteen minutes. I knew that I had made the right decision to allow a loving family, whom I had picked, to adopt her. They clearly adored her from the moment they saw her. I have never seen her again. To this day, I dream about her.

"It is so strange that my dreams change as she grows up. In the beginning, I dreamed of her having a bath in the kitchen sink, then the first steps she took. I could almost see her brushing her hair, riding her bike for the first time. Now I see her getting all dressed up for her first prom or hanging out on the front porch with her girlfriends. The only thing that I have ever asked God for is to keep her safe and let her know that she is deeply loved. Giving her up was the hardest thing but also the most unselfish thing I have ever done in my life. I feel as though there is a hole inside of me that cannot ever be filled or healed. That is okay; in an odd way, the pain keeps me connected to her.

"Nevertheless, you know me, Emily, the overachiever. I do not believe in having pity parties, so I have moved on and tried to help others not make the mistakes I made. I kept to myself, worked hard, and tried to make a difference. Then last week, I left the job that had been my entire identity. I went from being a winner to a loser. Once again, I find myself alone with little money and no place to go.

"About the same time, I received a letter from my father's lawyer advising me that the house, which was the only thing I inherited after my mother's death, was in dire need of repairs. So I decided to move back to Fergus Falls, the place where it all began. I plan to fix up the house and then sell it. Then, perhaps, I can figure out what to do with the rest of my life. I hope that while I am here working my butt off to get this place in shape, I will find a new start.

"Well, there you have it. See, Grace, you have nothing to be ashamed about. I think so far, I win the prize for being the biggest loser of this sisterhood."

This time they all leaned close to Emily. Lindy said, "Wow, what a night at the Larsons. This Asti stuff has made honest women out of all of us. Emily, welcome to my world—the world of ordinary!" They all laughed as they toasted each other.

Grace nudged Rebecca, telling her that it was now her turn to share one of her secrets. As Rebecca sat on the pillow on the floor, she sighed, looking at each of them directly in the eyes. Then she softly began to speak. "It is not that I have not had my share of mishaps over the years, because I most certainly have. I have been in love with two men that were both wrong for me. However, that story is for another day. Just two days ago, I moved back to Fergus Falls after having Mom's house remodeled. I can tell you that I have adored teaching at Holy Angels. I believe that it was my calling. I have had such a wonderful career.

"The secret I want to share with you has to do with the future, not the past." She stopped talking, taking a deep uneven breath. After she took another sip of Asti, she looked at all of their faces staring at her. "You must all promise that at least until I have my talk with Mom, that this stays within these four walls." All of them silently nodded, and no one said a word. Then Rebecca continued, "You all know that ever since I was born, I have had many health issues. Being a frail little girl was no fun. As a grown woman, my health has always been a barrier to doing many things that I have dreamed of experiencing in my life. Just as Emily dreams about her daughter, I dream about being healthy. I dream of running through a field, pedaling a bike for miles, swimming, skiing, and walking down nature trails. None of that is possible for me. I have learned how to accept my limitations. I enjoy all that I can do.

"However, this past year, it became obvious to me that my problems were becoming more serious. After many tests, my doctor has told me that there is nothing more that can be done. It seems that both my heart and my lungs are deciding to give out at about the same time. My only choice now is to go to bed and wait to die or to live the last few months of my life trying to squeeze in a few more adventures. Either way, my future can be counted in months instead of years.

"Please do not feel sorry for me. I am really quite okay with it. I wish with all of my imperfect heart that I did not have to cause my mother the pain that she will endure at my death. If I have any regrets, that is it. So, girlfriends, my wish is that I have some fun. I believe that God has put me here in Fergus Falls with all of you as one of my final gifts. So let's make the best of it, and help me go out in style."

They were all sobbing as they reached for Rebecca. Grace finally said, "Rebecca, I want you to know that you can ask me for anything. I promise to be there for you in whatever you need." Emily simply took Rebecca in her arms as they rocked in rhythm with their sobs. Lindy sat remembering all the pain of Larry's death and hoping that in some way it would help her to help Rebecca.

It was just before sunrise when they all decided it was time to get some sleep. Without anyone saying a word, they lay on the floor in front of the warm fireplace. They knew that they would not go to their separate bedrooms. They all needed to be close to each other tonight. Their old friendship had now blossomed into a friendship of adult women, with far more depth and meaning to all of them. As they wrapped themselves in their precious, twenty-year-old quilts, they fell asleep.

Chapter Twenty

A New Day

It was one of those crisp autumn days where the air feels cool and clean against your face. Lindy was the first one awake. She slipped out of the house without anyone hearing her. It was almost noon when Emily, Grace, and Rebecca awoke to the rich aroma of a fresh pot of coffee. As they slowly walked into the kitchen, they all paused in the doorway laughing. There was Lindy dressed in a bright red sparkling pants suit with a gigantic yellow hat, which had yellow feathers sticking out in every direction. The table was set, and in the middle of it was a platter filled with two dozen donuts of every kind and flavor. Emily was the first to speak. "Lindy, where did you ever find that wild hat? It hurts my eyes, or maybe it is just part of my hangover from last night."

Lindy told them that Larry had bought her the hat when they were in Aruba. As he had gently placed it on her head, he told her that no one else on the planet would ever be able to wear it in the style that Lindy could. It had become her good luck-thinking hat over the years. She had worn it when they had written some of the songs that would later be in their Broadway show, but that was a story for another day. She figured that today she needed to do some heavy-duty thinking. She was so thankful she had thrown it into the RV just before they had left on their trip.

Grace asked Lindy what was bothering her. Lindy sat down at the table, crossing her arms across her large chest, and said, "Well, here is how I figure out what happened last night. First, we finally all got honest with each other. In addition, surprise of all surprises, we discovered that not a one of us is perfect! Now I could have told you that twenty years ago, but it would not have been the same back in those days. Each of us has experienced some painful turning points. At least, we have all arrived here and are together. It seems as though this was our destiny for whatever the reason. Personally, I like all of you a lot better as grown women than as high-strung high school girls. The big news to me is that out of the four of us, three of you are going to be living here in Fergus. That leaves me once again as the odd duck. Well, you know me—I can't stand to be left out of the action.

"After thinking about it for all of two minutes, I decided that I don't want to miss anything that is going to happen. So, I got up early and went back to the hotel. I explained to my parents that I have decided to stay here for a while. As it turns out, my sister, Lana, needs to get away from a failing business and a divorce. It just so happens that the timing is perfect for her to hitch a ride back in the RV with her kids. She is going to live in my condominium and has promised that her kids will not destroy the place. With all of that done, it seems like everyone in my family is going to be happy with the new arrangement.

"Now, I just have to find a place to live, which brings me to my dear pal, Emily. I don't mean to hurt your feelings, girlfriend, but this place has turned into a real dump. I was thinking that maybe I can stay here with you. I swing a mean hammer, know how to use a paintbrush, and can wallpaper anything that does not move. The one thing I did not tell you all last night is that when Larry died, he made me a multimillionaire. I have spent the last months trying to spend the money, but it never seems to go down. Therefore, here is my offer, Emily. I will be happy to help you with any expenses you need to fix this joint up. You can consider it payback for the hundreds of nights that I slept here and ate everything in the kitchen. You would be doing me a huge favor because I really need to feel useful again. I figure this might be the place to find some new purpose. I also promise not to play my country-western music too loud.

"Now onto my dear sweet Rebecca. I am an incredibly good nurse. I knew from the first moment I laid eyes on you that there was a serious health problem going on. If Emily lets me crash here, I promise to be with you in any way that you will need. You know the old saying, in sickness and in health. Well, I am here to tell you that I do both of them pretty well. So, what do you all think of my plan?"

Emily jumped out of her chair and gave Lindy a hug, getting her raspberry-filled donut all over Lindy's arm. She laughed as she said, "God sure does have a great sense of humor. Just look at what has happened to us. Me, Emily, the rich and pampered overachiever, is now almost broke and living in this dump. Lindy, who never had more than two nickels to rub together, is now a multimillionaire, and she wants to help me! My oh my, how life takes us all on some interesting twists and turns. Lindy, I would love to have you stay with me. Your offer to help is truly appreciated. As soon as we are done and the house is sold, I promise to repay you for whatever money you lend me. In addition, girlfriend, if you can find some wallpaper with glitter, sparkles, or glow in the dark, you go for it! I need you and your wonderful can-do attitude in my life.

"I feel so blessed that all of you have forgiven me for being such a self-centered brat when I left here twenty years ago. I will be forever grateful for your friendship. Yes, Lindy, I agree with you that I think I like all of us a lot better today than when we were the girls of SOLA. I am truly amazed at what incredible women we have all become. However, we will always be the Sisterhood of Lake Alice. SOLA still has a wonderful charm to it."

Rebecca then softly told them that she, too, was so happy that they had taken her news in stride. She did not need to be surrounded with people who felt sorry for her or treated her like a china doll. She agreed with Lindy that they were all brought back to Fergus Falls for a reason. She wanted her future to be a rich time of joy, laughter, and meaning. Then she also turned to Lindy. As she held her hands, she said, "I am going to take you up on that offer to help me with the upcoming challenges that I know I am going to have to face. I cannot imagine trusting anyone more than I will trust you with helping me make good decisions. For the next few days, I want you to look at the health records that I have brought with me. After you have a good understanding of what is going on, perhaps you can come with me for my first visit to the doctor here in Fergus Falls.

"However, I have one huge favor to ask of you. Will you be with me and help me explain what is happening to my mother? I want her to know that you will be there for both of us. Also, I will be at peace knowing that you will make sure that my wishes for treatment are honored. I know that this is a lot to ask a friend that I have not seen for many years, but in my heart I know that you will be my anchor during this time."

Lindy quickly agreed to assist Rebecca in whatever her future held for her. They both agreed that they would spend some time going over the records. After they had a chance to discuss what Rebecca wanted for a course of treatment, they would then find a doctor who would work closely with both of them.

Grace sat there in total amazement at what was happening in front of her. In some ways, it was as though they had never left each other. Yet in another way, who they had grown up to be was such a wonderful surprise. Four girls had left Emily's house almost twenty years ago. Today, four compassionate and wise women sat around a table discussing how each of them would help each other. There was no doubt in Grace's mind: it was no accident that they were together again. Together they would help each other heal, grow, and find new purpose in life. For the first time in twenty years, she knew that she had three devoted friends— friends who had enough courage to be honest, humble, and loving with each other. After last night, she knew that there would not be any false pretenses. They would be able to trust each other with their virtues and their flaws.

She smiled as she looked into their faces and simply said, "So this is what it feels like to be with girlfriends. I did not realize how much I have missed your presence in my life until this morning. For the first time in a very long time, I feel free to just be me. We will do whatever we need to do for each of us. Rebecca, I want you to know that you will never be alone in your struggles. Emily, we now have an opportunity to see what was under all that expensive outer layer; I like what I see in you today. My Lindy, you will lead us into chaos and joyful adventures. Your love of life and delightful spirit will make us all reach for new heights. As for me, I don't know what I can offer all of you. Perhaps I can introduce you to the simple pleasures of living in a charming place called Fergus Falls. I just want you to know that I will stand by all of you. Plus, as a little added bonus, I promise that you can all buy clothes from Claire's at cost."

With that, they all clapped and told Grace that they were going to take her up on her offer. They laughed about buying matching outfits. Rebecca said that she would have to draw the line on wearing big yellow hats.

After two pots of coffee and eating all the donuts, they decided to go home and get some rest. They agreed to meet again at Mabel Murphy's for dinner. Lindy was going back to the Holiday Inn to pack her clothes and make the final arrangements for her parents' and Lana's family trip back home. She prepared a list of clothes, accessories, and special items that Lana would ship to her in Fergus Falls. Before she returned to Emily's house, she stopped by the car dealer and bought a new bright red SUV, which she drove off the lot. The salesperson was still in shock as he watched her wave good-bye to him while he held a check for $38,000. His boss had called Lindy's bank and was assured that the check was perfectly good.

Rebecca had again made everyone promise to keep her secret until she had time to tell her mother. She did not tell them that she needed to go home and rest for the afternoon. As soon as she got home, she went in her bedroom, where she used her rescue inhaler and took some of her stronger medications. After telling Monica all about the reunion and the sleepover, she excused herself for a well-needed nap. As she fell asleep, Rebecca felt at peace with all that she knew she would be facing in the future. She knew that her friends would be with her until the end.

Emily cleaned up the kitchen and den. She smiled as she walked from room to room in a house that had been cold and unloving. Now as she looked at each of the rooms, she imagined a new beginning—not just for the house but also for Lindy, her wonderful new roommate. She laughed out loud thinking if anyone was capable of finding wallpaper that did actually glow in the dark, it was Lindy!

Grace decided to walk back to her apartment by herself. She walked down the streets that were covered with an umbrella of trees in their full autumn beauty. She looked at the leaves in deep shades of gold, orange, and amber and smiled as she took a deep breath of the crisp air. Grace knew in her heart that there was a new beginning on the way. She thought about how good it felt to have Emily, Rebecca, and Lindy back in her life. Grace knew that they were going to make a difference in Fergus Falls. The girls of SOLA were gone. They had been replaced with four incredible SOLA women. Yes, life was good in Fergus Falls. Now there was a promise that it was going to get even better.

Chapter Twenty-One

Back Home

It did not take long for Emily, Lindy, Rebecca, and Grace to fall into a comfortable pattern in their daily lives. At dinner that evening, they worked on their schedules for the upcoming week. They agreed that every Friday evening would be a girls' night out with dinner and gossip, unless any of them ever were to have a date, which they all agreed was very unlikely. Then following their old tradition, every Saturday night they would have a sleepover at Emily's house. By the end of the evening, each of them felt as though they reconnected in a deeper way than ever before.

Lindy and Rebecca got together the next morning to start looking through all of Rebecca's medical records. By noon, Lindy had reviewed the files. They sat in the den with the door closed as they discussed what options were available for her. Aside from a complete lung and heart transplant, which they both agreed had very little chance of happening, most of her options revolved around medications and oxygen. For the most part, these options would keep Rebecca comfortable. There was no cure.

Lindy explained with great gentleness and honesty just how the disease would progress. In time, Rebecca would need to be on oxygen and then in a wheelchair. However, for the moment, they needed to find a good doctor and start working on a routine to keep her health as stable as possible. Rebecca spent time telling Lindy about how she wanted to live the balance of her life and that when the end came, how she wanted to leave this world. Together, they wrote down Rebecca's wishes. When that was done, Lindy gave Rebecca a hug and told her that she would honor all of her requests.

They decided that they needed to have the painful conversation with Rebecca's mother, Monica, as soon as possible. She was already concerned about Rebecca, and it did not seem fair to keep this information from her. Lindy agreed to join them for dinner that evening. After their dinner, they would have the talk. Rebecca was both emotionally and physically exhausted as she left to go home. She planned to spend some time praying and resting for the afternoon. Both of them were anxious but prepared to gently break the news to Monica. Rebecca knew this would be one of the most difficult conversations she had ever had. However, with Lindy's help, she knew that it would somehow turn out okay.

The evening at Rebecca's house went better than either Rebecca or Lindy had expected. After a delicious dinner, Rebecca and Lindy insisted on doing the dishes while Monica got to rest in her new leather recliner and read the newspaper. When they walked into the tiny living room, they found Monica sitting in her favorite chair simply staring out the window. Before they could say anything, Monica spoke. "Girls, I know something is up. I need to know what is going on. Rebecca, ever since you came home, it seems as though you are always trying to avoid me. I know it is not polite to talk in front of company, but I just cannot take the stress of not knowing any longer. Anyway, Lindy has always been just like family. So please, I beg of you, tell me what is the matter."

Rebecca sat on the armrest of her mother's chair as she told her that she was sorry for causing her any stress. She had thought that she had been hiding her anxious feelings pretty well, but it was always hard to fool a mom. For the rest of the evening, both Rebecca and Lindy told Monica all about the serious health issues and the options that were available to Rebecca. Monica sat listening with tears streaming down her face as she gently rubbed Rebecca's hand. She asked good questions. Lindy tried to answer as many as she could.

After a lot of conversation, they were all emotionally exhausted. Monica got up and asked them to come into the dining room for a piece of her homemade apple cobbler and ice cream. As they sat down to eat their dessert, they all realized that they were relieved that the entire truth was now out in the open.

Monica sighed and said, "Rebecca when you were born, the doctors did not give me any hope of you surviving more than a few days. After you showed them that you had a lot of spunk, they changed the gloom and doom to a couple of months. Nevertheless, I knew in my heart that they were wrong. From the moment I laid eyes on you, I knew that you were a survivor. I have thanked God for each day that he has given you. The sorrow inside me right now fills my entire being. However, I am going to be grateful for all the days we have and not let this pain take away from our time together.

"I am convinced that Lindy was brought back to Fergus Falls to be with you and me during this time. We will do whatever we need to do. I promise you that I will honor your requests for your treatment. I also promise you that for whatever time you have left, I will spend it rejoicing in your presence. You have been God's special gift to me."

Lindy left the DuPree house that evening knowing that the love within the four walls of that tiny house was going to be enough to get them through the pain that was to come. As she slowly drove home, she looked into the houses on the tree-lined streets of Fergus Falls. She saw families watching TV, dogs lying on front porches, teenagers walking down the sidewalks. When she pulled the car into the driveway, she got out and walked across the street to the grassy shore of Lake Alice.

As she looked out over the lake, she was stunned by the sight of the full moon lighting up the water. It sparkled and shimmered as the moonlight danced across the still water. A pair of loons dove under the water, creating a ripple. Then, they popped up on the opposite side of this perfect little lake. Yes, it was all going to be okay. No, it was not right that Rebecca was going to be taken away from them. Nevertheless, the girls were here together. Each one of them would help the others in their own special way. It was what it was, and together, they would survive.

Lindy and Emily had plans, lists, and paint samples spread all over the massive oak dining room table. As they went through the list of repairs and projects that Charlie had given to Emily, they sorted the tasks into projects they could do and what they needed to hire someone to do. Charlie came over with a list of contractors whom he trusted. Within a short time, the master plan for restoring the house was completely put together. If all went just as scheduled, the house would be remodeled and redecorated for the Christmas season. The two biggest jobs were the electrical work and plumbing. By some good luck, both men that Charlie had recommended were immediately available. Work was going to start the following morning on the bathrooms and kitchen.

By the end of the week, there were gallons of paint, rolls of wallpaper, samples of fabrics, and carpeting stacked neatly in the corner of the dining room. Contractors were coming the following week to repair the walls, ceilings, and hardwood floors. Emily and Lindy were going to Minneapolis while that work was being done. They planned to purchase new furniture, carpeting, and accessories. They prayed that the outside of the house painting could be finished and the new windows and doors could be installed while they were away.

Within a few weeks, the electrical and plumbing work was done. The house was ready to be transformed with the artistic flair of Emily and Lindy. The once-abandoned house was now a scene of busy people running in all directions with great purpose. If all went as planned, the house would be even more beautiful than in the past; however, this time the house would have a warm, cozy glow to it, instead of being the cold showcase of the past.

Both Emily and Lindy were so excited about how everything seemed to be falling into place. They truly enjoyed each other's company and worked well together. Each evening as they relaxed in the den with a glass of wine, they would recap the adventures of the day. They quickly discovered that between the two of them, they had a wonderful balance. Emily had a flair for elegance that mixed with Lindy's talent for the unexpected made their color scheme of rich burgundy, emerald green, and royal blue a stunning and lively combination. With Lindy's money, they were able to find beautiful silk and unusual woven fabrics for the drapes, furniture, and bedding. Each of the five bedrooms was going to have its own theme.

The Monday morning after the reunion weekend, Grace arrived at the shop late for the first time that she could remember. Jodi and Candice were waiting anxiously on the bench outside the store. They both asked her if she was okay. Jodi told her that they were getting very concerned when they arrived and the shop was not open. Grace smiled and told them that she had not slept so well in a long time; it was a simple matter of oversleeping. As Kelli and JoAnn arrived at the shop, they also noticed that Grace had more spring in her step and a big smile that made her face absolutely radiant. For the rest of the day, Grace talked about the wonderful reunion that had brought her three best friends home to her.

As the customers came and went, they all remarked about how happy Grace looked. Several of the women made comments, asking her if there was a new man in her life. Grace told them no, that it was even better than a new man—she had her three best girlfriends back in town. She even found herself humming as she worked on the books. Grace felt that the reunion had been a turning point for her. She was not sure what that meant, but she did know that her life had instantly become fuller with the addition of Rebecca, Lindy, and Emily. Yes, life seemed a little easier today.

Chapter Twenty-Two

First Snowfall

The autumn days in Fergus Falls were a wide variety of clear, blue skies one day and cold, dull windy days the next. Grace and Rebecca got into the habit of stopping by Emily's almost every day to see the latest progress on the house. Most of the time, they sat around the kitchen table just sharing a cup of tea and talking about what had happened to each of them during the day. Without fail, Lindy always seemed to have some funny story to share with them.

Emily and Lindy had banned Grace and Rebecca from the second floor of the house until all of the work and decorating was completed. Grace commented that the house seemed to have an aura of warmth and friendship that had never been there in the past. Emily quickly agreed, saying that it was because for the first time, there was love and true adult friendship within these four walls. They all just nodded in agreement.

Fall quickly turned to winter in Fergus Falls. The first week in November, they had their first snowfall, which ended up being four inches of the light powder type of snow that was terrible for snowballs. The town looked like a Currier & Ives painting. As the snow began to fall, they decided to take a walk around Lake Alice.

They walked in silence, which was very unusual for them. It just did not seem right to do anything but take in the beauty of the lake and trees sparkling with the white snow. As they were coming back to the house, they stopped and quietly watched as Warren Brooks played with his daughters. Without giving it any thought, Lindy ran up to them and told them that it was time for snow angels. She promptly lay down and created an angel by moving her arms and legs in the snow. Everyone quickly joined in, laughing as they made their angels in the snow. No one noticed that Warren had run into the house, quickly returning to photograph the looks of four women with pure joy on their faces, lying and laughing in the fresh, white snow.

Emily invited everyone back to her house for some wonderful hot chocolate. Within minutes, they were all in the house gathered around the old kitchen table. The first snowfall had proven to be a happy event.

As they all stood around talking, Melissa recognized Grace as the lady from the shop where they had bought their school uniforms and other clothes. Warren thanked her again for all of her guidance in getting the girls ready for school. Grace laughed as she told Warren that perhaps it was time for another trip, to purchase warmer hats, gloves, and warm socks. They agreed that they would come to Claire's on Saturday. Warren insisted that after their shopping was done, he wanted to take Grace to lunch with them as a small way of saying thank you.

Lindy told the girls that they also needed to get Pops to buy them some ice skates. While six-year-old Sarah sat on her lap, Lindy told stories about how they would ice-skate for hours and always come back to Emily's for Isabel's perfect hot chocolate and warm chocolate chip cookies. Before too long, Rebecca and Grace were mixing the cookie dough while threatening to lock Lindy and Emily out of the kitchen if they did not stop eating raw spoonfuls.

Warren went home and returned with a pot of chili that he had made for dinner. The rest of the evening was filled with good food, laughter, and friendship. After the kitchen was cleaned, they all went into the library, where Emily had a fire going. As they sat on the floor on big overstuffed pillows, they continued to tell the girls stories about growing up in Fergus Falls. It was after nine o'clock when Warren and three very tired girls left.

After they left, everyone started teasing Emily about rekindling the old high school crush. Emily slowly turned to Grace and said, "I do believe that the spark in Warren's eyes was not for me, but for Grace. I watched you two together. I must admit that you both looked comfortable together. Grace is a much better match for Warren than I could be." Grace blushed as she denied knowing what Emily was talking about. However, later on she found herself thinking about Warren and his daughters.

At ten years old, Melissa needed the guidance of a woman to help her create her style. Katherine, who had just turned eight, appeared to be coming out of the tomboy stage, and Sarah was a spirited little girl who needed to cuddle. She had forgotten how blue Warren's eyes were, and she liked his smile. She was also very impressed with his parenting skills. A man raising three young girls was a huge undertaking. Perhaps she could help him a little with the girls by offering a gentle woman's touch that they needed.

With the snow on the roads not yet plowed, Grace and Rebecca decided to sleep over. The mood of the evening had brought so many memories to the surface that none of them wanted to be separated from the others. That evening, they slept in the library again, surrounded by the memories of the past. The first snowfall had proven to be a wonderful success and a time that they would remember for many years to come.

Chapter Twenty-Three

One Day at a Time

The days flew by so fast. The Thanksgiving celebration was at Rebecca's house. Monica had spent days making lefse for the dinner. As they crowded around the small dining table, they held hands and said a prayer of Thanksgiving. Each of them took turns giving thanks for their special blessings this year.

Emily smiled as she gave thanks for losing her job, which helped her find her way back to Fergus Falls and to her friends. With tears in her eyes, Lindy gave thanks for having Larry in her life and all their loving memories. Then she paused to regain her emotions for a moment and proceeded to give thanks for bringing some life and color into the Larsons' dreary old house. Grace gave thanks for her shop, all of her staff, and this wonderful girlfriend reunion, which had brought them back into each other's lives. Rebecca softly prayed her thanksgiving prayer to her special mother, good doctors, and for enjoying more laughter with her friends than she had ever dreamed possible. She also thanked God for giving her the courage to face each tomorrow. Monica cried as she thanked God for every moment of Rebecca's life.

They all sat in silence for a moment before Monica passed around a box of Kleenex and then began serving the meal. It was a wonderful day filled with many reasons to be grateful.

This was the busiest time of the year for Grace at the shop. She had already warned Emily, Lindy, and Rebecca that she would not be able to spend much time with them until after the holidays. Grace had spent a full weekend after Thanksgiving decorating the shop and the front windows for Christmas. Each year her windows were decorated with a large nativity scene surrounded with hundreds of twinkling lights that appeared to be stars in the sky. Every year, she added a few new pieces to the scene; this year she introduced a pond, geese, and horses.

Claire's shop offered three special *men only* shopping events, where the shop was only open to the men of Fergus Falls looking to buy special gifts for their wives, sweethearts, mothers, or daughters. There were also three Sunday afternoons reserved just for the children to come and purchase gifts for their mom, grandmother, and sisters. On those days, Grace had baskets overflowing with scarves, pins, ribbons, small bottles of perfume, and purses, all under ten dollars and including free gift-wrapping. The shop hours were extended until nine o'clock each evening and all day on Saturday.

Although Rebecca was feeling weaker with each passing day, she knew she needed something to keep herself occupied. So she volunteered to help Grace at the shop. She enjoyed having a reason to get up, get dressed each day, and be in such a wonderful Christmas place. Rebecca was officially in charge of the gift-wrapping department, where she could rest if she needed to during the day. The excitement of the shop kept her mind busy. She truly enjoyed reconnecting with many of the people whom she had not seen in years.

Rebecca did not tell Grace that she now required oxygen each night as she slept. The only person who knew about it was Lindy, who had helped her make all of the arrangements to have the oxygen delivered to her house. Each evening as she went to bed, Monica would come in and talk with her for a while, always making sure that she was settled in for the evening. Rebecca did not know that at least twice during the night, Monica would tiptoe into her room just to check on her breathing. Each day Rebecca struggled to find a little more energy. She knew that this was all part of the disease that her doctor had discussed with her. She continued to count on Lindy to answer her questions about what to expect.

What surprised Rebecca the most was that the weaker she became, she noticed that she had a stronger sense of peace that had overcome so many of her fears. As she lay in bed each night, she prayed that she could continue to make each day that was given to her a good day. So far, she had been able to do that. For that, Rebecca thanked God each night as she fell into a deep sleep.

The rule of not allowing Rebecca or Grace on the second floor remained in place all during the remodeling. Because the major work to restore the house was now done, all that was left were the decorating and finishing touches. Emily announced that for the week before Christmas, they were not allowed to visit. She mailed both Grace and Rebecca a handmade invitation to join her and Lindy for Christmas evening service at Bethlehem Lutheran Church, followed by a special dinner, gift exchange, and sleepover. Both of them quickly replied that they would be there.

Lindy had already sent boxes of gifts to her family in Florida. Rebecca's mother had volunteered to work the midnight shift and Christmas day at the nursing home so that others with family could celebrate together; she planned to sleep there as well.

A few days before Christmas, Pastor Meissner called Grace and asked if the Girls, as they were known throughout Fergus, would consider singing a few hymns before the start of the candlelight service on Christmas Eve at Bethlehem Lutheran Church. Because they were still not allowed in Emily's house, they met at church to practice some of their favorite Christmas carols. They were looking forward to singing in this beautiful, old church with its stained-glass windows, oak pews, and majestic pipe organ.

On Christmas Eve, the snow began to fall about five o'clock, and the temperature dropped to twenty degrees. Lindy and Emily took Lindy's SUV to pick up Rebecca and Grace for church services. On the way to church, they practiced their songs. The service was breathtaking, with hundreds of candles and the freshly cut giant evergreen tree decorated with handmade ornaments by the children from Bible classes. As the people filled the pews, they sang. Soon the entire church was filled, and everyone sat quietly listening to their wonderful blended harmony as SOLA sang one song after another. Lindy finally asked them all to join in as they closed with "Silent Night." Pastor Meissner started his sermon by saying that he would never forget the beauty of all the voices singing "Silent Night" as it was sung tonight.

As Emily, Lindy, Grace, and Rebecca took their places in the front pew, they all said a special prayer of thanksgiving. Holding hands and bowing their heads, they prayed together. They were all at peace. It was good to be home in Fergus Falls.

Chapter Twenty-Four

The Larson House

Before going to Emily's house, Lindy took a quick drive around Lake Alice to see the houses all decorated, with the snow gently forming a white haze over the lake and trees. They arrived back at Emily's house after the church service to find lights shining from almost every window. From the outside, the house seemed to glow with special Christmas warmth. Lindy asked them to go in through the front door tonight instead of their usual kitchen entrance; however, they needed to wait until she had parked the car so they could all go in together.

Emily smiled as she slowly opened the front door, painted a deep shade of red with a beautiful etched glass panel and a decorated evergreen wreath. As they walked into the front hall, they saw a woman standing in the shadows of the winding staircase waiting to take their coats from them. The wood floors had been polished to a high shine, and in the center of the large foyer stood a round marble table with a huge Christmas floral arrangement done in red and gold flowers. Overhead, a new three-tier crystal chandelier hung from the second floor to midway down to the first floor and softly illuminated the area.

Grace took off her coat and handed it to the woman without looking directly at her. She suddenly sensed something was different about the woman. As she turned to the woman, she was shocked. Isabel smiled at her with tears welling in her eyes as she quietly waited for her girls to recognize her. In seconds, everyone was talking and hugging at the same time. Emily and Lindy had decided that this was the perfect Christmas gift to give Grace and Rebecca. They laughed as they realized they had successfully pulled off their surprise.

When Emily had finally tracked down Isabel, she told Emily she would love to come for a visit. She asked if she could bring her husband Rolf and her twin daughters, Anna and Beata, age nineteen, with her.

It had been twenty-four years since she had last seen Emily; however, as they hugged each other, it seemed like yesterday. Emily and Isabel had only a few moments together before she needed to leave for the church service. Isabel and her family had flown into Minneapolis and were then whisked away in a limo that Emily had arranged to bring them to Fergus.

Isabel was in her mid-forties and the mother of five children. Her life had been a good life, filled with the joys of raising her children alongside a loving husband. Rolf inherited the family bakery shop, where the whole family worked side by side. The young girls were the last children at home. She had told Emily over the phone that she especially wanted them to meet the girls from Fergus Falls. From their early childhood, Anna reminded her so much of Grace that she was thrilled that she had chosen the name Anna, which meant grace in Norwegian. Beata meant blessed and reminded Isabel of Emily in so many ways. Beata had many musical talents and was planning to study in Oslo to become an opera singer.

She went on to explain that as her way of saying thank you to Emily for the wonderful and generous trip that she would prepare and serve a very typical Norwegian Christmas dinner for them. She would do all the special planning because they would bring some of the food with them from Norway. That explained the unusual smells that now came from the kitchen. Isabel called her family to come in and meet the girls, whom she still talked about so often.

As they came into the foyer, each of them was warmly welcomed. Rolf was a big man, who stood over six feet five inches tall. He had blond hair, blue eyes, and rosy cheeks, with a warm smile. Anna looked just like Isabel had looked so many years ago. She was quiet and sweet with long, blonde, braided hair. Beata looked more like Rolf and instantly went to hug Emily, Grace, Rebecca, and Lindy. She told them that she had not slept for a week before they flew here yesterday. She also told them that the house was even grander than she had ever imagined.

After a little while, Emily explained that she was now ready for the official unveiling of the Larson house. The first stop was the formal living room, which was decorated by Emily in rich colors of burgundy, emerald green, and royal blue. All of the furniture was overstuffed and comfortable. This was no longer a stuffy room filled with antiques. In the middle of the bay window stood a live evergreen tree that touched the ceiling. The tree was covered with thousands of tiny, multicolored lights and hundreds of gold bows.

Next, Lindy led the group into the dining room, which had been her project. This room was also done in rich shades of burgundy, emerald green, and royal blue. The striped silk drapes softened the oak paneling and floors. There was a colorful Persian rug under the massive oak table, and each of the eight chairs was upholstered in a different color. The light fixture had been inspired by Chihuly, with clusters of lights in the shape of flowers all lit in different colors, giving the room a soft rainbow effect. The cove in the ceiling was painted sky blue with soft clouds.

Rebecca had tears in her eyes as she took in the beauty of the room. She turned to Lindy and said, "You have created more than a room; this is an oasis from the world. You have captured a sense of peace." They stood in silence for a moment before Emily told them it was time to reveal the second floor.

As they walked upstairs, Emily explained that each of the five bedrooms now had a name and a theme. She laughed as she told them that they would quickly be able to figure out who decorated each of the rooms. There were new bathrooms, connected between two rooms for even more convenience. All of the doors were closed, and each had a small brass plaque on it.

Emily decided to show Grace's room first. The plaque on the door read, "Amazing Grace will be with you here. Enjoy your time in this space dedicated to peace." Emily asked Grace to open her door. Slowly, Grace opened the door.

The room was designed in soft pastel shades of yellow, pink, purple, and blue. As they walked into the room, they sunk into thick, plush, off-white carpeting. There was a graceful, antique canopy bed covered in a beautiful handmade quilt. In the corner by the large window, there was an off-white chaise lounge, with a soft pink cashmere throw and many fluffy, pastel-colored pillows. There was a small desk with a crystal lamp. On the wall was a large framed picture of Grace and all of her family, including Denny. On the desk was a framed handwritten prayer that

Denny had written many years ago. Grace's mother had given it to Emily to become part of this special room.

Grace could not speak as she sat at the desk hugging Denny's framed prayer. Emily knelt down close to her and simply held her hands as the two of them cried. Finally Grace regained her composure and softly said, "How can I ever thank you for the gift of honoring my family in such a loving way? I am so blessed to have found your friendship again. But now it is time for the rest of the rooms to be unveiled."

The next room had a plaque that read, "Rebecca's haven, for those who know that music feeds our weary souls." Rebecca opened the door and walked into her special room.

This room was decorated in many shades of blue. The big oak sleigh bed had a royal blue plush duvet, with musical notes embroidered in the middle of it. The sky blue walls gave the room a feeling of instant peace, and the lace curtains added to the softness. There was a small window seat with cushions, each with a different musical note embroidered. A guitar was leaning against the wall. In the corner was a full-size harp with a small, silk-covered chair. There was a violin in a stand on the dresser. The mirror, which hung over the dresser, was lit with tiny twinkling lights that gave the room a playful quality. The indirect lighting that encircled the room could be dimmed for another special mood.

Rebecca was as deeply touched as Grace had been. She went to the harp, with her hands stroking the fine polished wood that been shaped into a perfect instrument. Then she sat in the chair and began to play "Silent Night." They all gathered around her as they sang in sweet harmony with tears rolling down their faces. It was Lindy who finally broke the spell by telling them it was time for her surprise. As difficult and tempted as Lindy was, she never peeked into the special room that Emily was creating for her.

Lindy's room had a plaque that read, "Lindy, the lover of life, laughter, and love. May you be blessed with all of these gifts as you rest in this room." As Lindy opened the door, she screamed and danced with joy.

The room was decorated in an animal theme, with rich, thick, green plush carpeting. Three walls were covered in natural-colored grass-cloth wallpaper. One entire wall was filled with a mural of many different animals, including elephants, lions, tigers, camels, giraffes, parrots, and dogs. The ceiling was painted similar to the dining room, with an appearance of a bright sky of blue with soft, floating clouds. The lighting in the room made the mural almost seem to come alive. A bed had been built into the corner with a gauze net hanging over it. Two huge leather chairs and an ottoman created a comfortable seating area and were surrounded by an assortment of giant stuffed animals.

Curled up in the corner of the room was an overstuffed wicker basket with a real puppy sound asleep. Lindy picked up the envelope that was taped to the front of the puppy's basket. When she opened it, she read it to the group: "Hi, Lindy. My name is Linus, and I need some extra loving and a good home. Please be my friend, and I promise to be yours forever." Lindy gently picked up the tiny puppy and said, "Well, little guy, you have come to the right place. We're going to have a good time together." As Grace, Rebecca, and Emily gathered around Linus, they all knew this little puppy was a very lucky dog!

Lindy finally turned to Emily and told her how happy she was about her special room. She also told her that she was shocked at her wild creativity. Now it was time for Lindy to show Emily the room that she had designed just for her.

Emily's door had a plaque that read, "As you enter Emily's room, you are sure to find grace, peace, and friendship. Enjoy your stay." Emily walked into her special room and instantly felt at home.

The color scheme was rich burgundy, royal blue, and emerald greens. One entire wall was lined with oak bookcases filled with her favorite books, and a few wonderful pieces of artwork mingled among them. A rich, emerald green silk comforter softly covered the bed, with special reading lights on each side. There was a down-filled chaise lounge, with a small table that held a CD player and stacks of soft jazz CDs. The soft gauze pleated blinds on her windows did not obstruct the view of the weeping willow tree in her backyard. The room was truly a haven for her.

Lindy giggled as she showed her the final touch to the room as she clapped her hands and the lights went out. With another clap, they came back on. They all laughed, saying they knew that Lindy had to do at least one unusual thing. Emily hugged Lindy as she told her that for the very first time in her life, she had a friend who truly understood her lifelong search for peace.

Emily then took them down the hall to the last room. She asked Isabel to open this door and read the plaque. The plaque said, "Isabel's place of wisdom, love, and caring. Begin your life anew today as you enter this room." Isabel was holding her daughters' hands as she walked into the room.

The light was soft, and the colors on the walls seemed to blend from one shade to another as if a rainbow had been captured. There were two twin beds covered in handmade quilts just like the ones she had given to the girls so many years ago. Emily had them lovingly duplicated by a woman from church who was a master quilter. There was a large rocking chair in the corner and several large paintings of Norwegian scenes on the walls. The furniture was very rustic, and the room had a wonderful, fresh pine smell to it.

Isabel turned to Emily with tears in her eyes as she said that the time spent in Minnesota with her had truly made her into the woman who now stood in front of her. "My children have been blessed with the love that I discovered as I cared for you those many years," Isabel said. "It is such a joy to reunite with you again as women. Even though we have only been together for a short time, I know that you are all women of substance with noble spirits and gentle hearts. I saw those qualities in you as little girls and knew the qualities would serve you well as women. Thank you, Emily, for giving me this wonderful opportunity to witness this with my family. Anna and Beata have had to listen to my Minnesota stories all of their lives. Now they see that my stories are true. Fergus Falls is a very special place with very special people."

They once again came together with tears flowing and embraced each other in a big group hug. Isabel's daughters looked around the room in awe at how well Emily had captured their mother's taste and spirit.

As they all were about to head down the staircase, Emily said that she had one last surprise for them. At the end of the hall, there was one more door with a small plaque on it. She asked Rebecca to go over and read it.

She started laughing as she read the plaque, which simply said, "When you need an extra lift, here it is." As she opened the door, she found a small elevator.

Emily told them that she figured someday they would all be in need of this type of lift. They all laughed as Emily told Rebecca that she should be the first person to use this latest addition to the Larson house. Rebecca asked Isabel to accompany her on the maiden trip. All the rest took the staircase as Rebecca and Isabel took the elevator, which brought them to the back hall right outside the kitchen.

Chapter Twenty-Five

The Friendship Gifts

Isabel told the girls that it was time for them to go into the living room, where they would find cheese and crackers and, of course, a bottle of Asti. One by one, they each offered their comments about the beauty that had been created in this house. Grace said that she was sure this was how the original builder must have pictured it many years ago. The house was now a warm, welcoming home. Rebecca told Emily that she should take great pride in her accomplishments and thanked Lindy for once again bringing that extra special sparkle to the house that only she could do.

Emily told them that she had such mixed feelings about ever returning to Fergus Falls because of her unloving parents. However, by the grace of God and one Grace O'Malley, now she knew that she was meant to come home. Once she arrived, she saw the house in an entirely different way. Perhaps it was because she was a woman with more of life's experiences. She just knew that she had what it took to turn this place into a home at last. With Lindy's lighthearted help, this was now a place with lots of living to be done. For whatever reason, Emily knew deep in her heart that she would never live anywhere else but in Fergus Falls from this day forward. The thought of selling the house was no longer an option. Now she just needed to figure out how to make a living in Fergus Falls so that she could stay here. Lindy had already made it very clear to Emily that she did not want to be repaid for any of the expenses for the house. She had money to burn, and this project had given her more joy than she had felt in a long time. Lindy did not want these feelings tarnished with any talk about money.

Rolf announced their Christmas dinner was ready and waiting for them. As they entered the dining room, they saw the table had been set in beautiful, hand-painted dishes, with a different Norwegian pattern at each place setting. There were tiny votive candles spread all around the table. By the doorway, they were greeted by Rolf, Isabel, Anna, and Beata, who were all dressed in their native outfits. Rolf escorted Emily to her place at the table, while Isabel took Grace to her place. Anna took Rebecca's arm, while Beata hugged Lindy and then showed her to her special place. Then Isabel and her family sat down in the remaining empty chairs, so that each of them was seated next to the lady they had escorted into the dining room. There was an instant sense of comfort as they all admired the beautiful table.

In a matter of moments, all eight of them grew quiet gathered around the table. Rolf cleared his voice and asked permission to recite a typical Norwegian prayer of blessing for this special meal. They all said yes at the same time. They held hands as he proceeded in Norwegian first, followed by the English translation.

"I jesu navn gar vi til bords,
Spise, drikke pa ditt ord.
Deg Gud til aere, oss til gavn,
Sa rar vi mat I Jesu navn. Amen.
In Jesus' name, we sit down.
Eat and drink on Your Holy Word.
To honor God and nourish us.
We get our food in Jesus' name. Amen."

At the end of the prayer, Isabel went in the kitchen and returned with a big platter filled with some very smelly and strange-looking food. She proudly announced that for this very special meal, she had brought all of the twelve place settings of hand-painted plates as a gift to Emily and Lindy for their generous invitation. However, even more important, she had also brought lutefisk, lefse, and lingonberry jam for their meal, all the way from Norway.

Lindy was laughing while holding her nose as she asked what lutefisk was. Anna proceeded to tell her that it was fish soaked in lye and in water for a long time, and you knew it was ready when it smelled this bad. Each of them took a small taste and then quickly passed on the platter. Rolf was pleased to see that he could have all the lutefisk that he wanted.

Lindy gave a toast, saying she was very thankful that lutefisk was not the main course. The dinner was filled with laughter, good food (except for the lutefisk), and memories.

After a wonderful meal, the girls decided to take a walk around Lake Alice to work off a little of their meal The night air was cold and crisp as they all bundled up in their heavy coats, scarves, hats, and gloves. Lake Alice had never looked more beautiful. For some reason, the colder the night, the clearer the stars in the sky seemed to be. With all the houses glowing with their Christmas lights and the stars above, it was a magical stroll. By the time they returned home, Isabel and her family excused themselves. They were leaving in the morning for their long trip back home.

After they went upstairs, Emily announced that it was time to open their gifts. Lindy said, "Well, girlfriends, I suggest we move our butts into the living room so we can begin." As Emily looked at Rebecca, she could see how exhausted she seemed to be. She suggested that they take a little break, get into their jammies, and meet back in the living room an hour later. As they headed for the staircase, Emily gently led Rebecca to the elevator.

They gathered back in the living room clad in the same flannel pjs, furry slippers, and warm robes they had bought together at J. C. Penney. There were stacks of gifts for each of them. Lindy sat with Linus cuddled in her lap as he happily slept.

Emily started by saying that never in her life had she experienced a more wonderful and meaningful Christmas. She was sure that the gifts would be wonderful; however, the best gift of all was their friendship. She would forever treasure this Christmas and their time together. They agreed as they sat quietly trying to capture the moment in their memories. She had already given them her gift, but now she told them that she hoped that they would all come and enjoy their special rooms whenever they wished.

Finally, Lindy asked if they could open her gift first. She pointed to the small gift with the large gold ribbon tied around it. On cue, they all started to open the box. Inside the red velvet box, they found a sparkling charm bracelet with four charms with their names engraved. For Emily there was a heart with a ruby; for Grace a dove with a diamond; for Rebecca a musical note with an emerald; and for Lindy a clown with a sapphire. They smiled as they put on their new bracelets. Rebecca told Lindy that once again she had given them a wonderful, sparkling reminder of why they were a perfect blend of friends.

Now it was Grace's turn to give her gifts, wrapped in two packages, to each of them. She asked them to open the smaller package first. They found an antique gold frame with a photo of the four of them playing out in the snow making snow angels. Lindy asked how she could have possibly gotten the picture. Grace told them that Warren could not resist getting the picture of four grown women having so much fun.

The second, bigger gift was the next to be opened. Again, there was a beautiful frame, with an embossed paper telling each of them that a star had been purchased and named for them. It included a map of the galaxy with a location of each of their stars, which were close to each other's. Lindy laughed as she hugged Grace and told her that now she had written proof that she was a star. Linus licked her face as if he was also saying thank you to Grace.

Finally, Rebecca handed out her gifts. There were four boxes each, and she told them that it was important to open them together and in the order that was on each tag. The first gift was a pair of expensive sunglasses, with each of their names in gold thread on the black velvet glasses case. Everyone said thank you; however, they all wondered why Rebecca had picked out that gift for them in the middle of a dark and dreary winter. The second gift was an elegant sequined jacket, each in a different color. The jackets were stunning, but as they all tried them on, they wondered where they would wear such a fancy jacket in Fergus Falls. The third gift was a colorful terry cloth cover-up, with their names embroidered on it. Once again, they all politely thanked Rebecca for the cute gift. The final gift was a small travel bag. Once they had all opened the gift, Rebecca told them to look inside the bag. At once, they all pulled out a large envelope, which had the Princess Cruises logo on the front cover.

Rebecca quietly announced that she had made all the arrangements for them to leave in two days for a seven-day cruise. They would be celebrating New Year's somewhere in the tropical breezes of the Caribbean, drinking their Asti and ringing in the New Year in style. They all jumped up and ran over to hug Rebecca at the same time. The frightened little puppy, Linus, didn't know what to make out of all the noise as he quickly crawled under the Christmas tree for safety.

Rebecca looked at a concerned Grace, who was thinking that there was no way for her to leave her shop at this time of the year. Rebecca told Grace that her staff had already planned their schedules and were happy for her to take some well-deserved time away from the shop.

For the next few hours, they talked, laughed, and planned the upcoming trip. A limo would pick them up and drive them to Fargo, North Dakota. They would fly in a small private jet to Ft. Lauderdale, Florida, and spend a night at the beautiful hotel Pier 66. Then they would board the Star Princess for seven days of fun in the sun.

Finally, Grace asked Rebecca how she could afford such an expensive gift. Rebecca smiled and told them that with some very wise investments, she was now officially worth more than $3 million. She told them all about the money and properties she had received from the father she had never known. She finished by saying that this had been a dream trip of hers for many years. The extra bonus was that she was going to share it with her best friends.

Shortly before going to bed, Rebecca said she had one more thing to tell them. Softly, she told them that her health had taken a serious turn for the worse. She did not want them to be worried; however, they needed to know that she would be on oxygen almost all the time. Arrangements had been made to have oxygen available for her on the flight to Florida and in her cabin on the ship. Lindy would be her roommate for the cruise. With Lindy's nursing experience and detailed instructions from her doctor, she was sure that she would be just fine for the once-in-a-lifetime vacation. As they went to sleep that Christmas Eve, each of the ladies was dreaming about the cruise and all the adventures that lay ahead of them. It had proven to be the Christmas to remember for all of them.

Chapter Twenty-Six

Fun in the Sun

The days flew past in a blur. They washed clothes, packed, unpacked, and packed again. They raided the storage room of Claire's and found some great summer outfits, the leftovers from last season. Lindy had her sister overnight some of her favorite summer outfits, complete with matching hats and shoes. None of them could stop talking about Rebecca's wonderful surprise vacation.

Before they knew it, they were piling their luggage in the trunk of the limo that would take them to Fargo. Warren and his daughters were on hand to take photos of his friends, all dressed in matching Hawaiian blouses, standing in two feet of snow beside the stretch limo. His daughters had happily agreed to dog-sit while their friends were away. They stood at the curb and waved good-bye to four very happy ladies.

It was cold and snowing all the way to Fargo. However, they sat comfortably in the back of the limo with hot chocolate mixed with Baileys Irish Cream and Monica's oatmeal chocolate chip cookies. After an hour of nonstop chatter, they arrived at the small airport and boarded their private jet for the final leg of the adventure. The pilot and copilot greeted them warmly, and within a short time, their plane taxied down the runway. As the plane lifted off the ground, they all cheered; then they settled back for a delightful once-in-a-lifetime flight.

Lindy cuddled close to Rebecca and helped her adjust the oxygen mask shortly after takeoff. For the first time, Grace and Emily realized just how ill Rebecca really was. Within minutes, Rebecca was asleep, and Lindy watched over her for the rest of the flight.

Three hours later, they stood in sunny Ft. Lauderdale, where they quickly shed their winter jackets and reached for their new Christmas sunglasses. The hotel was beautiful and unique with its round design; there were breathtaking views of the port where the cruise ships docked across the street. After they settled into their suites, Rebecca decided it was time for her to once again rest. Lindy tested her oxygen tank and adjusted her mask. Within minutes, Rebecca was sound asleep.

Grace, Emily, and Lindy decided it was time to take a walk around the property. They strolled past the winding, aqua blue swimming pool, complete with small bridges, and the palm trees. Emily hugged Grace and said, "Pinch me and tell me this is not a dream." Grace simply smiled as she assured her that this was very real. They found a small outside table overlooking the pool and ordered drinks as they enjoyed the sun warming their Minnesota-pale white bodies.

As the sun was setting, they slowly walked back to their rooms. Just as they entered the hotel room, Rebecca called to them to come quickly. They raced to her side asking what was the matter; she simply smiled as she pointed to the balcony, where they went to witness an incredible sunset over the water. The sky turned shades of yellow, then orange, and finally purple before the sun slowly faded into the ocean.

Because of their concern for Rebecca, they ordered room service for dinner that evening. They feasted on lobster bisque, shrimp, assorted salads, and a massive chocolate cake filled with chocolate mousse for dessert. After dinner, they settled into Rebecca and Lindy's room to watch the movie *The Way We Were* on TV. They decided that young Robert Redford was the man they were all looking for and would never find.

Grace and Emily were shaken as they watched Lindy help Rebecca with a handful of pills and get her comfortable in bed as she adjusted her oxygen level. Within a short time, they had all fallen asleep while the movie played on. It had been a long and very eventful day. By midnight, they crawled into their beds, once again dreaming and trying to imagine what the next seven days would be like.

It was nine o'clock when Lindy woke up Grace and Emily to tell them that breakfast was being served in Lindy and Rebecca's room promptly at ten o'clock. They quickly showered and dressed; they arrived just as the food was being rolled into Lindy and Rebecca's suite. As they stepped onto the balcony, they came to an abrupt stop. There across the street, the Star Princess Cruise ship was docked. It was beautiful and big, and seemed to glimmer as the water and sun bounced off her.

They sat in awe eating their breakfast and trying to take in everything that surrounded them. Finally, Lindy raised her glass of orange juice to offer a toast, "May this time bring us meaningful memories, lots of laughs, great looking pictures, and an opportunity to celebrate our incredible friendship." As they clinked their glasses together, each had a tear in their eye and a smile on their face.

At 1:00 PM, the very handsome cruise director named Kevin O'Brien escorted Grace, Emily, Lindy, and Rebecca onto the ship. He had been advised that this party of four was to be given VIP status for the entire cruise. He presented them each with their keys to the Presidential Suite, a long-stemmed red rose, and a gold lapel pin, which he told them that he hoped they would wear while on board. This pin would alert all of the ship's staff to their special VIP status and give them priority treatment wherever they went on the ship.

They had their welcome aboard photo taken, and then they took the glass elevator with a view of the nine-story, sun-filled atrium. They giggled like schoolgirls as they were led down the hallway on the Baja deck to their suite. Kevin stopped in front of double oak doors, which had each of their names on a small plaque next to the door. As he opened the doors, a soft light came on overhead. Lindy insisted that Rebecca be the first to enter their home at sea. However, Rebecca insisted they all hold hands and enter together.

The first thing they saw was the highly polished Italian marble floor, with a golden starburst design embedded in the middle of the floor. Just off center sat a white grand piano with a sparkling crystal chandelier hanging over it. It cast a soft golden glow over the large entrance area. Behind the half wall, there was a beautiful living room with a butter-colored soft leather sectional, which filled almost the entire room, and glass tables. There was also a glass dining table with another crystal chandelier and a small private kitchen area filled with all of their favorite foods. The wall of windows led out to a large veranda furnished with four plush chaise lounges and a table for four; tucked into the corner was a large hot tub. To both the right and the left of the living room, there were two large bedrooms and gleaming marble bathrooms with two vanities and gigantic whirlpool tubs.

As they whirled around the suite, Kevin cleared his throat and told them that he wanted to introduce their staff. Joseph, their butler, assured them that he would provide all of their dining, snack, and drink requests. He handed each of them a packet with all the excursions that would be available in the ports. He would personally arrange for any excursions, or he could also find other options. He could arrange for appointments at the spa, beauty shop, or special exercise classes. He finished by saying that he wanted to make sure that this was a perfect vacation for them.

Maria and Theresa were introduced as their private attendants, who would make sure that their clothes were unpacked and pressed, as well as keep their suite spotless. Kevin explained that there would be someone available to them 24/7 and that they should never hesitate to ask for anything. They had an option of having their meals in their suite or in the main dining room, whichever they preferred.

After Kevin left, they all ran around the suite giggling like the little girls they had been long ago. Lindy said that she felt as though she had just won "queen for a day." Little did anyone know that they were just four simple girls from Fergus Falls!

At 4:00 PM, they all stood on the veranda toasting each other as the ship left the dock. Once again, they thanked Rebecca for this awesome gift. Lindy added that she was very grateful for Rebecca's wise investments and asked her to teach her the secret of successful investing. Dinner was served on the veranda that night, with candles flickering as the world drifted away and their adventure began. They had already explored the ship and found the theater, casino, gift shops, and nightclubs. Each of them had taken turns wheeling Rebecca around in her wheelchair with a small portable bottle of oxygen attached to the back.

At 8:00 PM, there was a knock on the door. Grace answered it and greeted a very tall and handsome Italian man who introduced himself as the ship doctor, Dr. Sal D'Amato. He came to check on Rebecca and make sure that she was comfortable. After a brief examination, he left, taking Lindy out in the hall with him. Lindy confirmed all of the information that had been forwarded to him. She promised to keep him posted of any changes, and they arranged to talk each day. Dr. Sal smiled as he left and asked Lindy if she would like to join him for dinner some evening. She quickly agreed, and they promised to share dinner sometime during the cruise.

As she walked back into the cabin, all eyes were on her. Lindy blushed as they laughed, teasing her that the ship should be called the *Love Boat*. The rest of the evening was spent out on their veranda. They were overwhelmed by how black the sky turned with the absence of any city lights and by the thousands of stars that filled the sky. Their adventure had just begun.

Their first day was at sea, so they moved around the beautiful ship and had manicures, pedicures, and facials, while Rebecca had her breathing treatment. A wonderful lunch of fresh fruits, salads, and warm brownies, swimming, and a game of cards filled the afternoon. The ship was even more beautiful than they dreamed possible. The next day followed the same routine except in the afternoon; they all went to a pottery class where each of them decorated a special plate to celebrate this incredible vacation. As usual, Lindy's plate was full of swirls of bright colors, while Grace's and Rebecca's were more focused on the cruise theme. Emily asked for each of their handprints on her plate, and in the center she simply drew SOLA with the date.

On New Year's Eve day, by 4:00 PM, they all decided to take a nap before the beauticians arrived at 6:00 PM to fix their hair and apply makeup for their dinner with the captain in the main dining room. Promptly at 7:45, Kevin, the cruise director, arrived to escort them. As they entered the dining room in their matching sequined jackets, Kevin led them to a table where a waiter stood behind each of the eight chairs. Captain Giovanna arrived a moment later, along with Dr. Sal and the Chief Operations Officer, named David L'Heureux. The meal was a delightful time, with great food and friendly chatter. Lindy and Dr. Sal agreed that this did not count for a quiet dinner and made plans to meet again the following evening for a more private dinner.

After dinner, the girls were escorted to the front-row seats in the main theater for the Broadway-style musical show. After a full day, they pushed Rebecca back to the suite, singing and dancing down the hall. From their veranda at midnight, they toasted the new year's beginning as they watched the beautiful Caribbean sea gently float by them. Silently, they all felt an overwhelming sense of peace and a deep appreciation for their friendship.

The view of Old San Juan, Puerto Rico, greeted them when they awoke the next morning. Kevin arrived to escort them off the ship to their private van, which took them on a tour of the enchanting island, from the rainforest to a butterfly farm and then to the old city of San Juan. After dropping Lindy and Rebecca off at the ship, Grace and Emily still had enough time to go shopping before the ship sailed in the late afternoon.

That evening, they watched Lindy get dressed for her date with Dr. Sal. Grace helped her pick the perfect dress for the evening, loaning her some of her favorite earrings. Emily styled her hair and applied her makeup. By the time Dr. Sal arrived, Lindy's face glowed with a day in the sun and with a sparkle in her eyes that they had not seen in a long time. Grace, Emily, and Rebecca had dinner out on the veranda again, breathing the fresh sea air and feeling the soft, tropical breezes against their sun-soaked skin. By 9:00 PM, they were sound asleep. They never heard Lindy quietly come in at midnight.

Lindy's evening with Dr. Sal was a wonderful surprise. They quickly discovered that they had much in common and truly enjoyed each other's sense of humor and sense of adventure. Lindy danced for the first time in years. As Dr. Sal gently glided her across the dance floor, she felt truly happy for the first time in a very long time. As Sal brought her back to the suite, he gently kissed her and asked her if they could spend some time together the next day while they were in St. Thomas. He wanted to be the person to show her Megan's Bay, one of the ten most beautiful beaches in the world. Lindy answered with a smile and told him that it all depended on how Rebecca was feeling.

As Lindy got ready for bed, Rebecca woke up and asked her how her date went. Lindy answered without thinking, "I think I just fell in love."

Rebecca insisted that Lindy keep her date with Dr. Sal the next day while she spent her time resting and enjoying some shopping with Emily and Grace. She promised to use the wheelchair and return if she felt too tired.

Lindy and Sal spent the day at Megan's Bay floating in the sparkling, clear blue water and resting under a giant umbrella, telling each other the stories of their lives. Sal told Lindy that this was his last cruise. He had grown tired of the adventures of a life at sea and was looking forward to getting a "real" land-based job. Although he had been born in Venice, Italy, most of his family now lived in Chicago. They were excited to welcome him to the Windy City. They all had a single woman that they wanted him to meet, marry, and have cute little bambinos with.

Lindy talked about her life in Fergus Falls and New York City and all of the happy memories as well as the painful times she had faced. She told Sal about the girls' reunion and their wonderful Christmas together. She talked about her love of nursing and her plans to get back into her career. However, for the time being, it was on hold until Rebecca no longer needed her. They talked about Rebecca's serious health concerns. Lindy told Sal she was dedicated to helping Rebecca's last days be days of blessings. Sal admired her commitment to her friend and her gentle, loving care. By the time they came back to the ship, they both felt they had found a new and meaningful friendship.

Emily and Grace spent the day wheeling Rebecca in and out of the narrow cobblestone streets of St. Thomas for shopping. By noon, Rebecca had her lap, her arms, and the back of her wheelchair filled with bags of perfume, watches, linens, and clothes. They had lunch overlooking the harbor at the Green Door Cafe and then headed back to the ship for an afternoon nap on the veranda.

Just before the ship was ready to sail, Lindy came bursting into the cabin with a smile on her sunburned face. For the next hour, she talked nonstop about Sal. As they all sat quietly and listened to Lindy, there was no doubt that she was one happy lady!

St. Maarten was their next delightful port. They discovered that the French side of the island had white, sandy beaches and quaint sidewalk cafes for lunch; the Dutch side provided more shopping and exotic rum drinks, which were served in huge coconut shells. When they returned to their cabin, there was a beautiful Waterford vase filled with red, yellow, and pink roses, with a card to Lindy that read, "Thinking of you. May I have the pleasure of your company at dinner this evening? Love, Sal." Lindy quickly called Sal and thanked him for the beautiful roses but declined his invitation for dinner. They were planning a quiet dinner in their cabin, and it was important for her to be with her friends tonight. Sal understood and told her he would call her tomorrow.

That night's dinner was steak and lobster, served with their favorite melting chocolate cake with ice cream for dessert. They spent the rest of the evening out on the veranda looking over all their purchases. Emily gave each of them a charm bracelet with a charm from St. Thomas, St. Maarten, a ship, a wine glass, and a heart. She giggled as she told all of them that the heart was for Lindy's newfound romance with Dr. Sal.

Then they had another delightful day at sea planned, with a private tour of the ship's bridge and kitchen, appointments at the spa, and then a session with a personal trainer. However, before dawn, Lindy woke up to a strange sound coming from the bathroom. She raced into the bathroom and found Rebecca lying on the marble floor in the midst of a seizure. Lindy cradled Rebecca's body while she yelled for Emily to call 911.

Within minutes, Dr. Sal and two nurses arrived. After what seemed like an eternity, the stretcher carried Rebecca to the ship hospital, with Lindy and Dr. Sal at her side. The next few hours were critical because of Rebecca's serious health problems; her oxygen level remained under 60 percent. She fell into a coma. The only reasonable option for additional care was to have Rebecca airlifted from the ship. However, after much discussion, it was determined that it was safer to keep her on board and under their care until the ship docked in Ft. Lauderdale. During the entire time, one of them sat at Rebecca's side holding her hand and talking to her in a soft whisper.

When the ship docked in Florida at 6:00 AM, an ambulance was waiting to take Rebecca to Ft. Lauderdale Memorial Hospital. After several hours, the ER doctor felt Rebecca had stabilized, yet she was still in a coma. He signed orders for her release and approval for her to fly back to Fergus Falls, but only with an agreement to take her directly to the hospital. Dr. Sal announced that he wanted to accompany Rebecca on the flight. In comparison to the earlier flight, this one was quiet and tense. Rebecca lay motionless on the stretcher, which was strapped in the back of the plane. For the entire flight, both Dr. Sal and Lindy sat with her, monitoring her vital signs.

As soon as the small jet landed in Fergus Falls, the paramedics entered the plane to assist in loading Rebecca into the waiting ambulance. Within minutes, Rebecca, Dr. Sal, and Lindy were on their way to Lake Regional

Hospital, where Rebecca's mother anxiously awaited her arrival. Lindy made Grace and Emily promise to go back to Emily's house. She would call with a status report as soon as she had any news.

As Emily and Grace came into the dark kitchen of Emily's house, they were flooded with emotions of the past few weeks. They made it as far as the kitchen table before they both collapsed in deep sobs. They cried for the lost dreams of tomorrow for Rebecca and her weak, fragile body. Grace made a pot of coffee and offered to go over to pick up the Christmas puppy, Linus. Perhaps this cuddly little dog could help them pass the hours of waiting that they knew lay ahead of them.

Grace heard Linus barking and lots of giggles as she rang the doorbell at the Brooks' home. When Warren opened the door, he told her that he was surprised that they were already home. He stopped in mid-sentence as he looked into Grace's eyes. He asked, "What happened?"

All Grace could do was to fall into his arms, as once again the deep sobs overwhelmed her. He held her, rubbing her back and softly whispering in her ear that he was here for her. After a few minutes, Warren led Grace to the sofa and offered her a glass of water. After a few sips of water and some deep sighs, Grace told them what was going on. The girls sat quietly listening to Grace tell them that Rebecca might be dying and what a comforting presence Lindy had been to all of them. The girls promptly offered to continue to watch Linus. Grace decided that with all the chaos of the next few days, that was a great idea.

Warren walked Grace back to Emily's front porch, where they lingered for a few more moments. He reached for her, and she fell comfortably into his warm embrace. Finally, her hands gently reached for his face and she kissed him. Then without a word, she turned and walked quietly into the house. Warren remained in place for a few minutes, trying to understand what had just happened. For whatever reason, he knew that Grace had just opened his heart, which had been tightly closed for a long time. As he walked back to his house, he knew that his life was about to change.

Chapter Twenty-Seven

Rebecca's Challenge

Upon arriving at the hospital, Rebecca was given a battery of tests. Her oxygen level remained dangerously low, as well as her pulse and respiration.

Lindy stayed with Rebecca while Dr. Sal went to turn in the medical records he had brought from the cruise ship. Then he called his parents in Chicago and explained that he was in Minnesota. He told his disappointed mother that he would be delayed for several days.

Sal found Lindy in the hospital café, staring into a cup of coffee. The exhaustion of the last few days had finally taken its toll on her. Sal slid into the booth beside her and cradled her in his arms. Lindy simply rested her head against his chest and wept. After a little while, they walked back to the ER, where they were told to wait for the attending doctor to return with the test results. Lindy called the house and told Emily that this might be a long night and that they should go to sleep. She promised that as soon as she knew what was going on, she would call regardless of the time.

After a two-hour wait in the ER waiting room, a nurse arrived to inform them that Rebecca was being moved to ICU and that her mother would be waiting for them in the ICU waiting area. Lindy and Sal walked down the hall in silence, thinking the news was not good.

As they rounded the corner, they saw Rebecca's mom waiting for them. Lindy ran to her. A nurse led them to a small, dimly lit private room. Sal chose to wait in the open waiting room and not intrude. Monica explained that she still had no information and feared the worst. While they waited, she asked Lindy to tell her all about the cruise. To their amazement, they sat laughing about the cruise and all the fun they had. Monica thanked Lindy for helping Rebecca enjoy these last precious days with her best friends.

There was a soft rap on the door, and two young doctors and a nurse entered the small room. The grim look on the faces meant that this was not good news. After reviewing all of the tests, which included an MRI and CAT scan, it was determined that Rebecca had severe heart damage, her kidneys were beginning to shut down, and the seizure might have caused irreversible brain damage. The prognosis was very poor, and they did not expect Rebecca to survive the next forty-eight hours. They did not believe that she would regain consciousness.

One of the doctors asked if she had prepared a living will. Calmly, Monica advised them that no extraordinary measures were to be taken. Rebecca wanted to pass away in peace and dignity. Lindy agreed as Monica signed papers stating her decision.

The nurse took them down the hall to the ICU area. Monica, with Lindy at her side, entered the small dark cubicle where Rebecca lay. The only noise came from the beeping of the monitors. Aside from the oxygen mask, Rebecca looked as though she was sleeping and at peace. Lindy reached for Rebecca's right hand, while Monica held her left hand. For a moment, they simply looked into Rebecca's pale and gentle face. Then very softly, Monica began to pray the Lord's Prayer as she gently rubbed her daughter's hand. Lindy joined in and felt as though her heart was breaking.

The nurse appeared after a short time and told them that they should go home and get some rest. She promised to call them if there was any change. Together, they walked down the dimly lit hall back into the waiting area. Lindy saw Sal sleeping in a chair in the corner. When she woke him, he took Lindy's hand and agreed it was a good idea for her to go home and rest.

With very little discussion, Lindy decided that they should all go back to Emily's house. Monica quickly agreed, saying that the thought of being alone tonight was just too much to bear. Lindy assured Sal that they would find a place for him to sleep as well.

When they pulled into the driveway, they saw that the kitchen lights were still glowing and it had started to snow. As they walked into the warm, cozy kitchen, they could smell the coffee and saw a mound of freshly baked chocolate chip cookies spread over the table. Both Grace and Emily turned in silence before they rushed to give Monica a hug. The rest of the night was spent talking about the cruise, eating the cookies, and drinking pots of coffee.

When the telephone rang at 7:00 AM, they were all still awake. Emily answered it and said that she would make sure to pass the information on to Monica. The news was better than it had been last night. Rebecca's condition had become stable, and they had even detected some eye movement. The attending doctor, Kevin Tolzman, had asked to meet with the family at 9:30 AM to discuss what options were available for Rebecca. Monica insisted that all of the girls come with her to hear firsthand what was going to happen.

At 9:30, they were anxiously awaiting Dr. Tolzman's arrival. Each of them visited Rebecca in the ICU for five minutes. They understood how serious her condition was.

Dr. Tolzman was a tall, young doctor with a compassionate tone to his deep voice. Slowly he reviewed all the test results and Rebecca's current vital signs. He held Monica's hand as he told her that he had also reviewed Rebecca's living will. In order to honor her very specific requests, there would be no extraordinary means used to keep her alive. However, he felt that she was comfortable and pain-free at this time, and the staff would do everything possible to keep her comfortable. He then told Monica that the next few days were critical; if she survived, he could recommend a nursing home, seeing as there was no hospice facility in Fergus Falls.

Lindy asked if it was possible for all of them to be with her at the same time. Dr. Tolzman nodded and told them to follow him. As they entered Rebecca's dark cubicle, they quickly gathered around her bed. Each of them gently rubbed her arms, hands, or legs. Monica leaned over and put her hands on Rebecca's pale face. Then she whispered to her that they were all here for her. One by one, they told her how much they loved her. Each of them told her why she had been so special in their life. Softly, Lindy began to sing "Amazing Grace." They joined in perfect harmony as they sang through their tears. As they finished, the nurse arrived to advise them that she needed to take Rebecca down for one more MRI to check for brain activity.

They left Rebecca's cubicle as they had entered, one by one in silence. Then they all left the hospital together. Once they were outside in the cold Minnesota air, they broke down in uncontrolled sobs of agony. How could this happen so quickly? Why now after they had all come back together and found true friendship? The drive back to Emily's was painfully silent.

Once they were settled back in the kitchen, Sal announced that he had rented a car and was leaving in the afternoon to head to Chicago. He promised he would return to them if they needed him. Lindy drove Sal to pick up his rental car and have a private moment. He told her that he knew that the days would be painful. He also told her that her strength would be a source of comfort for Monica and her friends. He felt strongly that God would give her whatever she needed to get through this difficult time with grace and understanding.

As they embraced and kissed, Lindy asked when she would see him again.

Sal softly lifted her face to his and said, "Anytime you need me, I will be here. Chicago is not that far away, and I will do whatever it takes to be at your side. Lindy, before I leave, you need to understand that I am completely in love with you. This is not a quick shipboard romance. I intend to come back for you. I believe that we are meant to be together, and my goal is to make that happen. So, my sweet Lindy, be prepared to be romanced, loved, and a permanent part of my life in the future."

Lindy was speechless. All she could do was smile, nod, and tell him that she was looking forward to his romancing. As his car pulled out of the parking lot, he waved and told her would be back soon. Lindy stood smiling and crying at the same time as she watched Sal's car disappear onto the highway that would take him to Chicago.

Chapter Twenty-Eight

The Homecoming

Almost all of the next few days were spent at the hospital for the girls, each taking turns to be with Rebecca for a short, five-minute visit once an hour. Emily and Lindy had talked Grace into going back to work. When she was not at the hospital, Monica slept in Rebecca's room at Emily's. Every time she walked into the room, she was amazed at how it had perfectly captured Rebecca's love of life and music. She felt a special peace as she slept there, knowing the loving care that had gone into this special place for her daughter.

It had been four days since Rebecca had been admitted. Dr. Tolzman advised Monica that although they had found some brain activity on Rebecca's last MRI, his recommendation was that she be transferred to Pioneer Nursing Home by the end of the week. He told her that the staff would make the arrangements and give her more details about the transfer.

Monica came back into the ICU waiting room looking shaken as she told them about what Dr. Tolzman had recommended. She sobbed as she told them that this was not how she wanted Rebecca to leave this earth. Although the nursing home was a good place for many, this was not where Rebecca should be. What if she woke up? How could Monica explain to Rebecca why she had allowed this to happen?

The answer was simple, but the problems they faced to make it happen were massive. Lindy worked for two days to make sure all of the arrangements were made to have Rebecca transferred to Emily's house. Lindy signed documents stating that she would be Rebecca's primary nurse and a temporary nurse had been hired to fill in the times that Lindy needed to sleep. Seeing there was a do not resuscitate order, the rest of the issues had already been resolved. Monica planned to stay with Rebecca in her peaceful room.

Finally, the ambulance pulled into Emily's driveway to bring Rebecca home. The little elevator proved to be a wonderful solution for getting her upstairs. Quickly, Rebecca was in her own bed surrounded with her love of music and all those whom she loved.

They took turns being with her, bringing their coffee mugs and meals to her bedside. They talked constantly, laughed about all of their adventures over the years, and prayed with her. They wiped her face with a cool washcloth and brushed her beautiful hair. They played her favorite songs and sang. They simply wanted Rebecca to feel their presence and for her to know that she was loved.

Monica was sleeping on the chaise lounge in Rebecca's room when she awoke to a strange sound. She sat up to see if Linus, Lindy's puppy, had once again snuck into the bedroom. Instead, she saw that it was Rebecca making the sound. She yelled for the others to come. Rebecca lay there, wide-awake. She looked as though she had just awakened from a long night of sleep. She stretched and coughed as she tried to raise herself up. Monica told her to lie still until Lindy came to help her. Rebecca wanted to know how she had gotten here, as her last memory was on the cruise ship.

All at once, there was chaos as Emily, Grace, and Lindy came running into the bedroom. They stopped short and stared in amazement at Rebecca's pale blue eyes and her smile. Rebecca cleared her throat as she softly said, "Well, girls, you have some explaining to do. How did I get from the ship to my bed without knowing it? Why do all of you look so surprised? What is going on? Lindy, talk to me." They gathered around her bed as Lindy told her all that had happened the last week. She finished by telling her that they never left her side through the entire ordeal.

Rebecca had tears in her eyes as she told them that she had, indeed, felt their presence. She told them that she had been dreaming of floating through a blue sky and seeing Grandma Ruby waiting for her with her arms outstretched. She felt freedom, joy, and great peace. She felt herself soaring in and out of clouds that made her feel warm and loved. Then she looked up into each of their faces and asked, "Did you sing "Amazing Grace" for me? I heard it so clearly. Did you know that I sang along with you? We had such perfect harmony, and the words were dancing around me." Grace told Rebecca how they stood beside her bed, each of them touching her as they sang to her.

Lindy left to call Dr. Tolzman and tell him about the miracle that was taking place at Emily's. He told her that he would come over and that he needed to talk with Monica. He arrived ten minutes later. As Emily showed him into the living room, she was shocked by the grim look on his face. She expected that he would be happy that Rebecca had come back to them. Yes, he was wrong in his diagnosis, but he should be happy for the surprise recovery. He quietly asked for all of them to gather so he could talk to them together.

Monica was the last to enter the room; for the first time in a week, she had a smile on her face. Dr. Tolzman cleared his throat; he really did not want to tell these special women what he had to tell them. "Well, I am so glad that Rebecca is in this lovely home, surrounded by her mother and friends. However, I need to tell you that this is probably Rebecca's final hours. The medical books do not have a solid explanation for this, but it often happens just before death. The body has one final rally. It is as though the patient wills herself to be awake and spend the last few moments of life with her loved ones. Some who have faith call this God's final gift of life. Scientists have tried to prove otherwise and cannot seem to find a physical explanation. Regardless, I am here to tell you to not waste one precious moment that you have been given. Say what you need to say and have no regrets. I am officially off duty for the next forty-eight hours but would like to stay here with you."

Monica said that she knew that this was God's last gift to Rebecca while she was on this earth. "Let's use every moment to celebrate Rebecca's life and time with her. I think each of us should have some alone time with her. Emily, will you go to her first? Let us not waste time with tears; we will have plenty of time for that later. Now is the time to share joy with her."

As Emily climbed the stairs to Rebecca's room, her legs felt heavy. Before she reached for the doorknob, she took a deep breath, brushed her tears away, and put a smile on her face. The visiting nurse had helped Rebecca to sit up with the help of piles of soft pillows. Her hair was brushed, and she wore a new blue, satin nightgown. Emily thought to herself, *She looks like an angel.*

Rebecca patted the side of her bed and asked Emily to come sit with her. As Emily grabbed Rebecca's hand and looked into her sweet face, the tears began. It was Rebecca, who dried her tears and tried to comfort Emily. Softly, Rebecca told her that she knew that she was dying and that it was perfectly okay with her. "God has given me a preview of heaven, and I am happy to be going there. I have never felt such peace before. I am so happy that I have faith in him and that I know the joy that is waiting for me. I know you will be sad and miss me. I will miss you, too. I want you to know that I know you will be an important woman. You are blessed with gifts of leadership. Use them well and make me proud. Your life has been a painful journey, and you will have the opportunity to make this a better place for others. I have valued your friendship. You have given me the gift of fortitude. You have been my example of how to move on when I thought I could not move one more step. I thank God for the day, so many years ago, that he brought us together. Be at peace and know that I will be your joyful guardian angel."

Then she squeezed Emily's hand and told her to go bring Grace to her.

When Emily came into the living room, they were all amazed at the look on her face. Instead of tears, they saw a gentle smile. Emily looked relaxed and at peace as she told Grace that it was her turn to go to Rebecca.

Grace left the room without a word and ran up the stairs to Rebecca's room. Rebecca saw Grace standing at the door, and she lifted her arms to receive Grace's gentle hug. Rebecca asked for a sip of water. After she drank a little, she turned to Grace and began to speak. "I don't think I have ever told you, but Grace is the perfect name for you. You are full of God's glory and show his love through your gentle and kind ways. Fergus Falls was always meant to be your home. I know there were times when we all left you behind and that it was painful for you. However, look at what you have done for Fergus Falls. It is so much more than your delightful clothing store. You have given Fergus Falls spirit, laughter, and happiness. During the long winter nights, your bright talents have made people come to be entertained. You use your talents so well.

"For many years, I was jealous of your family. I watched you as you all sat around your living room, playing games and simply enjoying each other. Even after Denny's death, you all knew how to care for each other. I have also watched you grow into a compassionate woman. You so freely and without hesitation simply enjoy life. I want you to know that I am ready to go to God and looking forward to that blessing. Do not mourn for me, but celebrate what we have discovered as women—the gift of friendship, laughter, and honest conversations. You, my dear friend, have a lot of love in you; give it away and watch it come back to you in many exciting new ways. Now I think I need to talk to Lindy for a little while."

Rebecca closed her eyes as Grace let go of her hand and silently left the room. Before she closed the door, she turned to look one more time at Rebecca. Yes, Grace said to herself, *That is what an angel looks like.*

Lindy was sitting at the top of the stairs, knowing that it soon would be her turn. As Grace walked up to her, she just put her hand on Lindy's shoulder and continued to walk down the stairs. Lindy was well aware of what death looked like and how no two people left this earth in the same way. Some fought until their last breath, while others found a peace to almost welcome their passing. She knew Rebecca would find peace.

When she walked into the bedroom, she noticed a glow around Rebecca's face. Rebecca quickly took Lindy's hand and said, "Well, my bigger-than-life friend, we both know that this is the end. I hope that you can see that I am ready. You have been so much fun for me. Where I am dull, you have added color and sparkles. When I was timid, you transferred your big love of the adventure to me. You helped me to be strong. You showed me how to be brave, and yes, at times, you gave me the joy of learning how to act silly. God has given you a very special gift of bringing comfort and honesty to the sick. I know these past few weeks have been very difficult for you. You have been my nurse as well as my friend. However, I need to thank you for being both. Without your assistance, I would have never been able to take the cruise. Oh, what fun we had being pampered, spoiled, and treated like queens. Thank you for making fun-filled memories for all of us. Use your gifts wisely; bring comfort and joy to those who need your special, gentle touch. Your gifts are needed by so many. Now it is time for me to see Mom. Promise me that you will be with her and care for her after I am gone."

Lindy could not get the words out of her mouth. She simply nodded, gave Rebecca a hug, and left the room.

Monica was waiting outside Rebecca's room. Although she did not mean to, she overheard the conversation that had just taken place. She knew that she was saying good-bye to her daughter. There was nothing that she could do to stop what was happening. Monica would have gladly traded places with Rebecca, but that was not how this day was going to end. Her last gift to her precious daughter would be to tell her it was okay to leave.

When Rebecca saw Monica at the door, she thought that Grandma Ruby was standing beside her. She motioned her to come to her bed. Monica kicked off her shoes and climbed into bed next to Rebecca. She held her as she had held her as a little girl, gently rocking her and kissing her cheeks and forehead. Rebecca sighed and then started to speak.

"It is so strange that even as a grown woman, I still need your hugs and gentle kisses, and most of all, I need you to know how much I love you. You always made me feel that I was loved, wanted, and could do anything I put my mind to. You gave me a sense of purpose in my life. You could have been bitter about how life treated you, but instead, you found happiness in our precious little house on Bancroft Street. I learned to honor others because of Grandma Ruby and the entire heritage she passed on to me. You have sacrificed for me. No one could have given me a better life than you did.

"I know how painful this is for you, and I wish with all my heart that I could take away the pain this is causing you. I want you to know that I am ready. I am ready to see God and soar to heaven. I cannot wait to tell him what a wonderful woman you are. Think of me as being in the arms of God, with Grandma Ruby at his side, and know that it is okay. I love you so much, Mom."

Monica just continued to hold Rebecca, gently rocking her frail body. Softly, she kissed her cheeks and told her that it was okay for her to go to God. "I am going to be all right," she told her over and over again. "Rebecca, go to God and rejoice in his glory and grace. You have earned a special place with him. You have been my gift. Now I give you back to him."

Monica fell asleep with her daughter resting gently in her arms. When she awoke an hour later, Rebecca was gone. She stood up and looked at her child, fixed her hair, and straightened her nightgown.

Slowly she left the room and told the others that Rebecca was gone. Then she took her purse, put on her coat, and left. She walked down the streets of Fergus Falls back to her little house on Bancroft Street. She made a cup of coffee and ate her daughter's favorite oatmeal chocolate chip cookies. She knew that somehow, tomorrow she would begin to find a way to fill the deep hole within her. She also knew that she would find some way to honor Rebecca's life.

Two days later, they gathered at Bethlehem Lutheran Church for a small, private memorial service. Rebecca's body, per her request, was donated for research. Dr. Sal had come to be with Lindy. Emily, Grace, and Lindy sang "Amazing Grace." They knew they would never sing that song together again.

Chapter Twenty-Nine

Two Years Later

Emily

Emily truly adored the home that she had created. The once-cold house had been transformed into a loving home for her and Lindy. They hosted many fundraising parties. There always seemed to be someone at the kitchen table sharing a cup of coffee.

After Rebecca's death, Emily decided to become involved in city politics. She knew that she would never sell the house or live anywhere else but in Fergus Falls. She served on a committee to bring new business and industry back to the downtown area and helped to organize a fundraising drive for the expansion of the high school. She had been successful in bringing a new vitality back to Lincoln Avenue. Emily felt that she had finally found her purpose in Fergus Falls.

To her great amazement, she was asked to run for mayor. The local bank and many prominent business owners quickly endorsed her. They loved her exciting, new ideas to bring Fergus Falls back to its days of glory. In November, she won the election and became the first female mayor of Fergus Falls. The morning she was sworn into office, her two best friends, Grace and Lindy, held her Bible as she promised to fulfill the duties of her office.

Shortly after Christmas, her doorbell rang. Emily opened the door for a long-awaited visit from the McMahons, who had easily found her on the Internet. She stared with wonder into the face of Rebecca Grace McMahon. Her name suited her well, with her curly auburn hair and big blue eyes. It did not take long for Emily to realize that although Rebecca had Danny Driscoll's physical features, she also had the gentle and caring nature of Emily.

For most of their two-day visit, they all sat around the kitchen table and talked for hours. The McMahons brought their photo albums to show how Rebecca had grown over the years. Rebecca told Emily how much she enjoyed music and her choral group in high school. Emily shared with them her childhood memories. She told them all about the girls of SOLA and how they had reconnected as women. She told Rebecca all about her namesakes and why she had chosen those special names for her. Before they left to return to Wisconsin, Emily drove them around Fergus Falls, stopping at the newly constructed hospice. Emily asked the McMahons' permission to take a walk with Rebecca before they left for home.

Together, the mother and daughter, separated since birth, slowly walked around Lake Alice. First, there was silence, and then Emily began to speak. "Rebecca, giving you up for adoption was the most honest act of love that I have ever committed. You need to know deep in your heart that it was because I loved you so much that I knew I had to make sure your life was filled with love and caring parents. At that time in my life, I had nothing to offer you. As soon as I met the McMahons, I knew my prayers had been answered. I am sure you might not understand my decision; however, you do need to know that I pray for you every day and you are always in my thoughts. Thank you for finding me and giving me a glimpse into your delightful life." Rebecca simply took Emily's hand as they finished their walk around the lake.

Just before leaving, Tom McMahon asked if it was possible to obtain a medical background on both Emily and Rebecca's father. Rebecca had some allergy problems, and their doctor had requested more family medical history. Emily promised to get as much information as she could find for them.

Rebecca and Emily's relationship was in the early building stage, but it held the promise of becoming a new dimension in Emily's life. Emily was so pleased to see what a caring young woman Rebecca had grown up to be. There was something in her smile that reminded Emily of the lady she had been named after. Emily had no idea where their relationship would go, but she was so grateful that the young Rebecca had come to meet her. After Rebecca left, Emily wrote a letter to the McMahons thanking them for loving and raising this very special young lady.

Emily kept her promise to provide family medical information to the McMahons. It did not take too long for her to find out how Danny's life had turned out. She Googled Danny Driscoll and found several articles about him. Sadly, she read stories about his arrests for drug possession. Emily sighed as she read an article detailing his standoff with Madison police and his suicide three years after she had left him. After many more hours of searching the Internet, Emily was never able to find any of Danny's family.

That night, she spent a long time in conversation with God. She thanked God for the beautiful daughter that she had been given. She also thanked him for giving her the wisdom to leave a lifestyle that was so wrong in so many ways. Finally, she asked God to forgive Danny for all his poor choices and to give him the peace that he had never found in his life.

Tonight was the second anniversary of Rebecca's death. One year ago, each of them simply tried to get through the day alone. It had proven to be far too painful. This year, they were all gathering at Emily's for a special meal and a celebration of Rebecca's life. Emily prepared the dinner herself with all of Rebecca's favorite foods. Monica was invited and told Emily that she would bring dessert. Emily knew it was time to move forward. As she set the dining room table with her special Norwegian dishes, she smiled and remembered a special time not so long ago.

Grace

Grace had wept for days after Rebecca's death. Then she realized that Rebecca would want her to get back to her normal life, although now there would be a "new normal." Life without Rebecca left a hole that Grace decided to fill by working as many hours as she could each day. She knew that she needed to get back to Claire's. It would soon be time to make the annual buying trip. She had responsibilities to her staff and her customers. A week later, she was in the window putting the finishing touches on the Valentine's Day display when she heard a tap on the window. She turned around to see Warren and his three daughters smiling back at her.

Warren invited her to join them for an ice cream sundae across the street at the Viking Café. Without hesitation, Grace accepted. From that day on, her life changed. She adored the Brooks girls, and they quickly became attached to Grace. She helped Warren with their clothes and took them to her hairdresser for stylish new hairdos. She taught them how to ice-skate on Lake Alice. On cold winter evenings, she taught the girls how to knit.

In the meantime, she also discovered that Warren was a wonderful man. They began to date on a regular basis, both with and without the girls. Quickly, they discovered that they had fallen into a very comfortable love. Grace spent many of her evenings and weekends at Warren's house, working side by side with him on his remodeling projects. Grace often smiled as she looked out Warren's front window to see Emily's beautiful house next door.

In May, Warren surprised Grace by stopping in Claire's and requesting a special outfit for each of the girls. As he was walking out of the store with new outfits and a big smile on his face, he asked if she would join them for dinner that night. Grace gladly accepted and told Warren there was no need to be so formal. He simply smiled and said, "We will see you at seven o'clock."

When Grace arrived, she found the table in the dining room beautifully set and fresh flowers everywhere she looked. The girls were all dressed in their new outfits and Warren in his best business suit. Warren offered her a seat in the chair by the fireplace. The girls were sitting quietly on the sofa as Warren carried in a tray with five Waterford crystal champagne flutes. Two were filled with Asti and three with apple juice. Before Grace could ask what was going on, the girls jumped to their feet, begging Warren to "do it now."

Warren handed the champagne to Grace. Then he knelt down in front of her and said, "Grace, I know you might think this is too sudden; however, I have a question for you. All of us would like to ask you if you will marry us and join our family. You have given us the love that we have been missing for such a long time. We want to begin a new life with you."

Grace simply said, "Yes, I would be honored to become a Brooks girl." They all had a group hug with tears in their eyes.

In August, they were married, in a church filled with friends. They took the girls with them on their honeymoon to a cabin on Ottertail Lake. When they returned to Warren's home overlooking Lake Alice, Grace and Warren began to remodel the last of the rooms in their home. Four months later, Grace announced that their family would be expanding. To their surprise, her doctor informed Grace that she was having twins. On a beautiful spring day, Grace welcomed Claire and Dennis Brooks into the world. Grace thanked God as she softly sang "Amazing Grace" to her two miracles.

Grace went back to work after six weeks with the babies. They had created a small nursery for them at the store, and they became the center of everyone's attention. Grace loved her new life and knew how truly blessed she was.

Tonight she was going to dinner next door at her best friend's house alone. She felt deep in her soul that Rebecca was part of her life. She prayed that her daughters would grow up to be loving, caring women, just like her friends. As she stepped onto Emily's front porch, she was overwhelmed with memories of the past. However, tonight, she also felt the warm, gentle presence of all the joy that Rebecca had given to her over the years. It was time to cherish those memories; the pain was almost gone. It had been replaced with a certainty that Rebecca was watching over them.

Lindy

Wow, what a busy day Lindy had today, but the timing seemed to be perfect. This morning, she attended Emily's swearing-in ceremony. This afternoon, Lindy and Dr. Sal had the ribbon-cutting ceremony and grand opening of Rebecca's Place. The hospice would accommodate twelve patients in their final days. The building was across the street from Lake Regional Hospital; however, you would never guess that this quaint building was a hospice. The one-story building was shaped in a large square. Each of the spacious and beautiful rooms faced a quiet courtyard that had a large statue of an angel in the middle of a pond. The courtyard would be filled with flowers in the spring and summer. During the fall, the large maple and oak trees would change colors; and at Christmas, Lindy planned to decorate the area with thousands of tiny white lights.

Emily and Lindy also decided that Emily's spare bedrooms would be offered to family members as a place to go and rest from their daily sorrow and pain at the hospice. Lindy had moved to the third floor of Emily's house and created a delightful loft, where she spent hours painting and creating wonderful pieces of art, which had now found a home at Rebecca's Place.

As the crowd passed through the hospice, people commented on the feeling of peace that seemed to surround them in each of the rooms. Dr. Sal and Lindy proudly greeted everyone as they arrived. After Rebecca's funeral, Sal had told Lindy that although Chicago was where his family was, he knew that Fergus Falls was where his heart was. They fell into a comfortable relationship. They worked side by side to design the special hospice. They were committed to working with a staff of dedicated and caring people.

Lindy had learned a week after Rebecca's death that she was named the executor of Rebecca's multimillion-dollar estate. Rebecca had written each of the girls a letter. In Lindy's letter, she told her to make sure that her mother, Monica, was always cared for; the balance of the money should be used to do something for others. She told Lindy that she was sure that she would find the right project and then do it with her special flair. As Lindy watched the people coming to see the finished dream, she knew that Rebecca was happy with her choice.

Once the last of the crowd left, Sal and Lindy were in a hurry to prepare for their first patients. A forty-year-old woman in her final days after a long battle with breast cancer was scheduled to arrive in two hours with her husband and two teenage girls at her side. They knew they were prepared to give this family a comfortable place to stay.

Sal found Lindy putting away the punch bowl in the community room. He turned her around and held her in his arms, giving her one of his wonderful hugs. Then he said, "My precious Lindy, we have completed one project today, and my wish is to begin a new one before sundown. Will you give me the honor of marrying me?"

Lindy fell to her knees as she screamed *yes* so loud that the staff came running to see if there was a problem. She proudly announced that she was *finally* going to be a doctor's wife. Lindy had felt Rebecca's presence all day, and she knew that her beloved friend was happy with how her money had been spent. Because of Rebecca's life, others will find peace and comfort in their last days. Now Lindy also had a chance for some true happiness and joy, which was long overdue. It all felt so right.

And so in typical Lindy style, she called Emily and Grace to inform them to change any plans they had for the next weekend. With all the arrangements made, they flew out to Las Vegas. Lindy and Sal were married by an Elvis impersonator, who was dressed in a white satin jumpsuit with a gold cape and sunglasses. Lindy wore the sequined jacket that had been Rebecca's Christmas gift to her. Lindy laughed as she told the girls that the minister was prettier than the bride and there ought to be a law against that. After an expensive dinner at the Wynn, they flew back home.

Sal and Lindy were now living on the third floor of Emily's house while their new home was being remodeled. It came as no surprise to anyone that they purchased an old house, which was on Lake Alice and in walking distance to Grace's and Emily's homes. Lindy always laughed about what a hoot it was that they all ended up with the same view of the peaceful little lake that had been such a big part of their childhood memories.

Lindy was now on her way to Emily's for a special dinner in memory of Rebecca. She felt proud of what she had created to honor Rebecca's short life.

Monica

After Rebecca's death, Monica felt pain like she had never experienced. The girls all gathered around and seemed to pop up whenever she needed a shoulder to lean on. Lindy came to her and asked for her approval on the idea of building a hospice in honor of Rebecca. Lindy kept her busy and very involved in all the stages of planning and building at Rebecca's Place.

Now that it was completed, Monica was going to be there every day. She would coordinate the volunteers and help in any way she could. Just before the grand opening, Sal, Lindy, and Monica took their own private walk-through of the beautiful building. Monica knew that sorrow would fill the rooms, but she prayed that some joy and peace would also be present for the people who came to Rebecca's Place. When they entered the courtyard, she saw a large, covered object in the middle of the small pond in the courtyard's center. Lindy and Sal led her up to the object and asked her to pull off the cover.

In front of her was a sculpture of an angel that stood eight feet tall. Her arms were stretched out as if she was welcoming you to come and be embraced. Her face looked just like Rebecca, and even in this bronze statue, you could almost see her eyes twinkling. She wore a gentle smile. Her presence gave off a sense of comfort and peace. A local artist named Leon had taken on the project, and although he never knew Rebecca, he had perfectly captured her spirit in this stunning sculpture. There was a brass plate on the base of the statue that had Rebecca's name, followed by, "*From the SOLA girls with love forever.*" It was the final touch to Rebecca's legacy.

Now it was time to give the gift to all those who would need to discover the comfort of Rebecca's Place. Monica would be there to welcome their first guests and for many days to come.

She was so pleased that she was going to share a dinner with the girls at Emily's house to celebrate Rebecca's life.

The Dinner

It was a typical winter evening in Fergus Falls. The air was cold and crisp as the snowflakes softly fell to the ground. As each of the guests arrived, they watched the ice-skaters as they glided across Lake Alice. Their sounds of laughter brought back memories of four girls many years ago.

The table was set just as it had been more than two years ago at Christmas. Each place setting had hand-painted plates and satin napkins, and candles and flowers filled the middle of the table. They hugged each other and then silently walked into the dining room that had given them all so much happiness in the past. Each of them took their turn lifting their glass to toast their beloved friend. They spent hours around the table. They laughed, they cried, they shared their memories, and they celebrated.

They celebrated the Brooks twins and Grace's wonderful new life. They celebrated Emily's new challenges as mayor and were anxious to see her in action. She bragged about her Rebecca and told them that they were planning a little two-day trip to Chicago to become better acquainted. They celebrated the opening of Rebecca's Place and Lindy's marriage to Dr. Sal. They celebrated their many blessings and their futures.

Finally, at midnight, they bundled up in their heavy winter coats, hats, and gloves and went outside. Emily carried the small bronze container that Monica had given to her with instructions to do whatever the girls all felt was best. Silently, they walked onto the ice of Lake Alice's center. Emily looked up and let out a gasp as she gazed at the midnight sky. There were thousands of twinkling lights in the dark winter sky. As they all gazed into the heavens, they saw four shooting stars. Emily opened the small container, which held Rebecca's ashes, just as a wind blew in from the west. The ashes flowed from the container, swirling into the sky with a gentle breeze that had not been there just moments before.

Without saying a word, Emily, Grace, Lindy, and Monica held hands as they began to sing "Amazing Grace" one more time. Their eyes looked at the heavens. They saw one shooting star after another; and when they finished singing, so did the shooting stars.

As they walked back to Emily's house, they knew that this was their last gift to Rebecca. The peace and joy that had spread over Lake Alice that night would continue to spread in the many years to come. They had gathered on this cold day in January and witnessed the joy of their timeless friendship once again. It had been their time to come together to celebrate their friend and to give thanks for their many blessings, both in the past and in the future.

Yes, life was good in Fergus Falls.